Go Back Jack

Maureen Kellar-Kirby

Second Edition

TotalRecall Publications, Inc.
1103 Middlecreek
Friendswood, Texas 77546
281-992-3131 281-TEL
www.totalrecallpress.com

Copyright © 2024 By: Maureen Kellar-Kirby
Edited By: Sigrid Macdonald
All rights reserved

ISBN: 978-1-64883-280-2
UPC: 6-43977-42802-8

Library of Congress Control Number: 2017949350

FIRST EDITION
1   2   3   4   5   6   7   8   9   10

"This work depicts actual events in the life of the author as truthfully as recollection permits and/or can be verified by research. The conversations in this work all come from the author's recollections, although they are not written to represent word-for-word transcripts. Rather, the author has retold them in a way that evokes the feeling and meaning of what was said and occasionally, dialogue consistent with the character or nature of the person has been supplemented. Names of some actual individuals have been changed to respect their privacy".

For my guardian angel, Angela,
who faithfully kept her promise to me;
my mother, who remained a constant friend;
my sister Kate, who willingly served as a channel
between the dimensions, giving me the
encouragement to see this adventure through;
my dear friend Jann Bailey, late Executive Director of
the Kamloops Art Gallery who always told me to
reach for the stars, and the world-renowned musician
and producer Daniel Lanois who helped me to
preserve and record the music without knowing the
story behind it.

About the Book

A young Canadian woman, through dreams, visions, and psychic information, discovers a past life as a black, male, American blues musician who lived during the Great Depression, "rode the rods" and died tragically before realizing his musical dreams. Flying to San Francisco, California in 1973, on a journey to retrace the footsteps of that past life, she becomes caught up in a karmic crisis. Will she overcome the temptations that led to her premature death in the previous lifetime or suffer the same fate once more?

Have you ever wondered about the ultimate purpose for your life? Why are some people so lucky, their every need seemingly supplied, while others struggle under impossible conditions meeting every kind of misfortune? The Eastern religions call it karma and possibly by seeking to know and understand the distant past, we can reconcile with ourselves and advance to a brighter future. This book is a search for truth by a young woman, not only for evidence of a previous lifetime, but also for the meaning of life itself. Come along with her on an adventurous journey and you will not only be fascinated, but you just might be inspired to "Go Back Jack" and find out the truth about yourself!

Table of Contents

"Those who cannot remember the past
are condemned to repeat it."
--*George Santayana (1863-1952) Life of Reason*

Old Photo of Hobo

Chapter One

Journey into the Past

Who am I?

Don't ask me who I am
Ask those who have lived before
Ask the leaves and the trees that watched me come and go
Ask the fields where I ran barefoot in summer, as a laughing
*   child*
Ask the rock whose crevice contains my diary, hidden still
Ask the tree that bears my initials
Ask them, and they might tell you
That I've existed since time began
Just as they have.

So long ago, it seemed like an echo in my memory, I heard a voice–I presume it was my own–pleading urgently, "This time, give me something to remember. Give me knowledge, so I won't make such a drastic mistake again. Let me help others to understand also, and give me a chance to help someone who is like I was."

Birds singing, winds gently whispering, nature in perfect innocence was enjoying an endless summer's day in paradise. A small group of people stood at the far end of a grassy meadow bordered by forest. Beside them, a shimmering, turquoise lake reflected a sky that seemed to glow with rainbow crystals in constant motion. A young, black, Hispanic man, Michael

Jacksonish in appearance, dressed as if he'd stepped out of a 1930s soup-kitchen line, was deeply involved in a heated discussion with Angela, a young woman, a vision of ethereal, blond beauty.

"Don't make me go back, Angela. I'll do whatever it takes. Just don't send me back!"

"You can't stay, Nick. It's not up to me. It's been decided. You have unfinished business—but I'll always be with you, even though you can't see me."

She gazed at Nick with sympathetic eyes and hugged him reassuringly, then vanished among the crowd of people he knew to be friends, slowly retreating.

"Please," he cried out in anguish to them, but he knew that he had no choice in the matter. He had been overruled by a presence higher than his own who knew what was best for him. He would begrudgingly call Them "The Council," but he would not call Them God. He was alone now with his thoughts, a sense of deep sadness in his heart, resigned to fate, and then he seemed to experience a falling sensation, as if he were tumbling down, head over heels, through a tunnel of darkness.

Steeltown Hamilton

In Steeltown Hamilton,
I see skyscrapers shrouded in low hung fog
Deserted, boarded up buildings haunted by airborne pollution
Furnace factories laboring through the night
Shift workers coming up Wentworth and James
A workman's town,
The lunch bucket crew
Loading up on beer when the working day is through
Jolly Cut on the mountain, coming down, hugging the hill at
    night

The city lights spread out below
Dofasco, Stelco, where sparks and cinders fly
Steel dust and smoke in my eyes
Both the steel and the city lights glow
In Steeltown Hamilton.

Christmas, pre-dawn, on Wilson Avenue, in Ancaster, just outside Hamilton, Ontario, 1954 suburbia. The moon shimmered silently over fresh snow on the front lawn. Inside the two-story brick and wood home, a massive Scotch pine in the living room twinkled with multi-colored lights and ornaments, almost entirely blocking the view of a snow-covered front lawn. Perched atop the tree, a delicate, golden star illuminated the shadows, now quickly fading into daylight.

A precious moment of silence was broken before the excited shouts of my eight-year-old brother, Bob Kellar, thumping down the stairs, burst into the room. A two-and-a-half-year-old toddler, Maureen Kellar, a.k.a. Minnie, I was in the arms of my father, Ken Kellar, standing beside my mother, Eileen, in front of this splendid Christmas tree, surrounded by huge piles of Christmas presents.

My eyes were focused on one tiny, red piano poking out from the branches at the base of the tree. Screaming in excitement, I ran toward it and grabbed it. My fingers found the keys and the touch, somehow, felt familiar. I banged the keys, "tink, tink, tonk", "tink, tink, tonk", amid the shouts and laughter.

Bob howled in delight, a new bike! He flitted about the room, ripping wrapping paper off gift after gift, and dumped his assorted treasures from the Christmas stocking, hung at the fireplace mantel, licorice candy, peppermint, oranges, a deck of playing cards, socks, coloring pencils, comic books. It was a veritable feast and a celebration this Christmas.

My gaze turned toward my mother, as she modeled a new Persian lamb fur coat for my father, who watched admiringly. She strutted across the room in Hollywood mode. My father, a handsome and self-made man, reflected the arrogant confidence of one who has overcome the poverty of his Irish farming roots.

My father, Ken Kellar, in his home office of Kellar Steeplejack's Ltd. In Hamilton, Ontario in the late 1950's.

His was a rags-to-riches story. Before serving as a radio operator in the Second World War, with the Algonquin Regiment, 4th Armored Division, he had crossed Canada as a steeplejack, climbing bridges and tanks, taking the most dangerous jobs, learning the ropes, before starting his own business and meeting my mother. She was a young mother, ten years younger and disillusioned by a previous marriage to a cheating husband. She was living with her father and her young son, Bob, working in a factory when they first met on a blind date, and it was love at first sight.

My father had also been married before, to a wife who squandered his pay while he was risking his life in the trenches of war overseas. They had parted, long before I was born. There had been no children from the relationship. I was Ken and Eileen's first child, born outside of a legal marriage. My father was already thirty-five and more than ready to start a family. It was taboo in the early 1950s to have a child out of wedlock–a disgrace, a rebellion against the norm–but my father was a natural rebel, and the lack of approval from the institution of marriage didn't sway him.

Legal marriage to my mother would have to wait a few more years, until the divorce papers were final, and without a doubt, she trusted him. However, it wouldn't be until six years later that they were finally given the green light and were officially married at City Hall, shortly before my sister Kathy was born.

I soon tired of playing with my little, red piano and saw a light shining from a crack from between the French doors at the far end of the room. It seemed to beckon to me. No one noticed as I slipped away, pushing my way through the doorway, into the kitchen. The light over the sink revealed a semi-opened cupboard door with an array of interesting bottles on its shelves. I saw a kitchen chair and knew how to maneuver it to the counter and climb up. I reached for the pretty, pink candies in one of the bottles, St. Joseph's Children's Aspirin, and climbed down, clutching my treasure.

I twisted the lid, which was loosely tightened. It slid off, without hesitation. Dumping the contents on the floor beside me, I picked up the pills, swallowing them one by one until they were all gone. Somehow, I sensed that what I had done was forbidden, but I was unaware of the danger.

Bob, now pretend aiming a new football at Dad, teasingly,

suddenly paused in mid-air, scanning the room for someone. His gaze fell on the little, red, toy piano. He picked it up, looking disconcerted.

"Mom, where's Maureen? Isn't this hers?" Mother hesitated for a moment, scanning the room, alarmed.

"She was here a minute ago, playing with her new piano."

The French doors that separated the kitchen from the living room were partially open. A dim light filtered through. My mother grabbed the handles and pulled them wide open to reveal me, pajamas covered with vomit and sobbing on the linoleum floor, the empty Aspirin bottle on the floor beside me. Behind, the chair, pulled up to the counter. The cupboard door hung open.

"Oh, my God, Ken! She's swallowed them all!"

My frantic mother, followed by my father, both stunned, watched as I vomited again onto the floor, crying.

"Christ, Eileen! You were supposed to be watching her! We'd better get her to the hospital right away."

Mother was panic stricken, disorganized.

"Bob, get dressed! Get your coat on. Hurry!"

Bob clung to his new football, reluctant to let it go. "Aw, Mom..."

How could everything so perfect have gone wrong so quickly? Perhaps it was then that I earned the Kellar family label of "shit disturber"–i.e., one who causes commotion, disruption, turbulence, in the midst of what should have been a peaceful interlude and enjoyment of life's simple pleasures.

"Bob...I need your help! Please!"

Not stopping to undress me, she threw a blanket over my shoulders. I was sleepy now and starting to fade away. Vaguely, I heard my dad revving up the car outside in the snowy driveway, and then I lapsed into complete unconsciousness.

I awoke to bright lights, glaring in my eyes. I was lying on a hospital bed in an operating room, amazed by the all-pervading light, and my stomach felt sore.

Outside in the corridor, a doctor reassured my parents.

"She's out of danger now, Mrs. Kellar. We pumped her stomach. Just watch her carefully."

And then I was three and kneeling down in front of my bedroom window on a hazy, warm, humid, Hamilton summer evening. I could smell the neighborhood scent of cut, green grass, hear dogs barking and Jimmy Day, next door, practicing saxophone with his bedroom window open. I looked up into the sky at dusk. The sun was setting over the tadpole pond, and still farther on, the woods, the ravine, and north to Dundas.

The sound of a train whistle shrieked, eerily familiar. Listening to it clickity-clacking in the distance, I was somehow fascinated and suddenly overwhelmed by a feeling of longing to go with that train, wherever it was going.

"Maureen, oh, there you are!" Mother had entered the room, searching for me. "It's dinnertime, luv."

"Mummy, the train!"

I pointed toward the window, eyes shining with excitement. She smiled at me, indulging the moment.

"Yes, dear, it's the train. It goes by every night about this time. Now come for dinner."

I looked up at her protesting, "But Mummy, I wanna go to the train."

She smiled and said, "Someday, dear, just not right now." She took me by the hand and guided me away from the window and downstairs to dinner, with the train whistle still tugging at me.

I hear that ole train whistle a comin' down the track
And I'm headin' for the track with a pack on my back
And I know that before tonight I'll see the lights of New York
*   City*
Comin' into sight.
Oh, train whistle in my mind
Oh, train whistle till I die
I'll be ridin' the rods, choking on dust
Ridin' the rods 'cause I know I must
I'll be ridin' the rods, baby, in my dreams
'Cause I'm the Billy Bo supreme!

Fast forward to the summer after I turned four, and I was climbing out of a dusty station wagon holding a plastic bag in one hand and my father's hand in the other. My face was a pale shade of green. We had arrived at the farm outside of Perth Road, Ontario, and I was going to spend the summer with my grandparents.

My grandmother Lottie, in a faded house dress and flour-dusted apron, silver-gray hair pulled back into a bun, welcomed the two of us with a smile.

"My Lord, I haven't seen you two in a dog's age. It's about time for a visit."

Then she noticed my pale face.

"Why, Ken, what's the matter with Maureen? She's greener than a swamp bullfrog."

My father replied with a slight edge of annoyance in his voice, "Well, Mother, she was sick on the way down. I had to pull over by a ditch." A look of exasperation crossed his face.

"She said she was going to throw up in the car, so I gave her a plastic bag, and she barfed in it."

"Did you give her some Gravol before?" Lottie asked.

"Yeah, the Gravol didn't work."

"Ken, were you smoking in the car again?" Lottie drilled him with her eyes, and he turned his gaze.

"Smoking? Yeah, still do, once in a while. I'm tryin' to quit."

"Well, I hope you do. It makes Maureen sick. Did you roll down the window?"

"Just a crack. Didn't want a gale wind blowing through."

Grandma Lottie shook her head, disapproval in her eyes. I hung my head nervously, glancing from one to the other, swinging the plastic bag full of vomit slowly, as if apologizing for being sick. Lottie beckoned to me, and gingerly taking the bag out of my hand, she deposited it into an old barrel beside the garage.

"Let's get you some nice, cold, well water to settle your stomach. You can dip the cup into the pail yourself. There's fresh, homemade donuts sitting in a barrel behind the old, wood stove. Don't you worry about a thing, dear. Grandma will take care of you now."

I followed my grandmother up the weedy flagstone path of a tidy, wire-fenced yard, carved out of cow pasture, sumac trees, and rock, past an old well pump and an outhouse perched on a rise on the front lawn. My dad stayed behind to pull luggage out of the trunk, then retreated to the shadows of the garage, watching them. Taking a cigarette out of his pocket, he lit it with a "Don't tell me how to raise my child" kind of look. Taking a few precious drags, then suddenly disgusted, he tossed the cigarette and ground it into the dirt.

Dad only stayed the night and left the next morning. I looked forward to spending the whole summer on the farm. I was the only one who ever wanted to go there. The poverty didn't seem to touch me. When snow drifted in between cracks in the old, log walls, I dived under the covers or warmed up at the wood stove. When flies buzzed about the kitchen, I helped Grandma hang sticky fly strips up from the ceiling to catch them. Ice cream was a real treat. Grandpa would bring out a brick and cut it into thick slices on Sundays. Grandma Lottie had a talent for baking and quilting and would sew while sitting in her rocking chair overlooking the cow pasture. The back kitchen smelled of pails of fresh cow's milk and smoke from the wood burning stove, and drifting in through the windows, the smell of cow's manure and hay. We were not only close to nature; we were essentially a part of it, drifting with the changing seasons–a world apart.

I loved the pastures, the trees, the lake, the horses, jumping into piles of hay in the hayloft with the two native Children's Aid boys that Grandma and Grandpa were fostering or spending time on the swing on the front lawn. I waded with Grandpa through a foot of cow manure in the barn to feed the pigs and sat on the hay wagon on its bumpy ride through the fields behind the draft team. Sometimes Grandpa let me ride on Queenie, holding onto the harness horns. But most of all, there was the old, upright piano in the parlor. I would spend hours plink-plonking away on its yellowed keys, sometimes picking out by ear old hymns like "Jesus Loves Me" or "Children of Salem" and other times trying to match the melodies in my mind to the keyboard in front of me.

One morning, I sat in front of a big, black, upright piano in the parlor, picking out a tune, and watching Grandma Lottie shove an apple pie into the old, wood stove in the adjoining kitchen. As my fingers wandered up and down the keyboard, I slipped into a trance-like state, almost as if I were dreaming.

Nick Jackson, a young, black man, early twenties, stood alone in a dark alley outside of an inner-city nightclub, left shirtsleeve unbuttoned at the cuff. His right hand grasped his left arm, and he leaned against the building, looking dizzy. Muffled sounds of laughter and music floated down the alley. Nick bent over and vomited behind a garbage can. A black teenager, resembling Fats Domino, coming around the corner, spied him.

"Hey, Nick, whats-a-matter? Are you sick?"

Nick nodded, his eyes closed, still leaning against the building for support.

"Are you gonna be all right?" The boy had a look of concern in his eyes.

Nick mustered a grin. "I'm okay, man."

A black musician, carrying a guitar case, stepped through the nightclub doorway leading into the alley, searching. He was a young Percy Mayfield. His gaze took in the boy talking to Nick.

"Hey, boy, your mama know you here? Nick, get a move on or I'll have to play piano for ya, and I've got a real lady waitin' inside for me...name's Isobel!"

He grabbed Nick by the arm and led him into the crowded bar where a drummer waited patiently. Isobel, the attractive black woman, all dressed up for Saturday night, sat at a side table, patiently waiting. Nick slid onto a stool at the piano and launched into the intro to his "Little Girl Blue."

Coming out of a trance, I hesitated for a moment, and as if pulling music out of thin air, I began to play the same intro. The music intrigued Lottie. She wandered over to the doorway, listening to it.

"I didn't know my granddaughter was so talented. Did you write that? What's it called?"

I could only shake my head mysteriously. "I don't know, Grandma, but I think it's called "Little Girl Blue."

Searching

Firelight in the tunnel
Energy races
Keep up the pace. Don't slow down till you've found what
*   you're searching for*
Find the door
Open up your eyes to a beautiful sunrise
We know we have been blind
See what we cannot find,
But locomotive rider in the night
Shadows in the mind, blind target found
On the edge of a precipice looking down into
Firelight in the tunnel
Curiosity propels us from flesh to dust
And beauty is in the word
And freedom, like the flight of a bird, eludes us
My friend, I cannot say there is an end, Peace.

Chapter Two

The Awakening

The rebellious teenage years.
Sitting outside our family home in Perth Road,
Ontario approximately 1968.

About a mile east of the tiny farming village of Perth Road, Ontario, a deserted rural road, bordered by split rail fences, horse pasture, and mixed Canadian forest ended in a rambling, country home, nestled among shade trees, bordered by rose gardens.

It was the summer of 1970, the year after Woodstock had rocked the nation. My father had retired early and hired local tradesmen to custom build this mansion on the site of a farmhouse that had burned down a decade earlier. Located a few minutes' drive from my grandparent's old log and stucco home, it was, what I considered, a slap in the faces of the simple people who populated the area, still struggling daily for basic survival.

Apparently, others felt the same way about it, judging from the way our school friends reacted when we brought them home. But my father hadn't considered the tragic history of the house that had previously stood there or realized its lingering influence that had already begun to touch every one of us.

Bob, who was a teenager when we left Hamilton, disapproved of the move the most. His reasoning was simple. The house was out of place in the area and would always be resented by those who felt that they couldn't compare to my father. Not only that, but it was "out in the boondocks" and socially inaccessible, unless you had your own car, which most teenagers didn't, making it a teenager's social nightmare. According to Bob, the local teens weren't the type you'd introduce your daughters to either, unless you looked forward to her having a future of milking cows and bringing in the hay. He feared for us. He often said that if he'd had that kind of money, he would have bought or built a house in a neighborhood of doctors and lawyers in order to give us better social opportunities.

Much as I'd loved visiting my grandparents at the farmhouse in the summers, I too had been upset by the move, reluctantly leaving my neighborhood childhood friends behind, in Hamilton. Kate was too young to have had ties with Hamilton, and Mother, who was Hamilton-born and a real city girl, kept a stiff upper lip and made the best of it. My brother Kenny was born several years after the "big house" was built and knew no other home.

I had become something of a poet, scribbling them down whenever they came to me, but a lot of what I wrote didn't seem to have much to do with me at all. Visions, scenes, scents and emotions all conspired to create strange prose that I kept, nevertheless.

Wanderer's Lament

I feel like a tumbleweed, racing
In a constantly drifting wind
Ecstasy is in the mountains everywhere I roam
But I can't stay long in any one place
Before nostalgic memories of other travels crowd in
And ruin my self-complacency
I don't remember belonging
Don't really care where I go
Can't remember finding peace like an ordinary man
I've covered many miles, St. Louis, San Francisco
Held no home for me
Still I keep on moving
Life's too short to waste away
On riding buses and watching television every day
New highways, new horizons now in view
I guess I'll keep on wandering—it's what I want to do.

But I wasn't a man, and I'd never been to St. Louis or San Francisco. How could I say that these cities held no home for me when I'd never trod their streets? And even stranger...

Waterfront Reflections

Something in this dark and rainy night
Brings me back to a creaking, lonely wharf
To the bumping of battered, wooden hulls
And the splashing of dark and restless waves
It brings me back to a lonely, ragged tramp
Sprawled against an empty, peeling shack
Wondering when he's ever going back
Watching the harbor lights shining on the water, black and cold
And suddenly feeling very, very old...

Who was this tramp who mourned a lonely life and estrangement from those he loved or who loved and cared about him? I would sit out in the wilderness, pad and pen in hand, and crazy words would pour onto paper, spoken deep from within my soul, that seemed alien to me.

Memories

Like Pandora's Box butterflies
Flit through my mind
Or like lightning flashes
Lifts the lid on earthly spring smells
And recollections of summer fourteen years ago
Time ceases to be the determining factor
Body ceases to be. I am a new form but an older me
Years like October leaves tumble away
My mind is enveloped in an electrical photo flash illumination
Before the scene begins to drift away.

The mystery intensified, but in the meantime, several of my poems were published in children's magazines, and time flew by, much of it spent on pony back exploring the wilderness alone.

I was now seventeen, petite but rebelliously boyish, my dark blond hair shagged short. Dressed in old bell-bottoms and a ripped, tie-dyed T-shirt, like others of my generation, I still stubbornly clung to the psychedelic '60s. My mother and I talked as we examined articles of my wardrobe spread out on the bed. Although it was the middle of July, Mother and I were already planning ahead for the fall so we could get going on shopping trips in August.

"What about this checkered skirt?" Mother suggested. "It would look nice with this beige sweater."

I protested, "Mother, but what about *winter*? Boys can wear pants. I'll freeze in a skirt and nylons!"

Mother resisted. "Maureen, Sydenham High School still has a dress code. Girls have to dress like girls."

This only infuriated me more. "Well, I didn't ask to be a girl, so why should I dress like one?" I grabbed the skirt off the bed and tossed it angrily onto an open closet floor, followed by the sweater in turn.

"I don't wanna wear these useless things!"

I stepped to the dresser drawer and pulled out a garter belt, nylons attached, and flung it behind me. I didn't see my father entering the room.

"What the hell is going on?" he roared.

I turned around to see him standing in the doorway, garter belt and nylons hanging from his shoulder. I reached up and pulled them off, laying them on the bed sheepishly.

Mother explained, "Oh, she never liked the dress code at Sydenham High. Some of the city schools are letting girls wear pants now."

Father rolled his eyes. "She was trouble from the day that she was born." He threw a look of disgust my way.

Mother rushed to my defense. "You don't understand her like I do, Ken. She's different from the others."

But father wouldn't hear it. "She's a kook, Eileen, plain and simple, catchin' frogs down in the swamp, stealing my hip waders...Why, she even studies astrology!"

Mother countered, "Frogs for you, so you can go fishing, hip waders to keep out the leeches and water snakes...and she taught herself astrology. She knows all of the signs!"

Father went on lamenting. "Pickin' blackberries and playing Mother's old piano, instead of working...there's chores to do around here. She hasn't been cleaning the dog kennels lately, I've noticed."

Mother replied, "Blackberries for your ice cream, and she plays 'Lili Marlene' on the piano, the song you love so much."

I'd heard enough. Eyes flashing, I yelled, "Stop it, both of you!"

Confronting my dad, I stared accusingly at him. "You'll never understand me!"

Bolting from the bedroom, I raced down the stairs, taking them two at a time. Exiting through a front door, I slammed it after me. At the end of the driveway, I ducked into the detached garage and grabbed a bug jacket, hanging from a hook on the wall, a frog box and hip waders. Pulling on the bug jacket, I strode down toward the pasture gate.

My younger sister Kate, age twelve, was grooming a fat, black, Shetland pony tethered under a shade tree beside the garage. Her head shaved and marred by black stitches, forming a semi-circle on one side of her head above her left ear, framed a pretty face. An English riding helmet sat propped up on a fence post beside her.

Bug proofed in my jacket, hip waders slung over my shoulder, I strode toward her, frowning. Kate looked up.

"What's wrong, Min?"

I sighed. "Everything's wrong. If you really want to know, it's Father...and the stupid school dress code. Mr. Thelan in Guidance said I've got phobias and an anxiety disorder."

Kate sympathized, "Hey, Min, I didn't know you were messed up. As the old saying goes, "You can catch more flies with honey than with vinegar."

"Yeah, well, it's gonna take more than honey to catch that fly...and Kate..."

Kate smiled, "Yeah, Min?"

I pointed to the pony's legs, a look of warning in my eyes. "Put that helmet on, and keep away from those hooves!"

Two years earlier, Kate had been kicked in the head by one of the ponies, and my parents had made a mad, life-and-death dash to the hospital in Kingston, a half-hour away, to attempt to save her life.

Luckily for us all, a neurosurgeon was on call in Emergency that day and operated on Kate, saving her life. Or was it all the prayers that we offered up to God that day that saved her? We'll never know. But what followed were years of follow-up operations and medications to control the seizures that now plagued her. Through it all, Mother stood loyally by Kate's side. I'm sure that she did her best to give us the attention that was left over.

Taking another worried glance at Kate, I headed off into the bush, searching for frogs. I'd been able to start a little bait business of my own, and in a rare moment of proud encouragement, my father had built me a "holding station"–a big, wooden bin that I would deposit the frogs into until I was able to sell them. Sometimes I caught them expressly for his own fishing trips.

Later that day, I wandered along a stretch of railway tracks along a cat-tailed, swampy edge of an inland lake, in oversized hip waders, breathing in heat waves of hot tar and railway ties, swinging the frog box, humming softly to myself.

Searching for frogs in the marshy grass, I spied a green leopard hopping, just the right size, not too big and not too small. Slipping in front of it, I reached forward and cupped my right hand over it, surprising it into surrender. Pulling it gently out from under with my left hand, I held it up by the legs, upside down. Froggie jerked wildly, trying to break free.

"Gotcha, ya little devil!" I shoved the frog into the box and listened to it thump, thumping against the wooden sides.

Suddenly, the shrieking whistle of a CN locomotive coming around the bend broke the silence. A freight train, loaded with flatcars and cargo containers, stretched as far as the eye could see. As it barreled down on me, in a startled moment, I dropped the frog box. Falling over my own feet, I scrambled up the rock face beside the tracks as the train thundered by, clinging for dear life to the jagged edges.

I was breathless, fascinated, focusing on the boxcars, piggybacks, oil tankers and hoppers, wheels and couplings, rumbling past. And as the train disappeared from view and I slide back down onto the grass flat, I gazed after it, almost as if it were the first train I'd ever seen.

It was late when I arrived home. Coming up the driveway, swinging the frog box, a big grin on my face, I was dirty and sweaty. The hip waders over my shoulders were covered in stinky swamp mud, but I was happy. The catch had been successful. The box was filled with green leopard frogs.

But my father didn't see it that way. Coming down the driveway toward me, he took one look and..."You've been down in the swamp again. Look at you! You're a Goddamn mess. Those are my hip waders. I've been looking for them."

My eyes averted his gaze, and I replied, "Yeah, I'll clean 'em off and..."

He interrupted, "You sure as hell better, and put them right back where you found them."

Startled, I responded, a hurt expression in my eyes. "The frogs are for you." I held the pail out to him. He took it, looked inside, and shook his head, dissatisfied. He handed it back. "Too big! The big ones'll eat the little ones, and the fish won't bite 'em. Let 'em all go."

Tears springing to my eyes, I cried, "After all that work? You build me a frog box, tell me to go look for frogs, and then criticize me for catching them? I can never please you! You let them go!"

I tossed the frog pail and the hip waders onto the gravel driveway. He missed the box, and it tumbled onto the ground, springing the lid open. The frogs, taking their opportunity for freedom, hopped away. Looking on tearfully, I turned and raced up the driveway. Yanking open the front door, I bolted inside and slammed it after me.

Running up the winding staircase, crying, taking the steps two at a time, I bumped into older brother Bob, standing on the landing. He gazed at me sympathetically.

"Did he call you a loser?" he asked.

"Might as well have," I replied, shrugging my shoulders.

Bob sighed. "Me too. I'm leaving tomorrow. Can't stick around here any longer. I'm going back to Hamilton to look for a job."

I wasn't prepared for this. "What about university? You're in mid-term."

Bob looked hopeless. "I'm dropping out."

"He'll be pissed," I warned. "He won't understand."

"Nothing new," Bob shrugged, smiled, giving me a big brother hug. "Look me up in Hamilton, if you ever get there."

I bolted into my bedroom and shut the world outside. Sprawling across the bed, I turned over onto my back, eyes begging the ceiling.

"God, why me? Why is he always so unfair? Things happen for a reason. I *know* they do."

My hand knocked a Holy Bible off the bedside table onto the floor. It dropped open at Matthew 7. Reaching down to grab it, my eyes rested on Verse 7. I picked it up and read aloud.

"Seek and ye shall find. Knock and the door shall be opened unto you."

Pausing for a moment, pondering the meaning of the message, I shut the book carefully and tucked it into the table drawer. Shivering, I pulled a sheet over myself and cried myself to sleep, still fully dressed as the daylight faded. Dinner went on without me.

Hours later, dreams came restlessly to me. A full moon illuminated the night sky through a window, curtains pulled aside. It lit up the room and reflected the glow of the tiny, silver cross on the necklace around my neck.

Nick Jackson sat at the piano in the back of a dusty, bare planked room, empty glass in his hand. Depression era crowd conversation drifted across the room. The door swung open and more black hobos wandered in, just off the trains, sweating, dirty, and tired. They slugged down beers at the bar. Nick stared at a pretty, young, black woman sitting alone at a table by the wall. An old black bartender, wrinkled and gray at the edges, smiled at Nick and plunked down another drink on top of the piano. "Here, Nick, dis'll chase your blues away."

Nick looked up and grinned. A front tooth was missing, and a silver cross that he wore around his neck reflected the light.

"Who she?" Nick asked, pointing to the woman.

"Oh, dat's Sandra. She allays in trouble. Her man beat her up."

Sandra, sensing that she was being discussed, turned and looked their way. A sad, pretty face was marred by a big, black eye. Nick smiled, "Well, I've got a song for the pretty lady." And he launched into the romantic, sentimental

"Little Girl Blue" singing:

I see you, little girl blue
Are you sad, are you sad, are you sad, sad and lonely too?
Have you been looking for some one
Could it be, could it be, could it be,
That that someone is me, girl?"

The words were still on my lips as I awoke, mumbling in a sweat, shaking. A wave of nausea swept over me as I jumped out of bed and dashed to the bathroom, vomiting into the toilet.

A moment of calm followed as I sat huddled on the bathroom floor. I wiped my mouth with a washcloth and slipped out of the bathroom, shutting the door behind me. I tiptoed down the stairs to the rec room and slid onto the stool in front of the old piano, singing "Little Girl Blue." A moment later, I looked up to see Mother, in robe and slippers, smiling and standing in the doorway.

"Maureen, you're still dressed! I thought you'd gone to sleep hours ago. That's a pretty song. I don't think I've heard it before."

I admitted, "It's been in my head since I was little, but I had a dream...I know the words now."

Mother looked at me, a puzzled expression on her face. "I've been listening..."

I went on, "I know. Dad just slams the door, so he can't hear me playing." I slumped on the stool, running my fingers through my hair, discouraged.

Mother paused a moment, choosing her words carefully. "You know, Maureen, your father really means well. It hasn't been easy for him since Kate's accident."

This hit home. I guess I could understand. "She should have been wearing a helmet..."

Mother argued, "Even with a helmet, things happen and your dad just lost the cottage on Slide Lake because of the government expropriation. He's not the only one they've done this to. There have been a few neighbors in this area but others got off scott-free and your father has suspicions about political maneuvering. I hear that they're going to call it Frontenac Provincial Park.

Mother gazed at me with sympathetic eyes.

You know, with all that's happened, he's just not been himself. He lost a fortune you know. He had plans for that land and for us."

I felt a twinge of guilt for targeting him. "Yeah, we've had some hard times lately."

Mother went on, "You've got a special gift for music, Maureen. Keep working on it...just not in the middle of the night."

"Yeah, thanks, Mom, I will."

Mother turned, her finger poised over the light switch. "Oh, and by the way, Maureen, the dentist's office phoned today. I'll have to take you in. You'll need a root canal soon."

I smiled, self-consciously, touching a finger lightly to a front tooth that was slightly darker than the rest. "...or I'll lose it. Imagine me with a tooth missing in the front. Scare off all the boys–I'll never get a date then."

I pulled away from the piano, giving Mother a big hug as she turned off the lights, and we made our way up the stairs to bed.

Maureen at her Grandmother's old piano 1960's barefoot
as Nick probably was growing up during
The Great Depression.

Summertime in the bush was the best time for riding. Like a bat out of hell, bareback on my gray, Welsh, pony cross-mare, I raced down an old jeep road, deep in the forest, dodging branches, clumps of dirt and stones flying.

A sagging, wooden gate rose ahead at the end of lane. With a slap of the reins, I urged the mare forward, and she took the fence effortlessly.

There were thick bushes overgrowing the road ahead, so she slowed from a gallop to a trot, now stumbling. As I brought her down to a walk, we maneuvered the bush, getting denser toward the lake appearing in the distance.

We emerged into a clearing. A log cabin nestled among the trees by an isolated lake looked out at a wooden dock, jutting out from the shore. A canoe was overturned on top and beside the cabin, a woodpile and outhouse.

Pushing through the bushes over the rocks, I picked up a piece of rotted plywood from the ground, examining it closely, then dropped it hurriedly and stepped back as a swarm of beetles emerged from the underside. I turned and approached the cabin. The shutters were closed and the door padlocked. I stepped back for a moment, admiring my father's workmanship, then jiggled the lock, but it held firm.

As I stepped forward, my foot kicked a metal sign, buried in the tangled grass. I moved the grass aside with my shoe carefully and studied the faded words, "Property of Ken Kellar." I sighed sadly and closed my eyes, as if in meditation. I could hear the wind swaying the branches of the pines around me, the waves lapping against the shore, a pair of loons calling out to each other, a bullfrog croaking. There was only precious silence, except for the sounds of nature and my pony snorting, swatting flies with her tail, ripping lakeshore grass.

Talking to my pony, I spoke aloud. "I used to swim across this lake, spend all summer in the woods..." I gave her a slap on the rump, looking pensive and continued, "Not anymore, girl. They took it away from us." The mare nodded her head up and down, as if in agreement.

I untied the reins, grabbed her mane, and swung myself up. Gathering up the reins, I took one last thoughtful gaze at the cabin and lake before heading back through the bush at a trot. Arriving back home, hair tangled wildly from the wind, dusty, and sweating, I pulled the bridle off the pony and turned her back out to pasture. I hung up the bridle on a hook on the side of the detached garage. The yard was deserted, and that was fine with me. I stomped in through the attached garage into the kitchen hallway, wiping the dust from my pants, kicked off my shoes, hung up my jacket and peeked inside. The kitchen was empty.

I hesitated for a moment, hiding a secret that I could not reveal. I was planning on running away to the Strawberry Fields Rock Festival with my friend Mike that weekend. The hippies were gathering for a celebration of peace, love, and music. I'd missed Woodstock in the U.S.A. the year earlier, but I wasn't going to miss this once in a lifetime chance to "be a part of the hippie scene," so I pulled open the fridge door and grabbed a mickey of Jack Daniel's and a can of ginger ale and slipped them under my shirt. I wasn't about to begin this adventure without a drink to celebrate.

Strawberry Fields Rock Festival

Chapter Three

The Strawberry Fields Rock Festival

Mind Experience

*Shimmering, rainbow colored airwaves are blown, fragmented,
   in the breeze*
Ringed round with blue and gold
*Distorted sound, touching tenderness, feeling, swelling,
   bursting with life*
*In the heat of the day, the hot sun beats down upon the dusty
   road*
Fire, water and music flow together as they always have before
My head is spinning. Time has slipped away
Heavy emotions drifting up from the oneness that is me
People cannot see, day trip, night trip, ego trip, any trip
I cannot speak, but wonder why too many times
*Female breasts, nude in the hot sun, male hair, flowing with
   sweat*
Star crystals in the sand
*God has reached down and touched the Woodstock Nation with
   His gentle, guiding hand*

Mike and I arrived at the Mosport Park Raceway, in Bowmanville, Ontario, the next day, following the signs and the crowds heading for the Strawberry Fields Rock Festival. John Brower, in tandem with John Lennon and Yoko Ono, had planned this festival for July of 1970 but running into problems, John and Yoko dropped out. Brower moved ahead, finally disguising the event as a championship motorcycle race with contemporary entertainment. I'd never been to a rock festival. In fact, I'd never been to a rock concert of any kind, but I felt I knew that the "hippie movement" wouldn't last much longer. Woodstock had been the big climax, last year on the American side, and I wanted to be a part of the action, even if just for a weekend.

I'd told my parents that I was going to spend the weekend at my girlfriend Beth's house but instead, picked up my sometimes friend Mike in Inverary, and we headed up the 401. It was the first time I'd driven the 401. In fact, I'd never been out of Kingston before, but the thrill of the adventure overrode any hesitation that we might have had.

Mike and I, wide-eyed and amazed, "babes in the woods," followed the crowds, in the heat of the day, over dusty roads, passing a kaleidoscope of hippie vehicles, campsites, peace signs and American flags, and parked under some shade trees, digging the tantalizing strains of rock music pounding in the distance. Our favorite bands booked to play were Procol Harum, Jose Feliciano, Ten Years After, Jethro Tull, Grand Funk Railroad, Crowbar, Lighthouse and more–all big named talents.

Mike was a young, James Dean type, always "riding on the edge of life," half-drunk, half-stoned, and "rebel without a cause." High on cheap liquor and excitement, he suddenly lost interest in me and decided to "take off." Shouting at me, with stars in his eyes, he yelled, "See ya later, Min, back at the car."

"Sure, Mike, sure," I mumbled, slightly annoyed as he disappeared into the crowd. I began my own explorations.

Just over the hill, I came across a hippie vending booth, manned by a long-haired American freak dressed in a Vietnam War field jacket and Hendrix T-shirt. He smiled down at me benevolently.

"Do you have any LSD?" I asked. I'd never used any, but it had a tantalizing reputation, and it was one drug I wanted to try. In fact, LSD *was* the hippie movement, a ticket to magic land, I'd heard.

The pusher leaned toward me and whispered, "Got Purple Micro Dot, girl. Made in a lab, real pure. Ran out of Sunshine this morning." He narrowed his eyes. "Be careful. You ever dropped acid before?"

I shrugged sheepishly. "Can't say that I ever have." The pusher explained, "You only want to do half a tab at once. It's pretty powerful."

I smiled, paying for the foil wrapped pills. "I'll keep that in mind."

I retreated to the shadows and took half a tab as he'd advised, but when a half-hour drifted by without anything to show for it, I popped the other half and started to feel strange. Walking down the grassy pathway was like tripping the Yellow Brick Road on the way to Oz. As I approached them, tree trunks started to melt in front of me, but it was all a part of the trip. Hippies approaching me, flashed their peace signs at me and smiled, their faces dripping like candle wax. The very atmosphere vibrated with a strange mix of rock music, idealism, and the bizarre. The air was filled with heat waves and dust. I plodded along on what seemed to be a never-ending journey, in slow motion past scattered tents, parked vehicles, campfires and flags.

Thoughts raced through my mind. "Why did you do this? Don't you know that this makes you crazy? This is the drug created in laboratories to bring sanity to the insane or insanity to the sane." For a moment, anxiety overcame me but it was lost over the desire to experience the unknown.

Over an open campfire, a half-naked American hippie, bare-chested and dressed in red, white, and blue striped pants, cooked a hamburger in a frying pan. I stopped to watch. The hamburger appeared to be alive! It was breathing as it was being flipped. And then mesmerized, I waved a hand in front of me, and five different colors flowed from my fingertips; I followed their trails across the sky.

I bent down to touch the ground, and tiny sparkle crystals skipped away like miniature snow crabs across the sand. I laughed delightedly, "Oh, WOW!" And then suddenly, I was in a shady glen in the woods, and through the bushes, I could see a pool of water and hear giggling and splashing. A group of naked men and women diving into the water were calling out to me. I waved to them as I struggled through the dense bushes shedding my clothes as I went but as I approached them, suddenly everything disappeared. Then I was on the motorcycle track, a motorcycle speeding toward me. It swerved, trying to avoid a collision but slammed into me. I felt no pain but saw fresh blood, my blood, red, pouring into the dirt and then everything went black. I was blind, but my eyes were wide open. I was conscious. I could feel my hands. I was breathing, and I was aware.

"God, *where are you?*" I screamed, into the total blackness! What had started as an adventure into a strange world of hallucinations had become a spiritual quest.

Slowly, a hand materialized in front of me, shattering the darkness, and the darkness dissolved into daylight. A face came into view. A blond-haired, young hippie with a peace sign hung around his neck gazed at me, a look of concern on his face. I glanced down and saw that he had a raging hard-on. Slowly my body, clad only in bra and underwear came into view. I felt as 'though I'd just died in a motorcycle collision and been reborn but there was not a mark on me.

Some holy rescuer this! I jumped to my feet.

What had we done, or had we done anything? A funny thought crossed my mind. What if I'd had sex for the first time and couldn't remember it?

Hippie smiled at me, a smile of relief.

"Girl, I thought I'd lost you! Found you wandering around alone in the woods, crazy right out of your head."

I gazed at him in astonishment. "Wandering around in the woods?"

"Yeah...I talked you down. That must have been some pretty heavy acid! Hey, where are your clothes?"

Dazed, still confused, I shouted. "Where are yours? Geez! I lost my pants! My car keys are in the back pocket."

"Well, girl, we'd better go and find them before someone else does."

Standing up, hippie slipped into his jeans and pulled me close, with a soul-searching kiss. I pulled back for a moment, then responded, instinctively melting, reaching out for his love, any love. It was something that I was starved for. We lingered for a moment. He caressed my hair. I could feel desire stirring my body, and I whispered breathlessly, "I think I'd better go...I don't even know your name. Where are you from?"

"Does it matter, baby?" he replied slowly. "What matters is the moment. That's all that really counts."

I considered this pensively. "I could live for moments like these."

Hippie took me by the hand and threw open the tent flap. We both slipped out into the night, alive with Sly and the Family Stone. Somewhere in the shadows, we found my blue jeans, and all was well again. The darkness itself was electrified magic. Every stranger was my friend, and we all loved one other, flashing peace signs and giving hugs. It was Heaven, like I'd always imagined it would be, and we'd all come together in a celebration of music to realize this oneness. I eventually drifted into the company of a mysterious stranger dressed in a long, black cloak, who gave me a warm, oval, stone crystal to hold in my hand, which somehow, I sensed had come from outer space. It pulsated in harmony with us as he told me a story about its supernatural powers the stone radiating a soothing, hypnotic, peaceful vibration, but then, when I turned around, it had disappeared from my hand, and the stranger was gone.

And then, slowly, the dream evaporated into reality. I found Mike sleeping it off on top of the car roof. I didn't ask where he'd been, and he was too stoned to ask me, so we stuffed a bag full of joints in the glove compartment and headed home on the weary heels of others heading for the 401. Coming down was excruciating. My head was full of another world that I didn't want to leave.

Later that day, my silver Vauxhall Viva, flower power sticker on the side, turned into the driveway, music blaring, windows rolled down. I was tired but sporting a huge grin.

My dad approached, from the garage, but he wasn't smiling.

"Where have you been?" he growled.

"Oh, I've been to Heaven and Hell and back again," I replied flippantly.

"Get in the house, and give me the keys. You're grounded."

I pulled the keys out of the ignition and tossed them out the window, onto the ground. I slid out and slammed the car door angrily and, as I was doing so, I indiscreetly pulled the small cloth bag from the glove compartment and slipped it into my purse as he bent down to pick up the keys. I marched into the house and back to my bedroom prison to trip the rest of the night away. I was still coming down, and I wanted to savor those final precious moments.

For me, the whole weekend and even the days following, remained a blur in my mind, but the magic of Strawberry Fields stayed with me, images, scenes, smells, sensations and memories of the people I'd encountered, if only briefly. For the first few days, I walked around on a cloud with a huge grin on my face that wouldn't quit. I became spontaneously creative and sat on the front veranda for hours on end sewing an old bedspread into a cloak and gathered bits and pieces of crayons to make candles. Nothing bothered me anymore, and the feeling of having touched Heaven, if only briefly, had released all of my previous fears and uncertainties. I was finally free to reach out and enjoy all that life had to offer without being held back by crippling neurosis. Little did I know it, but the LSD had also pried open the doors to my subconscious, and all sorts of strange and wonderful things were about to follow.

Chapter Four

Conversation with Jessup

In the two years following, I managed to buckle down, finish high school and one year of community college in Kingston taking general secretarial studies.

I fell in love with a married man who was separated from his wife. It took me two years to see him for who he truly was, and at that point, I knew that I'd have to set him free to go back to his wife and child. Riding on my conscience was the fact that I'd somehow been instrumental in taking him away from his family, although he'd reassured me that it had been his choice to "leave the nagging bitch," as he described her.

Still, I had nightmares in which Jesus confronted me, pointed His finger at me, and accused me of being "sanctimonious." I couldn't bear the thought of not being in God's good books, but this man was charming, he was sociable, and my family liked him, which put me in an awkward position. After two years of working and paying all of the bills on an apartment just to have a love nest for the two of us, nearly starving, while wandering across Canada with him, waiting for him to get a job, I finally understood why his marriage hadn't worked out. He wasn't willing to work and assume responsibility, and I wasn't willing to look forward to a life of supporting him, so I had to eventually turn my back on the only one who had ever shown me any real love. It broke my heart.

After that fiasco, I lost my job and drifted back into a psychedelic frame of mind, although I never took LSD again. Still, there was some comfort to be had from those memories. I found another secretarial job and moved back home again. Poetry was a way of comforting my soul, yet I often didn't understand the meaning of what I was writing until much later.

One afternoon, I sat at the kitchen table, Santana's "Black Magic Woman" drifting in the background. Grabbing my new set of pearl bongos that I'd recently bought, I jammed along with "Oye Como Va" until the song ended, then set them aside.

Making a sandwich at the counter, I sat down at the kitchen table, munching and doodling. Suddenly, the pen raced across the page scribbling parts of a letter. I looked on in amazement and read the first paragraph aloud.

February 1st, 1942:

"Jessup, do any of these strike a note with you? The Nick Jackson trio, Black Sambo Combo, South American engagements by boat. Playin' night gigs. Two on the road, four to go. Meet me in L.A., bring Sandra.

Nick

I paused a moment and then continued writing. Finishing the second paragraph, I read this one aloud also.

I'm on the road again. I'm headin' down to L.A. to pick a few up. I'm not flyin' high, man. I'm just solo flightin'. Georgia Street Blues, Belle's Bugle, and Fats Domino. No time to sleep. I upped a fifth yesterday and downed two more today. Purple pin-pricks on Sebastian Lane. You know it, man, but I'm hung up on a white cloud. Can't come down too fast. Don't wanna come down ever!

Startled, I dropped the pen and studied the page in front of me over and over again wondering where these words had come from. Who was this person, Nick, and what did he have to do with me? Was this God's answer to my prayers? Was He telling me something that I needed to know–something that would give me the reason for my years of suffering and being persecuted and misunderstood by my own family? I remembered the night that the Holy Bible had dropped open at Matthew 7, and in the wonder of it all, I sensed a plan that was coming together and meant just for me.

Kate's head injury treatment had continued with operations to replace the damaged part of her skull with a plastic plate. But through it all, she forged ahead like a trooper, never complaining, always up, although we knew that an epileptic seizure could happen at any time. We were prepared for it.

One day, I entered the book-lined den furnished with a brown leather couch and chair and built-in desk, to see Kate sitting there studying.

"How's it goin', Kate?" I asked.

Kate looked at me with a weird look in her eyes and shook her head, uncertain.

"I don't know, Min. I'm feelin' strange. Maybe it's the Dilantin again. They increased the dosage again."

Suddenly, Kate dropped the book, looking pale, and stared off into space. Her right shoulder and arm began to twitch, telltale signs of a seizure coming on.

I waved a hand in front of her eyes and eased her to the floor. I grabbed a pillow and slipped it under her head, loosened her clothing and pushed the coffee table and desk chair away from her. I knew the routine.

Kate continued to jerk convulsively, then stiffened. I opened the sliding door to the den and called out, "Mother, Mother. Kate's having a seizure!"

There was no reaction. Nobody was around. I continued to monitor Kate, watching her anxiously. She quieted, breathing more heavily. Her eyelids twitched, still closed, and then an expression of calm flooded her face, and she began to mutter in a tone of voice spookily unlike her own.

"Nick Jackson, a black musician, rode the rods during the Great Depression and died of a drug overdose."

Startled, I drew closer.

"What? What did you say, Kate?"

Kate continued, "The songs, the music will answer your questions."

I stammered, "I don't understand. Who are you?" And she replied, "Angela."

A pause and then Kate sighed. Her eyes fluttered slowly open and swept the room before coming to rest, focused on my face.

"Kate, Kate, are you all right?" I whispered urgently, but Kate brushed it off cheerfully.

"What? I'll be okay, Min."

"You just had a grand mal seizure!"

Kate smiled weakly. "I've had a few since the last operation. Sometimes it gets gray, and I don't remember."

I didn't want to interrogate her, but I had to know. "What did you mean, 'The music will answer my questions?' Who's Nick and who's Angela?"

Kate looked at me strangely, not registering the comment. "I don't know what you're talking about. Maybe you're having flashbacks from the LSD you took at that rock festival you ran away to." Kate giggled. "Maybe it did something to *your brain!*"

I shrugged it off. It didn't matter anymore if the family continued to persecute me. I was getting stronger.

"Are you sure you're all right, Kate? I called for help and

nobody came."

Kate looked at me gratefully. "You came, Min. You came."

Evenings in the countryside were always a time when nature made its presence known. The wind, the crickets, the bullfrogs, the cicadas, even dogs barking in the distance always lulled me to sleep, and I welcomed the chance to escape the day, but this particular night was restless. Parted curtains at the half-opened bedroom window waved in the fall breeze. Moonlight streamed across the bed. I tossed and turned. A train whistle shrieked eerily in the far distance and woke me up. For a moment, I was confused. My eyes scanned the room and rested on the familiar lamp, open closet, the desk, the bookshelf with my miniature china horses parading across it. No need to fear. All was well in the world. I leaned back on the pillow and fell asleep.

The next day, I was at Grandma's old piano in the rec room with a tape recorder running, practicing scales, when suddenly my fingers seemed to take on a life of their own, and I was playing a rhythm that I'd never heard before and an entire song, lyrics, and melody spontaneously dropped into my mind–something called "Morning Train."

Kate approached curiously. "Whatcha doin', Min? What kind of music is that?"

I wasn't sure what it was, but it was on tape now. I hesitated for a moment, then fumbled for a piece of paper on top of the piano. I handed it to Kate.

"I wrote this letter a while ago, but I don't understand any of it." I thrust it at her.

"Here, Kate, read it. Maybe you can tell me what it's all about. You have a talent."

Kate was surprised. "I do?"

"Just give it a try," I urged. "Will you?"

"Yeah, sure, Min, anything for you."

Kate took the letter and thoughtfully folded it, slipping it into her pocket. She dropped into an easy chair and smiled.

"Hey, Min. Let's hear some more of that boogie-woogie!"

Somehow, I felt that Kate might hold the key to the mystery of the letter fragments. How I knew this, I couldn't say. Call it a hunch or an intuition, but I really felt that Kate had a talent for visiting that gray space in between this world and the next, where information flowed, a direct result of the head injury she'd suffered. She could exist in two separate worlds, and I wanted the insight that came from her unconscious. In the interim, I was scribbling down miscellaneous, unconnected information in notebooks:

"You are the angel of my dreams. You are my heart's desire. You are the honey that draws the fly. You are my hope, my fire. So let's jug a few, baby. Let's say goodbye to our cares. We are the troubadours of time, and we can go anywhere! You ask me why I love you, but I ain't gonna try. I'd rather love and leave 'em, than face the world and die. You are my angel, my Heaven on earth. You gave the sun a chance to shine on the day of my birth." "Dimsie and Lisa (the drums). Bongo playin' in S.A."

"I was born on the bayou, babe—there, where the days are gray. We sing and dance and live our cares away, only we ain't waitin' for tomorrow."

Names of songs—"Wild, Wild Blue", "Ridin' the Rods", "White Puffy Cloud", "Little Black Girl", "Lonely Child", "Sweet Blackness", "Shadow", "Lady Blue", "Shuebey Street Blues" and "Hit the Road, Jack."

"We live fast in this business. No, I haven't had a square meal in two days. We've been gettin' it behind the counter. Sam does it. He's ours. Don't say a word or you'll have hell on

your tail. I made it man, didn't I?"

A week later, Kate settled herself into the brown leather chair in the den, pulled out the sheet of paper that I'd given her, and another one of her own, and shoved it at me.

"Here, Min, is this what you've been looking for? This might explain your letters. Yesterday I was writing an essay for school, but my hand wrote this instead." She looked puzzled.

I took the pages from her, switched on the tape recorder, and read the reply.

> **"March 15th, 1942**
>
> *Nick, South American engagements by boat is gigs at nightclubs in S.A. Get there by boat. Bring Sandra, Nick's girlfriend–1940-1941. The Nick Jackson Trio and Black Sambo Combo are bands that I, Luke, started with Nick. Two on the road, four to go are gigs. Meet me in L.A. is a song. You hung out at Santana in SF with a group called Blue Sky, one of your first songs. Don't pick up too much stuff, Nick, or you will never come down. Up a fifth, Nick! Don't try to fly, man."*

I turned to Kate excitedly. "Wow, Amazing! It completely answers the letter I gave you, and it seems to be a reply from a guy called Luke...must have been a friend of Nick's Kate? Kate?"

Kate had slipped into a trance, but this time it wasn't precipitated by a grand mal seizure. Her eyes were wide open, but Kate wasn't in there. She threw back her head, ran her fingers through her hair, and a mischievous smirk formed on her lips.

"Who are you?" I whispered.

Jessup: "Well, I'm Jessup, man. Dat's me! I'm Nick's brother."

"Well, then," I stammered, "who am I?"

Jessup laughed, "Ah, you're Nick."

"I am?" I gasped innocently. Something then tugged at unconscious, submerged memories. The dam broke. I struggled for just a moment but finally surrendered to the flow, and sinking back into my chair, I drifted with it. I was Nick, and I was back in the past.

I drawled in a heavy Southern accent, "Ya sure, Jessup? Ya sure, I'm Nick?"

Jessup: Confidently, "I'm sure."

Nick: "Is this the way it's going to be for the rest of my life, two people in one body?"

Jessup: "Well, listen, man, could be two, could be ten. I mean, dis cat, dis body you got, it's got a purpose!"

Nick: "What purpose?"

Jessup: "You're fillin' it!" Enthusiastically, "You rode dem rails! You was the best one to ride dem rails I kin' imagine!"

Nick: Beaming, "Dat's right, Jessup. I taught 'ya! Man, I wanna know–I wanna know what I looked like. Describe my physical appearance."

Jessup: "I's, you were small boned."

Nick: "Like me, like she?"

Jessup: "Yeah, not too heavyset–jus right, medium, d'ya. You were, well, how'd I say my broder's cute?"

Nick: "Good lookin?"

Jessup: "Yeah. He's the one that got most of the girls...oh well." Jessup pointed to a photo of me at age four, on the wall. "Who dat cat? Look like Nick!"

Nick: "With curls?"

Jessup: "Yes, you did." He takes a long, hard look at me, as if seeing me for the first time. "Boy, Nick, you sure have changed!"

Then Kate's face fell ever so slowly.

Jessup: "But, Nicky, you lef me in da middle of da street!"

Nick: "I'm sorry, man. Where'd I go when I first went to SF?"

Jessup: "You went straight to a nightclub called Santana and hung around with a lil boy group. What was they name? You sent me home. Dat's where you learned to play bongos, congas, and piano, some guitar too!"

Nick: "I did?"

Jessup: "Yes, and you send me home 'cause you didn't want your lil brother taggin' after ya."

Nick: "Well," I replied, "I s'pose some of the cats need company, back home. Someone has ta feed 'em!

Jessup: "Feed 'em what?"

Nick: "Oh, we used ta feed em rats...we cut 'em up."

Jessup: Laughing. "Sittin' dere cuttin' dose rats up, blood spurtin' all over da place. We set de ole dog on 'em. Remember Randy? Sic 'em, Randy, sic 'em. Oh, we sic dat dog!"

We both laughed uproariously, sharing the memory.

Jessup: "You wrote me a letter and you say dey show ya somefin' call Puffy White Cloud. Don' know what tha means. Anyway, you hocked dose bongos. I help ya."

Nick: "Yeah, we were lil rascals."

Jessup: "We were more'n lil rascals. We were juvenile d'innocents!"

Nick: "Oh, man, you gotta tell me, tell me who our Father was..."

Jessup seemed puzzled by this question. "Ah, who our Father is?"

Nick: "Yeah, our Father who Art in Heaven. Oh, I love that Pater noster qui es in caelis–"

Jessup: "Oh, you always like Latin. I remember you..."

Nick: "What?"

Jessup: "PRAYIN'!"

Nick: "Why?"

Jessup: "I dunno. I ain't got the faintest idea!"

The conversation between us was a joyful reunion at a soul level. I no longer felt strange or that I might be acting a part. This was spontaneous, and it was real, and I felt it. I leaned forward, pulling Kate close to me in a gentle embrace. Tears ran down my cheeks.

Nick: "I missed you, Jessup."

Kate closed her eyes, but tears were sliding down her face too. After a moment, she pushed back, and her head fell forward. She took several deep breaths and opened her eyes. Disoriented for a moment, she touched the wetness of tears on her face with confusion and stared at me as I wiped my face with my shirt sleeve.

"You've been crying, Min...me too, I guess. But you don't have to. I'm okay."

I smiled and let Kate assume it.

"I thought for a moment it was going to be a seizure...but it turned out to be something different," I said gently.

Kate smiled weakly. I turned off the tape recorder.

"Do you know what we were just doing?"

Kate shrugged. I unwound the tape to the beginning and played Maureen/Nick repeating the words, "Who are you? Are you Luke?" and Kate/Jessup in a deep, Southern dialect replying, "No, I'm Jessup, man! I'm Nick's broder!"

Kate looked startled, then afraid. "I don't know, Min. It sounds pretty weird. It sounds like a black boy talking. S'cuze me. I've got chores to do."

She grabbed her binder and dashed out of the room.

Chapter Five

South American Engagements by Boat

"Prior to World War Two, the use of heroin was limited, for the most part, to people in "the life"–show people, entertainers and musicians, racketeers and gangsters, thieves and pickpockets, prostitutes and pimps.

The major ethnic groups represented among these users were Italian, Irish, Jewish and Afro American (mostly those associated with the entertainment life). There were also heroin users among the Chinese, who had a history of opium use. The distribution of heroin by those who controlled the market was limited mostly to these people, and there was little knowledge or publicity about it." (From *It's So Good, Don't Even Try It Once: Heroin in Perspective* by David Eldon Smith.)

The strangeness continued, and it was as if a cloak of mysterious influence had descended over Kate and I that led us further into the depths of it. I carried the tape recorder with me, whenever I was home, because I never knew what I could capture next. One evening I sat at the piano, fingers flying over the keys, and burst into singing a song that I'd never heard before.

The West 56th Street Blues

You wake up in the morning
Flat taste in your mouth
You don't know which way you come from, north or south
It's all my fault, gettin' drunk last night
The Lord tells me what to do, but I can't get it right.

I'm walkin' down West 56th searchin' for a friend
I need someone to talk to with some time to spend
An old familiar weakness shakes me head to toe
I'm goin' to the corner where the street folks go
Chorus:
>   *56th Street Blues got me down again*
>   *Sun is gonna shine sometime, but I don't know when*
>   *56th Street Blues got me down again*
>   *Sun is gonna shine sometime, but I don't know when.*

I flicked off the tape recorder and played the song again. I shook my head, amazed. At the top of the stairs, I heard the door slam. It was Father, tuning me out, as usual. I sighed and turned to Kate who was sitting on the couch, doing her homework. Picking up an atlas lying on the floor beside her, I flipped the pages, searching for a map of New York City.

The Rand McNally had an insert street map of New York. I examined it closer and shouting at Kate excitedly, I pointed to it.

"Kate, guess what? There *is* a West 56th Street in New York City! Can you believe that?"

Kate looked up, a surprised look on her face. She was getting used to the weirdness or maybe just putting up with it. "No kiddin', Min."

One of those trance-like looks came over her, and she picked up the atlas and opened the page to a map of the U.S.A., Mexico, South America and the Caribbean. Taking a pen, she traced a route on the map, across the U.S.A., starting from San Francisco to San Diego, and following the U.S.A./Mexican border, to Brownsville, Texas.

She spoke carefully, as if she were giving directions to a stranger. I turned on the tape recorder again.

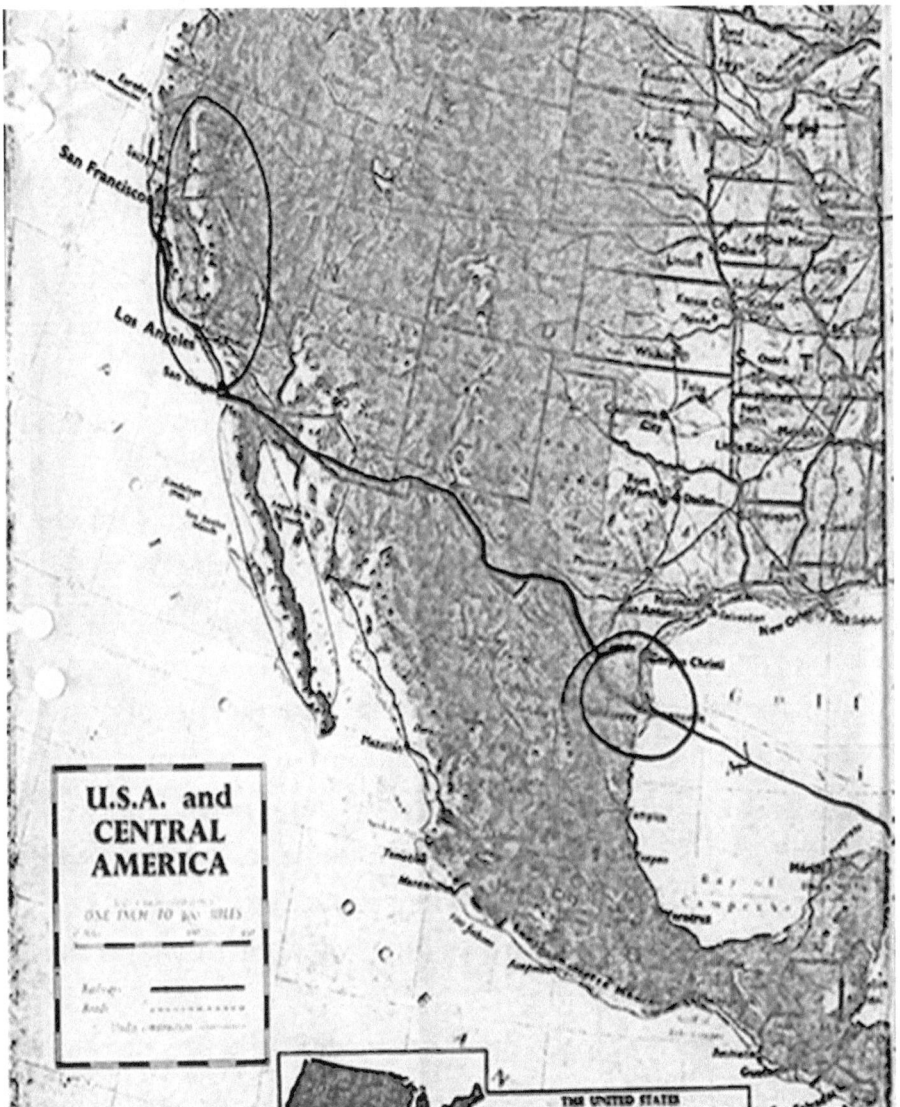

U.S.A. and CENTRAL AMERICA

"Coming down from San Francisco to San Diego, he crossed the border to Mexico at Brownsville, Texas, and boarded a ship bound for South America and the Caribbean." Tearing a blank page out of her school notebook, she scribbled down the names of cities–Tobago, Barranquilla, Columbia, Venezuela and Port of Spain, Trinidad.

She explained, "Nick played small towns on the southeast side of South America but only touched the coast with his music."

Making a semi-circle around the Caribbean and the Bahamas, she circled Puerto Rico and Miami. Her fingers flew as she alternately scribbled down names and traced a railway route.

"He toured the Caribbean and then headed for Miami, up the East Coast of the U.S.A. to New York City by rail."

She paused for a moment, taking a breath and continued on.

"But Nick never left New York. He died of a drug overdose in a hotel near Washington Square just off West 56th Street."

I looked at her, a little suspiciously. "How do you know that? You're not in a trance now."

Kate replied, "I don't know, but someone is guiding me to tell you this. Funny, but I keep hearing the song the 'West 56th Street Blues.' He bought his heroin in New York. That was what the song was all about..."goin' to the corner."

I jumped in, "And that's why the song will never be mine, but the music *does* answer my questions! It's not my song, and I couldn't write it because I've never done heroin, and I'm not a junkie. Don't you see, Kate? These songs prove the existence of someone separate from me. They prove Nick's existence."

Kate drew a picture of a road sloping down to a railway crossing between two cliffs and marked it with an X. Two cars were approaching each other from opposite directions on either side of the railway crossing.

I studied the drawing. "Wow! What's this all about–the map, the drawing?"

"Here is where Nick's diary is buried," she explained. "My hand just took off on its own again. Maybe it's Angela."

I pondered for a moment. "I think it's called automatic handwriting. I've read about it. It's an occult technique–a way for the spirits to guide us and give us information."

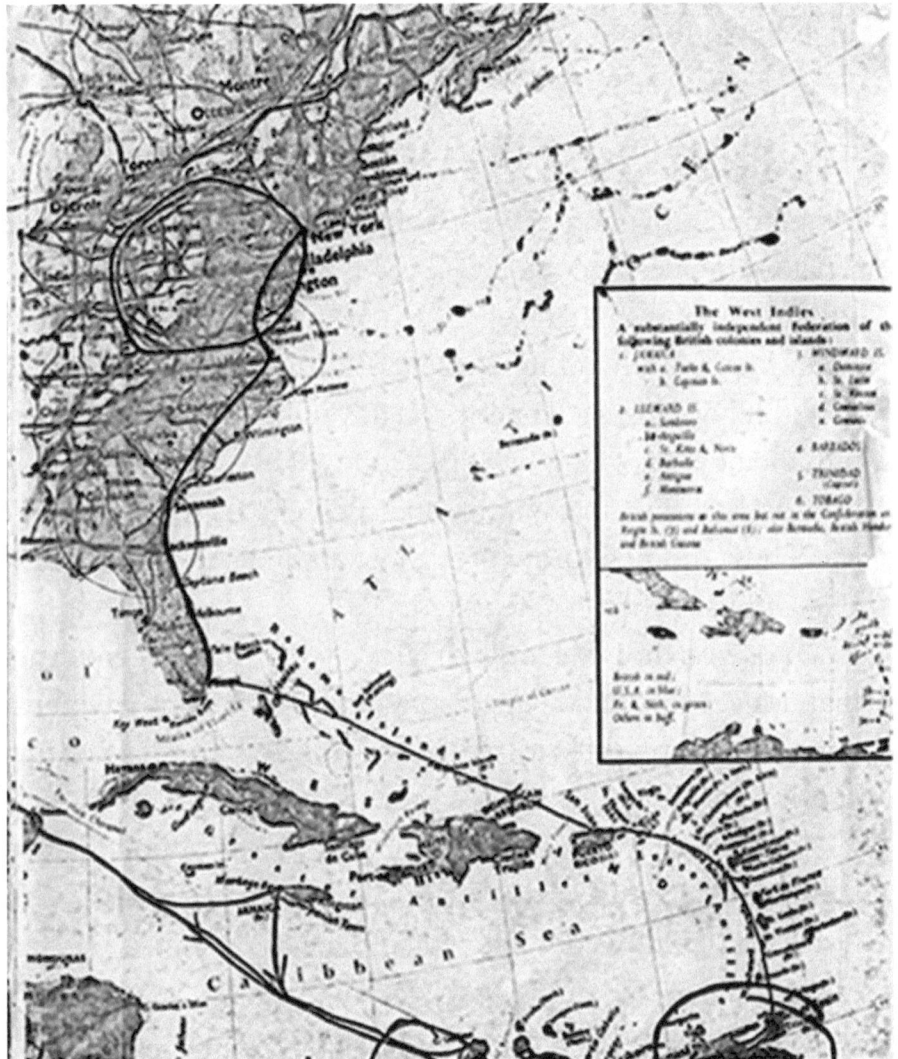

I paused briefly and reflected. "So, what am I supposed to do?"

Kate spoke slowly, a little uncertain. "I don't know, but I get the feeling that you're chosen to go. Someone's telling me."

A look of surprise crossed my face. "Chosen to do what, search for the diary?"

Kate replied, "I don't think so. Follow this route. Play his music. Go back, Jack, and do it again."

"So, you are saying that I'm being given a chance to go back and live Nick's life over again. Why should I do that?"

Kate continued, "It's called karma, I'm being told. Wipe his slate clean and set yourself free. You and Nick are one and the same."

I considered this. "And what if I don't? That's really dangerous, traveling alone to those places, and how will I know what to do once I get there?"

Kate sighed as if she were a teacher trying to get a point across to an uncomprehending student. "It'll just happen, Min, and if you don't do this, he'll haunt you throughout this lifetime or even into the next one! Don't worry. God will be with you!"

I paused, lost in thought, and then changed the topic. "Hey, Kate, how did you know that 'Meet Me in L.A.' was a song?"

"Did I say that?" Kate asked.

"Yes, you did. The reply to Nick's letter that you gave me says that 'Meet Me in L.A.' was a song, not a travel arrangement. The letter I gave to you said, 'Meet Me in L.A.,' but I never implied that it was a song."

I pulled a tape cassette out of my pocket, slipped it into the tape recorder, and turned it on. A hauntingly beautiful song, lyrics and melody complete, filled the air.

Meet Me in L.A.

Rollin' along down by the sea, moonlight in a dream
What does it all mean?
Meet me in L.A.
Ocean pass by, stars in a clear sky
Two on the road, four to go
Chorus:
> *Meet me in L.A.*
> *Whatcha be wearin'?*
> *Baby, I'm comin', baby, I'm comin' home."*

"What's that?" Kate asked. "I've never heard that before, and you've never been to L.A."

"That's the song 'Meet me in L.A.,'" I replied proudly. "It came to me yesterday afternoon when you were in school, and I recorded it."

Kate shook her head and smiled. "You're amazing, Min!"

There seemed to be a purpose to the strangeness that was gaining momentum and taking the shape of a plan. I had been chosen to be illuminated and given a choice. I could either "Go back, Jack" and do it again or continue on with my life as Maureen and hope for the best. If I went back, I might be able to pay off Nick's karma sooner and that would free me to continue on and begin a new life as Maureen.

At the same time, I was flattered. How many people had been given a second chance to get it right? How many people had been given the knowledge of their past life and an opportunity to correct their mistakes while being completely aware of what they were doing? It would be something like watching a movie and playing a part in it at the same time. The thought tantalized me.

I was also terrified. I was only nineteen, just a country girl from Ontario, Canada, turning twenty. I'd never been to California, Mexico, South America or the Caribbean and would have to do this alone, to boot! And I couldn't tell anyone why I was going or what I was going to do. They'd think I was crazy, and my family already had their suspicions. No one except Kate would ever know. Would they even let me go? They couldn't stop me. I was now legally an adult.

And so, I made my decision. I saved the money that I had made working as a typist in Kingston, got my shots and my passport, and booked my flight to San Francisco. Then, one day when we were gathered for dinner, I announced my plans to the family.

"Mom, Dad, I've saved up enough money for a trip to the U.S.A. I've finished school. I'm an adult now…"

Mother protested, "But, Minnie, you've never been outside of Canada on your own."

I reassured her, "Mother, I'll be fine. Lots of kids are on the road these days with a knapsack. It's the hippie movement!"

Mother was full of fears. "And dear, your stomach…you still suffer from car sickness!"

Dad cut in with, "What about finishing college?"

I hesitated, "Not now. I'm not sure what I want to do."

He continued, Kate's talking about taking a BA in Music." He turned to Mother, a look of suspicion in his eyes. "She's running away to another rock festival to take more drugs with the hippies."

"Ken," Mother shot him a warning look, "you'll never forgive her for that, will you? Don't jump to conclusions!"

I rushed in, "Mother, he's doing it again! He doesn't trust me!"

I jumped up from the table, knocking dishes flying, and dashed out of the dining room and up the stairs. Mother turned to Father angrily. "Why do you say such things, Ken? You know it upsets her. You'll drive her away, just like you did Bob!"

Tearfully, she pushed her chair away from the table and followed me.

Later that evening, I tossed and turned, restlessly. A clock ticked quietly on the dresser drawer beside my pearl bongos, its florescent hands pointing to midnight, and finally I fell into a deep sleep.

Outside New Orleans, on a share-cropping farm, Annie Jackson, a thin, tired-looking black woman, leaned out of the doorway of her shanty, searching for her twelve-year-old son Nick.

"Nick Jackson, where are you, boy? Neighbor Pete wants you to pick his cotton. Gonna pay us today. We got to eat, Nick."

Nick and Jessup, twelve and ten years old, giggled from behind a corner of a chicken shed, a short distance from the house, fishing poles in hand. Nick flashed a wicked grin to Jessup. He was missing a front tooth. Jessup was missing two.

Nick whispered slyly to Jessup, "Don' say a word, Jessup. Catfish jumpin' in da pond today. You know ole Pete ain't gonna pay us for pickin' no cotton. He neva pay."

Jessup agreed, "Yeah, you right, Nicky!"

Nicky continued, "One thing I know. Catfish'll fill our bellies tonight cause Pete ain't gonna. Let's go. Don' let Mama see ya."

"Okay, Nicky." Jessup giggled. "Comin' right behind."

The two boys made a dash across the meadow beyond the shed. Annie caught a glimpse of them as they disappeared behind the hill and yelled after them, "Damn it, Nicky! Gonna smack yo little black ass when I catches ya. Smack ya silly! Yess'n, I will!"

Nicky called out to Jessup as they took off over the meadow toward the pond, "Cep she won't catch me. I run too fas'." Soon they were splashing, swimming and diving, ducking and pulling each other under. Later they climbed back up onto the bank and got to work fishing for catfish. It was almost evening by the time they sneaked back across the meadow with a string of catfish, tiptoeing past Annie, who was snoring away in an old rocking chair out on the front porch, where she'd set up guard to watch for them.

They were almost past when Annie woke with a start. She grabbed Nick's hand, and the catfish thumped to the floor. Jessup made a fast beeline for the bedroom in the back of the shanty that he shared with Nick, leaving Nick prisoner, Annie still gripping him.

Annie's voice had a threatening tone. "That it, boy! You ain't nothin' but trouble, jus like yo daddy. I neva should a mix with a Mex', lazy, good fer nothin' mendigo."

She dropped Nick's hand, disgusted, and tugged at her sweater, folding her arms across her chest protectively as if she were shutting out the memories.

The insult wounded Nick. His eyes reflected the hurt, but he flashed an aim-to-please smile at Annie, nevertheless.

"We was catchin' dinner for ya, Mama. Got dese big dandy cats!" he said proudly, pointing to the fish lying in a heap on the floor.

Annie barely gave them a glance. "Catfish again? I was gonna buy us some ham hocks with the money you was supposed to make pickin' cotton."

Nick continued to placate Annie. "Lots of catfish, Mama. Don' need no ham hocks. Learnin' how to play boogie-woogie at the juke down the road. Joe teaches me. Wrote a song called 'Little Girl Blue.'"

Annie sniffed haughtily. "Play yo boogie-woogie, boy, and maybe you see yo daddy in the juke too or on the road to Tijuana. Don' you know it's a Depression happenin'?"

Annie looked Nick straight in the eye, a look of contempt on her face, and for a moment, it wasn't Nick she was looking at; it was Jack Juarez, her irresponsible husband, she was talking to.

"Hey, Jack! You listen real good. Hit the road, Jack, an' doncha come back no more!"

"But my name ain't Jack, Mama. I ain't my daddy," Nick pleaded to Annie, who was lost in the past.

"Yes, you is. You jes like 'im. He jus run off. That all he do."

"No, Mama," Nick reassured her, "he out lookin' for work. I knows it."

Annie snorted, "Hmmmph! He neva work a day in 'is life. You kin pack yo bags anytime, boy, and I won't be lookin' for ya no way neither!"

Annie stared ahead, stone-faced and silent. Nick turned away, defeated. Leaving the catfish on the floor for Annie to deal with, he opened the door to the shanty bedroom where Jessup was hiding out and closed it slowly behind him. Crossing the room, he stopped. His eyes rested on an old photo on the wall of Jack Juarez, a Mexican sharecropper, dressed in farmer's overalls, standing beside the shanty. He was holding baby Nick in his arms.

A shadow of a smile crossed Nick's face for a moment. Then his eyes swept the room and saw Jessup passed out on the old feather bed.

Tiptoeing past him, Nick climbed out of the open window and hurried down a dusty dirt road. Not far away, beside the bayou, a weather-beaten juke came into view. Nick rapped on the door, and an old, black man, Joe, leaning on a cane, poked his head out and smiled.

"Hey, Nick! Where y'at?"

"Kin I play some, Joe?" Nick asked.

"Sho can, boy. Nobody here. Come right on in."

Nick settled himself at the old, black, upright piano in the corner and played a few bars of boogie-woogie. Joe's pride was obvious.

"Jus like I taught 'ya. You learn fas', boy."

Nick grinned back, basking in the old man's praise. Joe stepped in and played a duo on the upper octave. As the two pounded the keyboard, it was obvious that Nick had found someone who truly believed in him.

After they finished playing boogie-woogie, Joe retreated to a corner of the room for a smoke, and Nick lingered at the piano for a moment, picking out a new tune and putting words to it.

Morning Train

I see the morning train
See through the misty rain, I hear it comin'
Mama says I'm too wild
I'm jus a homeless child, that's all I am
I'll hit the road someday
But I'll be back this way, oh, yes I will
I'll catch the mornin' train
I'll catch the mornin' train...
I'll catch the mornin' train.

A week later, streaks of red in the early morning sky blended into retreating shadows over a weedy garden, a rusty topped and tilted chicken shed, and the ramshackle farmhouse, as Nick and Jessup slipped quietly out the front door. Nick carried an old knapsack with his bongos perched on top.

They raced through the tall grass, catchin' up to a west-bound freight, shrieking and rumbling in the distance, blowing black smoke and loaded with open boxcars. The rooftops were covered with scores of dusty, ragged black men and others clinging or hanging out of rusty, open boxcars and still more rode the rods below.

Some of the men saw them coming and began to shout and wave at the boys, encouraging them on. The train slowed down, laboring around a curve, and the boys caught up. A hand reached down out of the boxcars and pulled Nick and Jessup in. Two more followed the dream. The hobo-laden freight rolled out of sight.

Days later, the train pulled into the San Francisco freight yard in the wee morning hours, and Nick and Jessup jumped out. Most of their fellow travelers had already left. They wandered through the streets, close to the freight yard, exploring the nooks and crannies of the big city, in awe and amazement until they approached a shabby nightclub. A faded sign, "Santana," hung above the door. A black musician lounging around in front beckoned them over.

"Hey, boy," he said, looking at Nick, who was holding tight to his precious bongos. "You a bongo player? Wanna play some music with da Blue Sky band?"

"Sure do, man. I play some good boogie-woogie too, but what about my broder, Jessup?"

The musician shook his head. "I sho like to hear dat, but he too young, son." He pointed at Jessup. "He can't come in."

Nick thought for a while, then turned to Jessup, who looked a bit forlorn.

"Ya gotta go back home, Jessup. Mama needs ya. Tell her I'm lookin' for work. Gonna make some money for us."

Jessup protested, "Awww, Nicky. We jus got here."

"Then you get back on de train and go home, afore somethin' happens to ya, Jessup. I'll write ya a letter." Nick pointed in the direction of the railway yard. He gave Jessup a push to send him on his way, handing him his knapsack.

"Look in dere, Jessup. Some money and some food will get ya home. It's all I got."

Jessup's eyes were tearing up, but he took the knapsack and turned away, saying, "I'll miss ya, Nicky." Nick gave him a big hug and replied, "I'll miss ya too, Jessup." That was the last time the two boys ever saw one other again.

Standing with my bongos on the back lawn of
our family home at Perth Road, Ontario in 1972,
looking much like Nick would have during
the Depression years.

The black musician watched the boys say their farewells and stepped forward to usher Nick around the corner into a side alley. He pulled a brown package out of his pocket and opened it up to reveal a white powder.

Nick eyed the powder suspiciously. "What dat?"

The musician explained, "Oh, dey call it Puffy White Cloud 'cause it make yo feel like ya floatin'. Ever seen any?"

Nick shook his head, wide-eyed.

The musician gave a big belly laugh. "We show ya, boy. Hey, yo mama know ya here?"

Nick shrugged. "Long way from home, and my mama don' care no ways."

The musician slapped Nick on the back, laughing, and motioned for him to follow. They disappeared through a side door. Subtly, the scene shifted, Nick dissolved, and then it was Maureen, holding her bongos, disappearing into the nightclub's interior.

I awoke, startled, and gazed around the room. The white disks of the bongos, sitting on the dresser, gleamed in the shadowy darkness. A cold breeze wafted across the room, and snowflake pellets pecked at the window. Off in the distance, a train whistle shrieked. Shivering, I got up and closed the window. Settling back into bed, I reflected, eyes wide open, listening to the train whistle moving through the night.

Chapter Six

Back to San Francisco

Three a.m., February 4th, 1973, Moon in Aquarius, and the frozen crust of Ontario snow blanketed the surrounding countryside. I awoke on the living room couch. Alternately queasy and strangely apprehensive, I thought to myself, "I'm going back to find myself. I'm going back to prove the existence of Nick Jackson."

Alone in the sleeping house, I knelt down on the living room carpet and prayed for the success of my mission. Once again, the words to the Lord's Prayer calmed me. My sleeping bag was spread out on the couch, knapsack packed and ready to go, my money belt, containing traveler's checks and my passport strapped tightly around my waist; even the bongos were tied on top tightly. Remembering something, I slipped out of the room and returned with a hunting knife on a leather belt that belonged to my father, opened my pack and tucked it deep down inside, along with two packages of birth control pills, in thoughtful silence. I had to be ready for anything, rape, self-defense–who could know what might happen? The Lord would be watching over me, so I knew that whatever came my way, I'd come out of it safely, one way or another. Through the large living room window, dawn streaked red across the sky through the gray, bare trees and snow-covered cow pasture.

My silver-gray tabby, Cindy, curled up in a chair, watched me as I paced the floor nervously, fingering the cross on a chain around my neck, somehow gaining comfort from its presence. I strapped on a leather money belt and grabbed my gear.

It was time now. My friend Doug, a real Perth Road neighborhood hippie with an Afro and an aimable grin, sat waiting in his 1969 red Mustang. I slid into the backseat with my gear and untied my bongos. As we backed out of the driveway in the dead of the night, leaving that big, isolated house where so many strange things had happened, I saw Mother standing in front of the window, my tabby in her arms, forcing a brave smile but obviously worried. She waved as we disappeared from sight, looking very unsure about the whole thing. I had told her about Nick and the research that Kate and I were doing, but I don't think she completely understood or, possibly, didn't want to.

In no time at all, we were rolling down the 401 to Toronto. "Do it Again," by Steely Dan came on the radio, and I untied my bongos and jammed along.

At the Toronto International Airport, I had some initial difficulty passing through Customs because I couldn't explain why I was traveling to the U.S.A. No business, no friends, no family, no real plans there...they let me through as a student with a promise not to remain long in the U.S.A. My journey was off to a bad start, but it was only one of many hurdles that I would encounter in the days ahead.

Once in the plane, I settled back into the seat and felt its power lift us into the sky. With Toronto below me and silently fading away, thousands of miles above the earth, what was one more miracle?

I fell into conversation with a businessman going to Acapulco for a holiday. He wanted to know about my journey. I told him about my mission to rediscover my past life. He was fascinated and wanted to hear more.

"I'll write a book about it, when I return," I promised.

"I'll buy it," he exclaimed.

I revealed to him that I had been told that I was a chosen one, and surprisingly enough, he agreed with me. "I do believe that you are," he said and smiled, and I know he wasn't humoring me. We talked all the way to Chicago, and then he had to leave to catch his plane to Acapulco, but before he left, he gave me the names and addresses of friends of his in California and the address of a good hotel in Acapulco.

And then, all too soon, I heard the words: "We'll be landing in San Francisco shortly, and thank you for flying American Airlines."

With my eyes still focused on the landscape below, I fastened my seat belt. There were tears in my eyes, and all I could think of was, "I'm coming home. I'm coming home, man." Canada was a frozen memory in the back of my mind, almost as if it had never existed. My life there seemed irrelevant now. Thirty years ago, I had left San Francisco as a black man called Nick, and now I was returning to this city as a white girl called Maureen. Yet inside, I knew I was still Nick. It was then that I realized that a miracle had occurred–something good and very wonderful. This truly was a second chance that God was giving me, and everything felt strangely right. I was doing what I was supposed to do, and I was going with the flow.

The jet rushed down to greet the water, and the water rushed up to slide beneath the belly of the huge bird. We touched down smoothly, rolled down the runway, and slowly came to a stop. The seat belt lights flashed off.

I picked up my bongos off the floor in front of me and stood up uncertainly, rather shaken by emotion and exhaustion. I thought, *I must be crazy. This is a strange city. I don't know anyone.*

I don't know where I'm going. I don't know what I'm going to do, but I'm not afraid.

Walking into the unknown, I went to claim my baggage, and as I headed off to catch an airport bus to take me downtown, a friendly, gruff voice called out to me, "Hey, girl, where are you goin' with those bongos?"

I turned around and a stocky, black man in uniform, a baggage porter, about forty was standing there, sporting a friendly smile.

"Oh, I don't know," I mumbled, slightly confused. "I only just got here. I thought I'd take a room at the YWCA."

"Well, what do you do with those bongos?" he asked me.

"Oh, I play them," I shrugged sheepishly. Maybe I shouldn't have been carrying them around in full view as if I was a professional.

"Well, I'll tell you what," he proposed, "and, by the way, my name is Charlie. What would your name be?"

"Oh, my name is Maureen, but my friends call me...and I hesitated a moment–"Nicki." *Might as well live the dream,* I thought wryly.

"Okay, Nicki," Charlie continued slowly, "I get off duty here at two, and if you're willin' to wait around, I can show you San Francisco and take you downtown to the YWCA."

I nodded hesitatingly, thinking, I'll bet Nick didn't stay at the YWCA.

So, I went upstairs to write a few letters home, and about 2 P.M., I found Charlie again and we headed for the parking lot. Soon we were on the freeway, and Charlie pulled several marijuana joints out of his pocket and lit one.

"Do you smoke?" he asked politely. I nodded, somewhat surprised. After all, this was broad daylight and he was driving, but wasn't it typical of Nick to run into drugs the first day he arrived in San Francisco?

I took a few drags, just to relax. I'd come to an agreement with myself that I would allow myself to use soft drugs like grass and hash but wouldn't touch the hard stuff. I'd never taken hard drugs before–only the LSD at Strawberry Fields, and that had been a once in a lifetime experiment.

Still, even smoking marijuana, I had a twinge of conscience as we sped along, dragging on that weed and rapping, totally carefree and barely hours off the plane. The sunshine, mingled with the sea breezes, erased my apprehensions. I still had my winter boots on, and maybe I hadn't even brought any shoes! My head was spinning. I was probably stoned, and words to Nick's song "Blue Skies" swept into my mind.

Blue Skies

Blue skies, all I got above are blue skies
Just as blue as your blue eyes
I've got blue skies above.

We got into a talk about astrology.

"This astrology thing really interests me," Charlie said. "I've been studying it for a long time, and I got the signs down pretty good."

Gazing at him, thoughtfully, I asked, "You're an Aquarius, aren't you?"

"Yeah, but how did you know? Nobody ever guesses my sign right."

I grinned. "Got a talent for it, I guess. By the way, where are we going? Isn't downtown the other direction?

Charlie had a plot brewing. "I know these guys who have a band here in the city. They call themselves Point Blank. You say that you play those drums, so I thought I could help you by introducing you to them. They're one of the biggest bands in the Bay area right now. They make a living playing gigs around town, and they got a record deal coming up. You'll like them. They're a nice bunch of guys."

As we drove along, Charlie kept busy pointing out different areas of San Francisco to me.

"This is South San Francisco, Brisbane, the Oyster Point Marina's over there, and Bayview's got the old Hunters Point Shipyards and Candlestick Park. Do ya like baseball?"

"Yeah," I answered with enthusiasm, "and I like football better than hockey. That's all you hear about in Canada, but I've never been a fan of winter sports."

Charlie made a turn off the freeway, heading into Bayview.

It seemed like in no time at all we pulled up in front of a dilapidated, little bungalow on Shafter Avenue and Charlie got out and knocked on the front door. It opened a crack. Charlie beckoned for me to follow. A tall, black man, sporting an Afro and a tie-dyed shirt, motioned us in.

I grabbed my drums and walked up the stairs, not knowing what to expect next. The blinds were drawn against the hot, midday sun, and it was dark inside the tiny, bare living room.

Charlie introduced me as I stood shyly, just inside the front door. Clutching my bongos and adjusting myself to the darkness, my pupils still wide from the San Francisco sunlight and open-mouthed wonderment at the situation that was quickly unraveling in front of me.

"Boys, meet Nicki! Nicki, this is James Richards, Eric Taylor, and Billy Moon. James is a talented Afro cat on congas, Eric plays keyboards, and Billy is a hell of a fantastic guitar player."

Billy Moon stepped forward to shake my hand.

"Hi, Nicki. We were going through a few songs that we've been playing at a club up on North Beach. Would you like to jam with us?"

"Sure, but I've never jammed with a real band before."

"Well, what are you waiting for? Follow me!"

Billy led me downstairs, the other band members following, to an area where the equipment was set up and ready to go. They all took their places and smiled at me, and the black conga player, noticing my drums, gave me a sexy wink. I sat down and listened to them play a few songs first and then joined in with them on drums. The black conga player and I wrestled for a harmonious duo, and when the song ended, I looked up for a sign of approval.

Eric Taylor then invited me to play his Fender Rhodes electric piano. I'd never touched one before, but when I launched into one of Nick's songs, his version of "Hit the Road, Jack," they all joined in with me.

Hit The Road, Jack

Well, I left my home down South one day
Ole lady kicked me out the door
But before I head off down the road, she said
Doncha come back no more
Well, I had my drums and I played 'em well
I thought I'd be a star
But after five years of playin' gigs I sure as hell ain't got far."

Laughter rippled through the room. James, Billy, and Eric looking amused but puzzled, continued playing, glancing across at each other with a "What the hell?" kind of look on their faces.

"Hey, Ray Charles didn't sing those lyrics. Where did you get that?" he asked me. Maybe he was a Ray Charles fan. I hoped I hadn't insulted him. I explained, "Well, I heard that it came from a musician by the name of Nick Jackson. I think that Nick, Percy Mayfield, and Fats Domino might have been club buddies back in the '40s in New Orleans. History says that Percy showed the song 'Hit the Road, Jack' to Ray, who made it a hit."

I looked mysterious for a moment and continued, "Wonder what ever happened to Nick?"

The boys didn't have an answer. I picked up my drums and turned to leave. Billy thrust a note into my hand as Charlie and I moved toward the door. I glanced at Billy, who answered me with a smile.

"It's my number. We'd like to see you back here again soon."

As Charlie pulled away from the curb, I was all smiles in the front seat.

"Do you think they liked me, Charlie?"

Charlie grinned, "Oh, yeah. They gave you an invitation to return, didn't they? They liked you, all right!"

Charlie turned back toward downtown and continued with his grand tour of San Francisco..."And this is the waterfront, and over there is Chinatown, North Beach...and that's Fisherman's Wharf. Can you see Alcatraz out in the harbor? Over there, in that direction is Haight Ashbury."

"Hippie heaven," I laughed.

"Not anymore," Charlie replied. "Only a few left. All boarded up now."

Charlie lit another joint, and we smoked as he drove past Fisherman's Wharf. We were both getting thoroughly stoned.

And now we were pulling up in front of a stylish San Francisco bungalow with a garage below. Charlie drove in and parked.

I turned to Charlie and asked, "Where are we now, Charlie? I thought you were going to take me to the YWCA downtown."

Charlie had a look of apologetic innocence on his face. "Well, Nicki, this is my place. I thought that you'd like to visit a while. You're welcome here...if you want to stay."

I wasn't too sure about that. "I guess, for a while."

"Here, I'll get your bags for you. I've got a nice, spare room. Sit down and make yourself comfortable. He went back downstairs to the garage, brought my knapsack up, and deposited it on the bed in the spare room. It was a clean, pretty, little room–lace curtains on the windows, single bed and dresser, closet, carpet on the floor.

San Francisco 1973

I satisfied my hunger next with a wonderful meal that Charlie, ever the gracious host, cooked for us. Afterwards, he pointed to the couch, and I settled into the comfortable, deep leather cushions. My gaze examined the room, a room obviously designed for entertaining, thick carpets, elaborate stereo system, mirror tiled walls, a casual bar off to the side.

I stepped out onto a little balcony, just beyond the kitchen, and gazed at the bungalows, shingles, pueblos, Victorians, a scattering of houses over a hilly landscape dotted with lights twinkling in the now evening darkness. In the far distance, Fisherman's Wharf and the black, moonlit waves of San Francisco Bay.

A wave of emotion that I could not justify swept over me. Tears welled up in my eyes, and I whispered to myself, "I'm home." This was *my city*, this crazy, put-together city, impossibly hilly with skies as moody as a woman. One of Nick's songs had put it aptly:

San Francisco Night

I lost my baby to a San Francisco night
Just strolling along the avenue
Just we two
I turned around and she was gone
Guess I lost her to the dawn of a San Francisco night
Stars twinkling down on a black harbor
Train bound for New York
The ships pull in
Ghosts in the dark of a San Francisco night
I love this town
It's in my blood
I am a hundred years of buildings to the sky
Guess that's why
I lost myself to a San Francisco night.

And I remembered the conversation that I'd had with Jessup when I'd asked Kate in a trance, "Where'd I go, when I first went to San Francisco?"

"You went straight to Santana and hung around with a lil boy group called Blue Sky. Remember dat? Dat was the name of one of your first songs."

My mind then realized the strange synchronicity of events, and it seemed that I must indeed already be fully immersed "in the flow." As Jessup used to say, "Don't fight the flow. Just flow with it."

Uniting Nick's consciousness from my own that night, I finally let myself drift with him and forgot myself. His memories merged with mine, into this immediate present, and he made love to my soul. He and I became one that night in San Francisco, the night that time stood still.

Chapter Seven

Stone Free with Point Blank

I awoke to bright sunlight streaming through the window of the spare bedroom. I lay in a sleeping bag, still fully dressed, and rubbed my eyes wondering for a moment where the hell I was.

A knock on the door and Charlie peeked in shyly. "Hey, baby, did I wake you up?"

"No, but I was getting up anyway." I slipped out of the sleeping bag and joined Charlie at the kitchen table. He was rolling a joint.

"Already," I thought.

Shaking his head in disgust, he said, "You know, Nicki, that girl across the street, man. She come lookin' for an outfit last night, 'an I say, 'Hey, girl, I don't keep none of that shit around here.'"

"All I got is my cocaine and some smoke, and I don't deal none of that junk, man."

He held out some of the white powder on a corner of paper and pushed it at me–"Here baby, try some of this white stuff."

I shook my head. "No, thanks."

He stepped over to the stereo and put on a Santana album–"Caravanserai," and we talked astrology and smoked for a while. "Black Magic Woman" floated in and out of my head. It was the song that I'd played at home, the night that I'd written down Nick's letter fragments. Charlie had put it on at my request.

"You're damn easy to get along with. You know that, Nicki? I like you."

"I like you too, Charlie. You're a good person."

Charlie warmed up to the praise and continued, "Well, I got my friends, but they give me a hell of a lot of trouble. Just like you said, Nicki, Saturn in Aquarius. I'm goin' down to the store. Can I get you somethin'?"

"Yeah, how about some, ah–True cigarettes, menthol," I suggested. It wasn't as if I was in the habit of smoking, but every now and then, I liked to toy with it, and American cigarettes were different.

"Sure, baby. Now you make yourself at home. Make yourself some breakfast–okay?"

I sat down at the kitchen table, drank some coffee, and generally got my head together. Charlie came back with the cigarettes. I lit one up and played around with it. I almost never inhaled.

"Where are you going today, baby?" Charlie asked casually, as the Santana album finished.

"Oh, I'm gonna visit Point Black again. Take advantage of their invitation."

Charlie agreed, "Yeah, you should jam some more with those guys. They're going places in the music business."

"That's what I'm lookin' for!" I exclaimed, grabbing my purse and bongos and heading for the door.

My desire for music was strong, and maybe it was more than that–maybe in San Francisco, I'd find the acceptance, admiration, and love that my family hadn't been able to give me. Using cable cars and buses, I found my way back to Shafter Street before the noon-day sun woke everyone up.

I knocked on the door, and Billy opened it, sleepily, yawning, his fingers running through his messy hair.

"Oh, hi, Nicki. We were wondering when you'd come back

and pay us a visit. Come in. We're just getting ready to rehearse."

I stepped inside and followed him downstairs where Eric, who was adjusting some knobs on the sound system, smiled. In the background, I could hear the Jimi Hendrix song "Purple Haze."

Publicity photo of the band "Point Blank"
taken in San Francisco

"Hey, Eric," Billy urged, "explain to Nicki what stone free is."

"Stone Free. Wasn't that one of Hendrix's songs?" I inquired.

"Yeah," Eric explained, "so to be stone free is to be free to do your own thing, but if one person is stone free, then everyone has got to be stone free, you dig? Free and beautiful, baby."

"Not sure I follow you," I replied wryly. "You're copying from Hendrix, aren't you?"

Billy chuckled to himself."

"I used to hang around with him in New York City."

"Oh wow, far out!" I exclaimed, "tell me all about it."

"Well, I heard there was this guy by the name of Jimmy James, playing guitar with his teeth at a coffee house in Greenwich

Village called the Café Wha, so I had to check it out. I went down to the club and saw Jimi for the first time and was amazed by his antics. I had to meet him. I was working there in the Village at a club just down the street from the Café Wha. The name of our band was The Eight Wonders, and we were the house band for the club. We had to back up performers that were featured in the club and had come to town without a backup band, so we had little time to learn the hit tune that the performers had on the charts to be ready for show time."

"That must have been tricky," I agreed.

Billy continued, "Anyway, after meeting Jimi, we hung out together getting high most of the time. He used to carry his guitar over his shoulder and usually had some girls following him wherever he went. After a while, we drifted apart.

"The next time I saw him was at a concert that was held at Central Park. It featured The Young Rascals. I went to see The Rascals, and the band that was on stage before them was The Jimi Hendrix Experience. There he was, direct from England, all dressed up in a yellow jumpsuit. He had a whole wall of amplifiers behind him. He did a fantastic set, and when he was done with his last song, he threw his guitar into the audience. The sound of the speakers when the guitar ripped off the jack chord was deafening. The people went crazy with applause, and it was quite some time before The Young Rascals could start their set. He blew everyone away. That was the last time I saw him. I was in California when I heard on the news that Jimi had died of an overdose."

I was overwhelmed. "Boy, I never thought I'd ever meet someone who used to hang out with Hendrix!"

James, who had been listening behind a big set of congas in the far corner of the room, then indicated to me that he wanted to play my bongos. I handed them over. He placed them on his knees and gave them a tap and frowned.

"Can't you get a better sound out of them than that?"

"I don't know," I shrugged. "See if you can." James took the key and tightened the rims a bit, tapped the skins, and smiled. "Sounds better now. Nice set of bongos. Pearl, aren't they? How long you been playing them?"

I almost choked on that question. "Oh, seems like forever," I replied, casually.

James soloed on the bongos for a few moments and then handed them back to me. I followed suit by playing a few beats from "Oye Como Va."

James smiled admiringly and commented, "Not bad. Just keep at it. Practice till you've worn down the palms of your hands like this." He turned his hands over and showed me how flat and calloused his palms were, the hands of a pro.

Billy rummaged in his pocket and pulled out a joint and handed it to Eric. I followed Billy back upstairs where a young, slender, black woman dressed in a white, fringed bikini, strings swaying, emerged from a bedroom.

"Nice bikini." I managed an uncomfortable compliment.

The black girl smiled and edged closer. "Hi, I'm Dana. Have you been down on North Beach since you got here? Have you taken in the 'music scene?'"

"Not yet," I replied, backing away slightly. Dana moved even closer, studying me and whispered in my ear, "You're cute." She stood in front of me, fringes swaying, then grabbed my hand urging me toward the bedroom, "I like you, Nicki. Come on."

I pulled my hand back. "Hey, that's not my scene. I'm just into the music."

Dana was disappointed. "That's too bad. You can be friendly

with me. No hang-ups."

At that moment, Billy took my hand and guided me into the bedroom and shut the door. I followed him mostly to get away from Dana, but following Billy probably wasn't the best move I could have made. This San Francisco scene was overwhelming for a green, country girl from the backwoods of Ontario and I wasn't sure I could handle it.

The shades were drawn, and in the dim light, I could make out an electric guitar propped up beside a messy bed. Billy slid onto the rumpled sheets and pulled me over beside him.

"Hey, you're kind of cute, you know, but you give off these little boy vibes. You could be quite a woman if you really wanted to be."

He took off his shirt and tugged at mine. I pulled away.

"Where are you from, Nicki?"

"Um, I'm from Canada—near Kingston, Ontario," I stammered.

Billy laughed. "We were in Canada once. Kicked out of, I would say. Stick around here, baby, and we'll star you in one of our shows."

Billy pulled down the zipper on my jeans. I pushed him away but I wasn't sure I wanted to.

"No, man. I'm heading down to Monterey and San Diego soon—maybe even Mexico."

"But why, Nicki?" Billy was disappointed. "You've got everything you need right here in San Francisco."

It was happening too fast. It was the movie of Nick Jackson in San Francisco with the Blue Skies band being played out in front of my eyes, all over again. This was wilder than I ever could have imagined, but more importantly, I was aware of the synchronicity and that meant that I had a responsibility and a choice to deal with it differently this time. I wasn't about to sell my soul to the devil music a second time around.

I jumped up and headed for the door, zipping my jeans up. "I can't do this."

Billy was amazed. "What's the matter with you, baby? Well, this is stone free. This is what it's all about."

"Yeah, but what it's all about is maybe what I'm here to deal with," I replied solemnly.

Billy shook his head, not understanding but he spoke calmly, "Whatever you say, baby. Make your choice." He smiled with arms outstretched.

This was an opportunity to enter the music business and to succeed where Nick had failed, and if I walked away, I may not ever have another chance like this again but the stakes were too high. I'd have to trust that God had another plan for me, bigger than this one.

I fingered the cross, hanging on the necklace around my neck, and made my decision. "I've gotta get it right this time," I cried, and bolted out of the room, clutching my bongos and slamming the door after me.

I ran across the street and into a Chinese restaurant, barely missing a collision with a car coming down the street. Huddled in a booth in the shadows of the restaurant, I shook from head to toe. A waitress approached, concerned.

"Are you all right, honey?" she asked. "Would you like to order?"

I smiled weakly, holding back the tears. "No, thanks."

Chapter Eight
Karmic Retribution

I didn't tell Charlie what had happened with Point Blank because I figured that he would find out sooner or later, and he probably wouldn't be able to make sense of it.

I took some time to explore San Francisco on foot. The city fascinated me. I loved the hilly streets and Spanish style architecture. Palm trees and grass were strange to me in February.

Downtown San Francisco! I wandered around exploring the stores, bought some shoes, and changed some Canadian money into American dollars until I heard music and was drawn to the corner to view my first street corner musicians. There were two black men, one on saxophone and one on congas. When the sax player grinned at me, I drew closer, intrigued. The beat of the congas pounded over the pavement, pulling people away, to watch. They gathered in a crowd to watch and throw money in a pot while an old black man shuffle danced in front. The rhythm of the congas seemed to fascinate and tantalize me. I liked bongos, but I loved congas, and I'd never had a set. The two black musicians reminded me of Nick and Jessup, and I smiled to myself.

Finally, I tore myself away from the crowd at the corner and headed down Market Street. I was walking along when a tall, young, Afro American man fell into stride with me.

"Hey, I just got in from Chicago, and I'm gonna start a little crap game. You mind if I walk beside you?"

"Hey, you wanna beer? Let's go and have a couple beers."

"Oh, I don't know, man," I said. "Thanks anyway, but I think I'm lost. Can't remember. Here to catch the bus home. In fact, I forgot where I live! Holy smoke, I think I'd better get a map."

I walked into the lobby of a hotel and asked for a map, but they didn't have one. By now, my fair-weather friend had decided to move on and left. I got on a bus that I thought would take me back to Charlie's house, but it didn't.

I was in a near panic. "Oh, hell," I swore at myself, "how stupid could a person be?" I'd been smoking too much dope and hadn't thought to write down Charlie's address and telephone number before leaving!

I tried to calm myself down. "Think, think, think!"

I went to a telephone booth and dug into the phone book searching for his phone number, but it wasn't listed. What if I never found him again—all my gear, my passport, my clothes and my traveler's checks were there. I phoned the airport, but they couldn't give out that information, and I didn't know which airline he worked for. I was near tears but made one more call instead, someone with the same last name. It turned out to be Charlie's son. I didn't know he had one, but by the grace of God, he did, and he was kind enough to give me Charlie's telephone number.

"Hello?"

It was Charlie, and I almost collapsed in relief.

"Hey, I'm lost. Where are you? Where am I? I forgot your address."

"Oh, baby," Charlie was all sympathy, and he gave me directions to get back to the house.

I was exhausted when I arrived, so I took a shower and changed my clothes. It was dark outside, and I thought, *I might still be wandering around the streets of San Francisco if Charlie hadn't rescued me.* Indeed, my guardian angel must be working overtime.

One evening, we were having dinner in the kitchen when there was a knock on the door. Four black women, obviously, friends of Charlie's, were stopping by for a visit. They were accompanied by a tall, black man, who was introduced to me as Jackie. Flashily dressed, he looked like a pimp.

As they sat around in the living room, smoking pot, listening to the blues and talking, I brought out the astrology book that I'd brought with me and did a few horoscopes for the ladies–what sign their Sun was in, their Moon etc. They were all fascinated by my knowledge.

Charlie's eyes kept shifting to me, up and down my tight blue jeans, and it made me uncomfortable. I excused myself and went into the kitchen to make coffee. One of Charlie's lady friends followed me. She pulled me aside and whispered, "Honey, I think Charlie's got a crush on you. Girl, you'd better watch your step. Be cool now!"

I wasn't sure exactly what she meant, but I replied, "Thanks for the advice, but I think I can take care of myself."

When they left, I hit the sack, not bothering to undress. The door opened wide and Charlie stood there, took off his pants, and tried to pull my blue jeans off.

"Hey, man, what the hell are you doing?"

"Oh, baby, I just wanna hold you. You're so cute," Charlie pleaded.

"Cute, hell! You better not touch me or I'll call the cops!"

Charlie bent over me with a strange glint in his eyes and a soothing drawl. "But baby, you wouldn't really call the cops on me, would you?"

"Sure as hell would," I exclaimed!

"So, I was right," Charlie exclaimed, "just like you wrote in your notebook, 'Biggest dope pusher in San Francisco!'"

I hesitated a moment, groping for understanding, then remembered the journal that I'd been writing in since leaving Ontario.

"What? Oh, my God! You've found my diary!"

"You were gonna accuse me of dealin' drugs, and I thought you were my friend. Well, I'll fix you!"

He strode out of the bedroom into the living room. I jumped up and followed him. He reached for the phone. I hung over his shoulder, panic stricken.

"Charlie, man, don't be stupid. I wouldn't do a thing like that. That was just a diary I was keeping. I'm sorry. I was wrong. I exaggerated, like I sometimes do. It's private. No one will ever see it."

Charlie couldn't be convinced. "Cops see that 'an take away everything that I've worked so hard for. No, girl, you ain't gonna get away with it. I'll make sure you don't."

He dialed a number.

"Hey, Jackie. Got a little trouble here. Yeah, you remember that chick I picked up at the airport? You met her here at my place. Yeah, that's the one. Get yourself over here. Gonna be trouble."

I grabbed the phone out of his hand, but Jackie had hung up. It hit the floor with a thud.

"Charlie, man. Don't be crazy!"

I bolted back into the bedroom and began throwing my clothes into the knapsack.

"Where you goin', Nicki?" For a moment, I couldn't tell if he was angry because I was planning to leave before Jackie got there or disappointed that I was leaving because he didn't want to see me go.

It didn't matter. I grabbed my bongos and tied my runners.

"I'm leaving."

Charlie followed, now pleading like a hurt schoolboy. "Nicki, you know I wouldn't let anything happen to you, baby."

"Doesn't sound like it!" I didn't want to argue.

"That there on the phone a minute ago. Jackie wasn't on the line. I was foolin' ya."

I made a beeline for the door.

"Well, let me drive ya where ya goin."

"I can take a cab," I retorted defiantly.

"No sense to that. I'll get the car."

In minutes, he was waiting at the curb. Should I trust him? Again, I had to make a split-second decision. Give him the benefit of the doubt? I jumped in and gave him the address, Aquarius House Hostel on the other side of Golden Gate Park.

It must have been the coke I knew he was doing. All coke heads are paranoid, I reasoned, but judging from the look in his eyes as he drove through the night, I felt that it was more than that. The black woman who had warned me that evening in the kitchen was right. Charlie had fallen for me whether I had noticed or not. But would he hurt the one he loved? Was he taking me to Jackie or to Aquarius House? I had to trust a hunch.

When he finally pulled up in front of Aquarius House, I grabbed my gear and jumped out, running up the steps, taking them two at a time. That was the last time I ever saw Charlie.

Chapter Nine

Aquarius House

The first thing they made me do at Aquarius House was to help wash the dinner dishes. A Tennessee lad, with a wired-up jaw and a foot in a cast, washed while I dried.

We got to talking, Tennessee and I, about him. I discovered a kinship between us. We were both Scorpios, and we were both horse lovers. His daddy had a horse ranch back home.

I wanted to know why his jaw was wired up.

"After I got outta the army," he grinned, "I got in a fight, and now I can't go nowhere until this heals up."

We talked a while about Vietnam, and then I asked him, "How did you get outta the army?"

"Wal," Tennessee grinned, and confided in me, "it was this way—we boys was on the bus, you know, our reg'lar training session and all that, 'an ever once in a while on one of these bus trips, I'd swaller a bit of castor oil from this bottle that I snook on board and whup! Pretty soon I'd be throwin' up and diarrhea all over the place."

I laughed gleefully.

Tennessee slapped his knee and belly laughed, "Sickern a dog. Now I wash them plates and rinse 'em well 'cause I learned in the army that if you don't rinse the suds off, you'll get the diarrhea."

The next morning, I awoke to the sound of knocking on the bedroom dorm door and a call for breakfast. I didn't feel hungry.

Good thing. I managed to get downstairs just as the last of the pancakes disappeared.

I spent part of that day at a laundromat, washing bed sheets, and the rest of the day writing a letter to Kate.

I settled into the routine of Aquarius House in the days that followed. I liked the coming and goings of young people, like myself, on the road. I liked talking to them and hearing their stories about where they'd been and where they were going. Some had been across the U.S.A. several times, while others had even been around the world.

A Gemini called Bill with blond hair and a happy-go-lucky grin told me all about his experiences as a wandering "hippie" from New York to San Francisco, north to Canada, and south to Mexico. He'd been everywhere there was to go in North America and even parts of South America as well.

I listened with great interest to his adventures of being imprisoned in a marijuana "ranch" somewhere down in Mexico with nothing to do all day except get high and hope that someone would open the door of the shed and let him out. Eventually, someone did, with a strict warning to keep his mouth shut and not to return that way again.

While his wanderings had covered most of Europe and the Middle East, he'd picked up a smattering of Spanish and French. He confided in me that he'd received over a hundred shock treatments in various mental institutions, "which," he said, "is a lot better than spending time in jail. Just plead insanity, and they give you a few shock treatments and let you go. You lose your memory for a while, but it comes back, and later on, you continue on your way, none the worse for it all."

Thanking him for the advice, in case I should find myself in a similar situation, I contemplated Bill's approach to life. His enthusiasm, despite his circumstances, was contagious, and he almost considered life to be some sort of joke, something my serious, philosophical mind found difficult to accept.

Two girls from the eastern U.S.A. kept popping in and out of Aquarius House, leaving gear, and then returning to pick it up. One was a fiery, argumentative Aries who liked laughing in the middle of battle, and her sidekick was a breezy Aquarius. They seemed almost disoriented, flitting back and forth between Berkley and San Francisco and invited me one day to hitchhike to San Jose with them. The three of us returned in the pouring rain carrying parcels back to San Francisco, and as I stood there dripping wet, by the side of the road, the radio in my mind played the song, "Do You Know the Way to San Jose?" When I got back to Aquarius House, I wrote the song, "The Windshield Wiper Blues," or maybe Nick had written it before in the past, and I was only repeating myself.

The Aries told me her fondest dreams for the future, which would include a nice, little home somewhere because she hadn't come from a happy household, which was one of the reasons she'd taken to the road.

I met a nice, young, Capricorn girl who had run away from home because her daddy didn't approve of her black boyfriend. She had been caught sleeping overnight at the local men's college residence where her boyfriend was going to school. Life had found her with a suitcase in her hand and a ticket for San Francisco where she was able to find, within a few days, a job as a live-in babysitter with a wealthy family.

And then there was a girl, five months pregnant, from the West Indies, who had just come in from Portland, Oregon, on a bus. She'd been living with a group of carefree hippies when she got into this predicament. She was still in love with the father to be, but apparently, he wasn't ready for parenthood, so she was alone.

I confided in her that I'd put myself on the pill before starting on this journey, just to be on the safe side.

"Oh," she said casually, "I forget to take those lil pills every night. They make me feel bad and get seek, you know. My boyfriend was in love with me, and we didn't think about things like that, you know. Now my skeen breaks out an' throw up, morning seekness you call it? But the baby–it makes me so happy to know that I am going to have a baby to take care of. I will find myself a lil apartment and settle down and look affer it and be so happy, but now..." She shrugged. "It's hard, you know. An' I want so much to have thees baby because the father is white, and that makes it special to me. She went on about her skin. "My skeen, it is all broken out, an' the doctor says it will go away in a few months when the baby gets bigger. All my dresses–they don't feeet me anymore, an' I don't have any money to buy more, you know."

I offered to give her some of my clothes, but she refused politely. "No, I don't accept second-hand clothes. I buy my own clothes, and I am proud that I can. He's gonna help me."

She pointed to Tennessee, who'd become very protective around her lately. It appeared that she and Tennessee were old friends from another time on the road, so she'd found someone to take care of her or so she hoped.

And then there was Walter. Walter was also an Aquarius but an embittered one. Having seen too much poverty in India and the selfishness of mankind, in his travels, he'd developed a hatred toward society. Water had worked all of his life and had nothing to show for it. He had had more bad luck, or so he'd said, than most and blamed society for it. He had wanted the color

TVs, the sports cars, the wealth, the good things of life and, somehow, was always cheated out of it. I found Walter to be stiff, reserved, and clearly an uptight individual, nearly intolerant of everyone at the hostel. Walter had something negative to say about everyone, and no one had anything good to say about Walter, but I thought, *It takes all kinds to make a world, and our little world was Aquarius House.*

One member of the group whom I particularly sympathized with was a gentle hippie with a ring in his ear from down south. He was a compulsive drug addict, heroin, chemicals, smoke–he'd done it all. But he didn't bother anyone and always tried to be cooperative and cheerful. Underneath, I could sense his desperation, and I wished that I could reach out and comfort him. He talked about getting a job in the city working with drug addicts, convinced that he could turn his life around, but the next day he'd come stumbling in, stoned on acid, and ask one of the others to trip out with him.

A tall, coarse-featured, big-nosed, black boy from Seattle wandered in one night asking someone to chip in for gas money to return.

"Have some dinner," I suggested. "You can probably get it free if you help with the dishes after."

"No thanks," he said. "I gotta get going," but he returned later and stayed with us for a few days.

They had a big, old, upright piano there at the house in the parlor that must have been as old as the house itself. Most of the keys stuck, but I needed to play a piano, any piano, so one night, when I had tired of watching a movie on TV with the rest of the group, I sat down and played "Little Girl Blue." Seattle Boy came running and stood in the doorway, his mouth agape.

"Where'd you hear that song?" he exclaimed. "It's beautiful!"

"Well, thank you. It's one of my own," I said proudly and played it for him again while some of the rest of the group drifted in to join him. Pretty soon, I had an audience, and Seattle Boy sat down beside me, and we played together, him taking the upper octave and me the lower.

A Hispanic fellow came in then with his harmonica, and the three of us played the blues. There was magic in the air that rainy night in Aquarius House amd I turned the show over to Nick playin' the blues, just as he used to in San Francisco, so many years ago.

The days flew by, and beyond having to do the laundry, clean the upstairs bathroom, cook meals and wash dishes, I continued to meet an assortment of drifters and oddballs, who entertained me with their life stories. Seattle Boy, whom I was teaching piano, fell in love with me and wrote me a love letter. Another confided in me about his life in New York City and how his buddy had ripped him off just before he left for San Francisco, leaving him only with the shirt on his back.

At the laundromat down the street, I met a man who was part Navajo Indian. He had blond hair, and looked the part of a California surfer, but he actually was a professional dancer, an artist, and Vietnam veteran. He now shared an apartment with a homosexual buddy a few blocks away and invited me over one night. I stepped inside to view a bloody gallery of paintings of Vietnam War scenes.

"It's the only way," he said sadly, "of making peace with the ghosts of the past. By painting these scenes, I can transfer them from my mind to canvas."

The next day, I set off with a camera to explore the San Francisco waterfront. I wandered along the deserted waterfront, past abandoned warehouses and empty docks, taking pictures and posing for a few that an accommodating passersby took for me. I sat on a dock at the Bay, just as Otis Redding had sung about, looking out across the San Francisco Bay at Alcatraz. Cries of seagulls circling overhead shattered the silence, and the waves lapped against the shore.

Sitting on the "dock of the bay" in San Francisco, chasing past life memories in February 1973.

A vision formed in my mind. Nick and the band were getting ready to leave on a cruise ship bound for South America. He was all smiles as he waved goodbye to his friend Luke and his girlfriend, Sandra, standing on the dock.

I blinked, my eyebrows knit as I stared intently at the abandoned waterfront, the subconscious recollection ticking at the edges of my memory.

"I've never been here before...have I?" I whispered to myself.

I continued wandering, farther along the waterfront, taking more photos, and turned the corner. A rusty boxcar sat deserted on a section of tracks no longer used.

I threw my jacket and day pack down in a corner and sprawled, leaning on them, from an angle where I could see outside.

A wooded landscape flashed by. It was 1936, and Nick was playing a harmonica song "Boxcar Blues" to a carload of hobos passing around a bottle of whisky. Another bo jammed along with him. One of the hobos in baggy pants, held up by suspenders, wearing shoes with gaping holes in them, joked with another older bo.

"Lots a whisky in Californiay, no more winter, and no more cotton fields," he grinned.

"Yes, sir, take yo place at the back of the bus. Yessir, not everybody please to see us comin'...course these young bucks..." and he pointed to Nick and his friend, continuing, "dey don't care one way'r nother. They just likes to go along for the ride."

Nick smiled and sang the words to "Boxcar Blues" while the harmonica player played melody.

Boxcar Blues

I've got the boxcar blues, just a rollin' along the track
I've got the boxcar blues, and I'm never goin' back
I lead the life I lead
Because I wanna be free...

My eyes slowly changed expression as the trance broke. I

jumped up, brushing train dust from my jeans, and hopped out of the open boxcar, continuing to the next street corner, and turning west, headed back to Aquarius House.

February 10th, 1973

Kate,

Yesterday while I was walking around San Francisco, through Chinatown and the area of Telegraph Hill, it felt familiar to me. I went through North Beach and the Broadway Strip where all of the nightclubs are and stood at the top of the high hill overlooking the ocean, searching for ships in the Bay. Down in the harbor area, where all of the docks "piers" are, I sat by the water looking out toward Alcatraz, listening to the seagulls. I wandered around in this warehouse that hadn't been used in years, and it was spooky and dark inside. I was all alone, and as I walked, I thought of Nick and of you.

A vision developed in my mind. It was boarding day, and Nick was leaving for South America. The band was going on tour. I could see them loading the instruments on board.

I followed the street down to the railway tracks and looked up at the street sign, and it read "Davis Street." Well, this kind of clicked with "Darby"–then it hit me "ten blocks west of Darby Ave. Turn left, two down on the right. Cocomo Road is home to me, babe. I'm going home tonight."

Some of the streets in SF are Market, Powell, Mission, Jackson, Union, Broadway (the nightclub strip), California, Taylor and Columbus. Some of the cocktail lounges are the Purple Onion, Sea Witch, One Hundred Club, Pier 23 Café, Red Lion, The Gaslight, Club 99, Black Fox, Club Sixty-Five, Jazz Room, Red Chimney, Trio Club and others. No Santana nightclub exists in 1973.

Maureen /Nicki

Kate sent me a letter in reply, that reached Aquarius House.

Dear Maureen/Nick:

We are downstairs. Watch yourself! Hard times ahead!
Don't do drugs much. I know you will. Don't be discouraged.
Names of places can change. Powell Street was one of the
streets, so was Capital, Frontier, Market...Some of these or they
could be in New York. Hope you're enjoying yourself. I haven't
gone to the music festival yet. Wish me luck, I'm getting help.
Sparky misses you. We all do, but fill what you have to do. Last
night I had a dream of you singing the "Boxcar Blues." I must
have been there with you! My powers are back!

Love,

Kate

San Francisco, rain darkness, street lit sidewalks glisten in my memory. I am walking to a little corner store to buy chocolate bars and cigarettes for the gang back at Aquarius House who are engrossed in a movie, but the adventures they see on the screen cannot come close to my own. Strange visions haunt me. I see the house on the corner that I am heading for, and there is a light on in the window. Someone is waiting for me. I climb the stairs and knock on the door. It opens a crack, and then someone whispers "Who is it?" and I answer, "It's me, Nick."

The door swings open and is shut swiftly behind me. A group of people are standing silently around a table in a dimly lit room. On the table is a little package, and that little package is the purpose of our rendezvous.

We divide the package and exchange remarks about it. Someone takes a sample. It's heroin, I think. There is much secrecy and suspicious undertones. I take my share and go out into the rainy, night streets of San Francisco—out onto the street lit sidewalks with pockets full of candy and cigarettes. It's late, and I walk up the steps to Aquarius House, open the door, and slip quietly in.

Chapter Ten

Hitchin' up to Monterey

In the middle of February, I picked up my pack, bongos, and sleeping bag firmly secured on top, and slipped my arms under the shoulder straps. The load felt heavier than before, way too heavy for a four-foot eleven-inch chick weighing in at a hundred-pounds total, but it was time to move on, and I planned on hitchhiking beautiful Route One to Monterey.

Hitching up to Monterey on Route One outside
San Francisco, February 1973, following the route map
that Kate gave me

Clutching my map of California, I walked down the front steps of Aquarius House and turned to see my friend Tennessee hobbling after me.

"Where are you going?" I asked, surprised. "I thought you were going to stay here with your girlfriend."

"Her!" Tennessee laughed. "I'm tired of her complaining and nagging. I'm going with you."

"You don't have to do that. I can take care of myself. Do you know how to get to Route One from here?"

"C'mon." Tennessee lifted the pack off my shoulders and swung it onto his own.

"If you want to go that way, we will," he cautioned, "but it's dangerous. The road has been washed out somewhere along the route, and it might be washed out before we get to Monterey."

"I heard about that," I said, "but I decided that I was going to try it anyway."

"Yeah," Tennessee agreed, "it's probably okay up to Monterey, and from there we can get back on the freeway again. It's faster and there's more rides."

We took a trolley together to the outskirts of the city. Right beside the ocean, I put down my pack, and Tennessee took a photo. The route began and ran parallel to the ocean all the way up to Monterey. I was sure of that by studying the map, and I'd chosen Route One because I'd read about it in a travel guide where it had been suggested as a beautiful drive.

We put down our gear and waited for a ride. I held up a sign with MONTEREY on it, but it didn't do any good. No luck.

"Why the hell don't they stop?" I complained to Tennessee. "They see us waiting here, and they know we need a lift, but do you see anyone stopping? No."

"Oh, be patient," replied Tennessee. "We'll get a ride, sooner or later."

It was a bright and sunny day, and the breeze off the ocean tangled my shag cut, but I didn't care. I felt very happy then, free and eager to be on the move again.

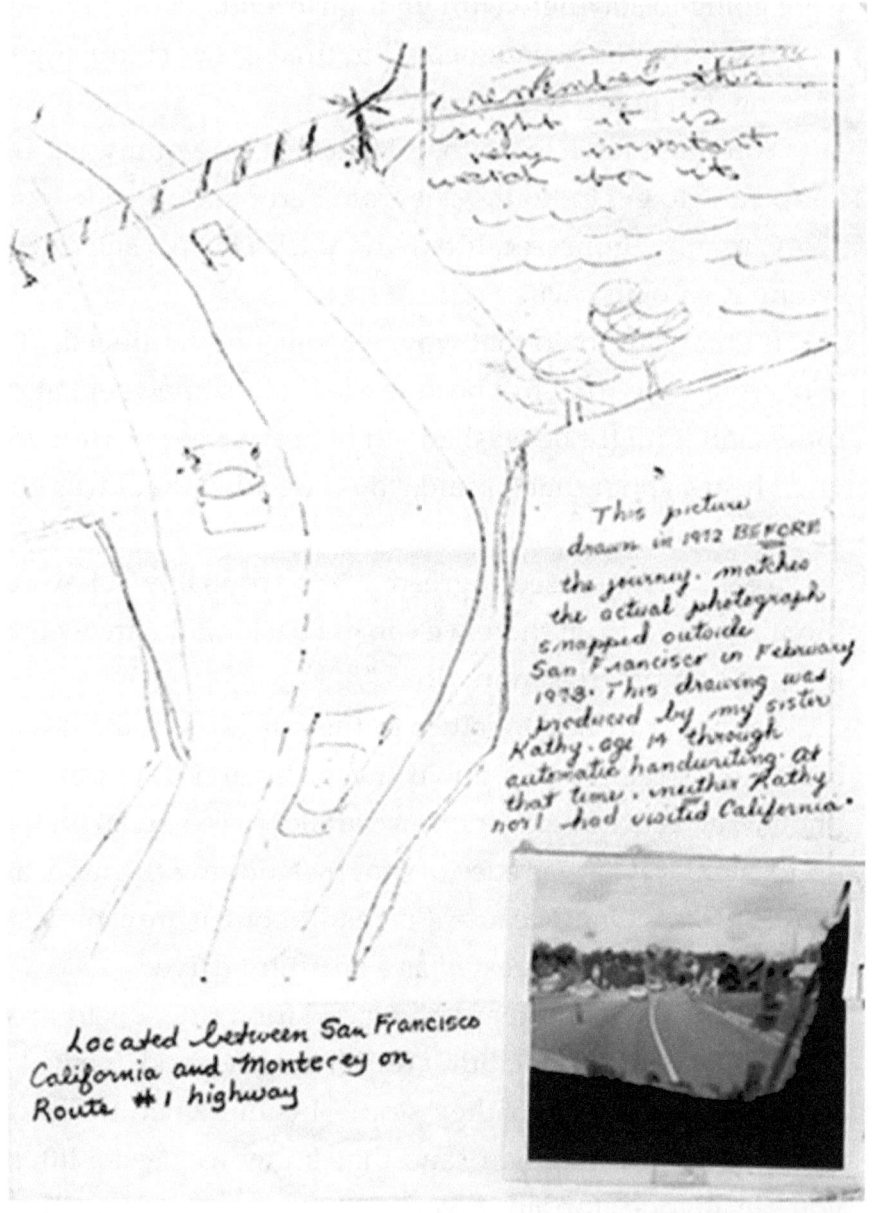

This picture drawn in 1972 BEFORE the journey matches the actual photograph snapped outside San Francisco in February 1973. This drawing was produced by my sister Kathy age 14 through automatic handwriting at that time. neither Kathy nor I had visited California.

Located between San Francisco California and Monterey on Route #1 highway

Finally, we got a ride. An ancient van pulled up beside us, surfboard stuck on top and an old dog with a festered eye, lying in the back on a dirty blanket. Tennessee took the front seat, and I crawled in beside the old dog. There didn't seem to be much room and yet, it was a ride, wasn't it?

Down the road to Monterey! Tennessee in the front with this tall, rangy, hippie-looking dude with a beard, silent and solemn. We passed houses perched on cliffs overlooking the ocean, beautiful places, and I had my camera out, snapping shots of the route while fending off the old dog, panting heavily, its injured eye in my face.

It came to my attention gradually that we were indeed running beside the railway tracks, and I began to get excited.

This must be it!

"Oh, my God! It was going to happen, just as I'd been told it would! This must be where the diary was buried."

I had a feeling of shock deep down in my stomach, mixed with a state of frozen anticipation. We were down over the hill. I leaned forward, between Tennessee and the driver and took a snapshot of it. It was perfect–just like the drawing. There was a railway crossing at the bottom of the hill and two cars approaching each other, on either side, a gray Volkswagen, similar in shape to the small car depicted in Kate's drawing. The ocean was close by but not in sight at that angle.

The camera was poised in my shaking hands, and as we approached the railway crossing, I took several photos as the van rolled over the crossing and on up the hill. A war was going on in my mind, part of me crying, "Stop and get out," and another voice advising me not to. I didn't have a shovel to dig with, and I might be left stranded without another ride for hours. I decided that the photos would be evidence enough for now.

It was mid-afternoon when we finally pulled into Monterey. I got out of the van and reached in to get my gear. When I turned around, Tennessee and the driver had vanished, and I was left alone, again.

More bewildered than frightened, I walked into a restaurant and ordered something to eat. While I dug into a plate of fish and chips, I tried to make sense of this crazy mixed-up day. For a few moments, my courage left me, and I was just uncomfortable, in a strange place, surrounded by strangers, another hippie girl on the run.

I made some phone calls from the lobby of a hotel and finally located a crash pad over in Seaside, a lady who was accepting transients into her private home overnight. I walked into a smoke shop to ask for directions. The man behind the counter smiled at me, "And what are you doing, young lady, with that big pack? You aren't hitchhiking alone, I hope."

"Yes, I am," I replied. "I lost my traveling companion, so I haven't got much choice right now."

"Well, you'd better be careful. There's been some girl hitchhikers around here murdered recently. If I were you, I'd leave this area. It's not safe—not like it used to be. This used to be a pretty quiet place."

"Well," I argued, "there's danger everywhere you go. If I was afraid of what might happen, I'd never go anywhere."

"True enough," he laughed. "Just be careful. There's sensible ways to travel—by car, by bus, and train. Just be careful, that's all."

I walked out of that shop feeling considerably more edgy than when I'd walked into it. It wasn't merely what the man had said, but something about Monterey rubbed me the wrong way. A feeling of uneasiness began to settle over me.

I sat down on a bench outside and waited for the bus. It was getting dark, and a young, hippie dude stopped and came over to me.

"Hey," he asked, "are you lookin' for a place to stay tonight?"

"Ah yes, I was, but I have the address of someone over in

Seaside who's taking in transients."

"Seaside!" the hippie dude exclaimed, "you don't want to go there. You can't walk down the street without being bothered. Why don't you come over to Carmel with me? I help transients from time to time. We have a really great place over there, and it's safer than Seaside."

"No," I refused, a hunch telling me to let this one go, "thanks anyway. I'm sure this place will work out just fine."

"Okay," hippie dude shrugged, "but if you should change your mind, come on over." He wrote down his address, and I shoved it into my pocket.

I continued to sit on the bench waiting for the bus, darkness falling, feeling more and more uncertain. Funny, the difference in places. I hadn't felt this way in San Francisco. Why this sense of impending danger here? I couldn't shake it.

Finally, a kindly, elderly lady told me that I was in the wrong spot to catch the bus I was looking for and that I'd better get a move on or I'd miss the last one going to Seaside. I headed up the street on the run and caught it just in time.

The driver let me off near the address, and I found the house without too much trouble. Nobody hassled me along the way, although it was pitch black when I finally got there. It was a small but cute house with a front yard, rather run-down, with children's toys scattered in front, but I took a deep breath and knocked on the door.

A tall, skinny Hispanic man opened the door and let me in. It was unbelievably crowded in there, messy and hot inside. I set down my pack, just grateful for a place to rest for a while. People introduced themselves–three ex-Marines on the run from the Vietnam War and one busy, flustered woman chasing a two-year-old boy with sandy blond hair.

The ex-Marines went on talking about draft dodging and asked me how the scene was up in Canada.

"Oh, there are quite a few of them up there all right," I agreed. "It's hard to get established when you're in a country illegally to begin with, but I've heard that they help draft dodgers in Montreal and Toronto."

They went on rapping about how they each had devised various ways of getting out of military service in Vietnam and how they'd duped the U.S. government.

I brought out my little astrology handbook and gave everyone the characteristics of their Sun signs. It was getting late, and there was no mention of a bed yet. Finally, I confronted the woman of the house, and she sent me into her little boy's room where there was a mattress lying on the floor, covered with a rumpled old sheet, next to a wall. I threw my sleeping bag on top, exhausted, blue jeans and all. One of the ex-Marines came in and sacked out beside me on the floor. I fell into a nervous sleep.

In the morning, the woman offered to drive me to the bus station because I'd decided that I was getting out of Monterey that day. I said my goodbyes to the other transients and wished them well. I was no sympathizer to the American government's involvement in the Vietnam War. It was every man for himself in this situation.

At the bus station, I bought a ticket for Los Angeles, but it wasn't scheduled to leave until later on that afternoon, so I wandered down to McDonald's for a hamburger, after putting my pack in a locker. I was in a music store, looking around, when a tall, young, sandy-haired, surfer type guy walked over to me and started talking.

He told me that he was just passing through Monterey and had run into car trouble. He was working at the army base temporarily, in the kitchen, to make some money to repair his car and would eventually be heading down to Mexico too. We discussed music for a while, and I asked him about the music scene around Monterey.

"Monterey! You kidding?" he exclaimed. "Why this is just about the most musical place around, blues, jazz, rock, country–you name it and you'll find it. Have you taken it in yet?"

"No."

He was surprised. "Listen, you haven't seen the half of it then. Why don't you stick around and I'll show you what's going on in this area? You can stay with me. I live on a commune with a group of young kids, great people. There's lot of space. You can have a shower and wash your clothes if you want. Stick around, and I'll show you some of the action."

He scribbled down the address of his friends and then apologized for having to leave for work, saying, "Meet me at the bus station at 8 o'clock tonight, and I'll drive you down there."

With that, he bent down and kissed me lightly on the cheek, turned, and walked away.

I left the music store and wandered down to the wharf snapping a few photos of Monterey Bay, which was beautiful, it's true, but not as beautiful as I'd imagined it to be. Then I walked out on the long dock to watch the boats and listen to the fishermen talking. An artist had her canvas up and was sketching.

One of the fishermen came over and sat down beside me, curious. "What is a pretty young girl like you doing alone, wandering around these parts?" he asked. "Aren't you afraid, and don't men bother you?"

"Yes," I replied patiently, "but I just ignore them and they go away."

"How come you travel alone?" the man asked.

"Well, actually," I explained, "I was traveling with someone, but I lost him here in Monterey, and now I'm alone again."

"Why do you travel?"

I shrugged. "I'm restless, don't like to be tied down, and I enjoy traveling alone."

"You don't sound like any woman I've ever known," the fisherman gazed at me perplexed. "They were always trying to get me to settle down. I have to give you credit for being brave, but don't be foolish. You say you are going down to Mexico. Do you speak any of the language?"

"No," I answered, "but I'll probably pick some up along the way."

The fisherman shook his head in wonder. "And when you get down to the Caribbean and need to get from one island to another, if one of the men says he'll take you if you *pay him*, what will you do?" the man asked slyly.

"If he wants money, I'll pay him what I can, and if I can't afford it, I'll wait for another boat or find some other way to get to where I want to go," I replied abruptly.

"Well," my friend admitted, "either you've got more guts than I've ever seen in a person or else you're *loco*."

"Is that your boat?" I asked, changing the subject and pointing to a small fishing boat, anchored along the dock.

"Oh, no," he answered, pointing to another, bobbing out in the Bay. "There she is, and I've got to go, but I wish you luck." We shook hands, and I continued on, exploring the waterfront.

I could hear Eric Burdon screaming, "Monterey" in my mind with the drums pounding above the salt sea spraying. Only several years before, Jimi Hendrix had burned his guitar, and Janis Joplin had made her great debut. The smell of dead fish and salt water followed me down to the train yards where I saw a locomotive with a few cars hitched up, ready to pull out. I drew closer, following a strong urge, contemplating hopping a freight, but the curious stares of several railway men frightened me away. Instead, I doubled back, making a wide circle around the area, back to the Greyhound Bus Station, and boarded a bus for L.A.

Chapter Eleven

Meet Me in L.A.

B y dusk, we were well on our way to Los Angeles. It struck me as funny that the area seemed much less populated than the outskirts of Toronto. High, lonely hills loomed around us and valleys upon which the only stamp of man's technology seemed to be the freeway that we sped along on and the super cars whizzing by. My eyes seemed hypnotized by the railway tracks, which were constantly beside us. Words flashed into my mind, "Santa Barbara, silver moonlight on the ocean, silver rail-way tracks," and the wheels of the bus hypnotized me to sleep and a vivid scene flashed into my mind.

There was a garden party in Santa Barbara, beside the ocean. Nick was playing in the band for this gig. He was dressed up in a flashy suit, walking by the ocean and talking to Sandra, who was dressed up in a full-length, party gown.

Chinese lanterns were strung up over the yard, glowing in the dark, and strains of Glenn Miller drifted across the beach. Waves pounded against the shore, and moonlight shone across the ocean. There was laughter and men dressed in military uniforms, strolling arm in arm with pretty girls, and the faint drone of military aircraft in the skies, coming and going from a nearby air force base.

Sandra gazed at Nick, a worried expression in her eyes. "Nick, I worry about you when you are so far away. It's always a gig to go to, and you promised me, we was gonna get married in the spring."

Nick smiled at Sandra and gave her hand a squeeze. "You know dis music business, Sandra. I gotta be free to follow da circuit right now. Not easy for a black man, playin' blues, and now swing. Ain't no boogie-woogie either. Gotta take every chance I can get. Better'n soft shoe two, doll, an' beats ridin' da rods!"

Nick pulled Sandra close to him, but she pulled away.

"Nick, you're not still doin'..."

"What," Nick exclaimed, "Puffy White Cloud? Girl, I ain't no junkie."

Sandra was not convinced. "I hear there's lots of it in South America and the Caribbean."

"Lots of it here too, if you know where to get it," Nick replied.

Sandra eyed Nick reproachfully. "It's jus' an excuse, Nick. You're runnin' from your mama and how you feel 'bout her."

Nick cast his eyes downward defensively. "She neva feel nothin' 'bout me, 'an I neva goin' back."

"Well, what about Jessup?" Sandra asked.

"Never mind Jessup. He fin' me," Nick replied stubbornly.

The couple turned up the beach toward the music and laughter. The drone of more military planes departing the nearby air force base filled the air, and Nick was singing.

Meet Me in L.A.

Rollin' along, down by the sea
   Moonlight in a dream
   What does it all mean
   Meet me in L.A.
Ocean pass by, stars in a blue sky
Two on the road, four to go, meet me in L.A.
Meet me in L.A., what you be wearing?
Baby, I'm comin', baby, I'm comin' home...

I awoke to dark waves pounding the shore beside us as we sped through the night. I yawned sleepily and turned to the passenger sitting beside me. "Did you hear something?"

"Hear what?" the passenger asked curiously.

"Glenn Miller music and airplanes."

The passenger looked at me oddly and shook his head. I scratched my head, puzzled.

"Funny, it was so loud." I shifted in my seat and pulled my jacket around me. Turning my gaze back to the dark moonlit waves, "Moonlight Serenade" in my mind lulled me back to sleep.

The freeway to Los Angeles seemed endless. Maybe there really wasn't a city called Los Angeles–just a freeway that wound through a suburban metropolis. We passed through North Hollywood at midnight, deserted and sinister in the dark. I remembered that Janis Joplin had died in North Hollywood, in a motel somewhere. It seemed like such a lonely place. We passed by the legendary Sunset Strip, and even there, the streets were deserted at that hour. At the downtown Los Angeles bus terminal, I waited for a transfer to another bus that would take me to San Diego. Suspicious faces stared at me from their plastic chairs attached to television sets, conveniently placed in the lobby. Drop in your coins, and watch your favorite show in the Home of the Stars. After all, this was the center of "show business," wasn't it?

I pulled out a map of Los Angeles and focused on the Hollywood area. Reaching into my pocket, I took out a pen and circled a neighborhood in the San Fernando Valley. Examining it closer, the Northridge area, I saw it–Darby Avenue! Why was there a Darby Avenue in Los Angeles and not in San Francisco?

But Cocomo Road was home and what was ten blocks west of

Darby Avenue. The only thing I could see there was railway tracks, and then it hit me. Of course, he was a "Billy, a bo, or a Billy Jack, an out and out outsider." Home was the railway tracks, and Nick had only come into Los Angeles to visit Sandra before jumping another train. That would seem to tie in with *two on the road, four to go, meet me* in L.A., *bring Sandra.* Maybe Sandra had lived in Los Angeles on Darby Avenue. What had her last name been? I wish I'd had been given that information so I could look up the family.

Cocomo Road

Cocomo Road is the pack on my back
Cocomo Road is in my brain
Cocomo Road is home to me
I see it through the rain.
Ten blocks west of Darby Ave., turn left, two down on the
*   right*
Cocomo Road is home to me babe, I'm goin' home tonight.
Many a traveler's gone the route
Many a night cab rider
A billy, a bo or a billy jack
A down and out outsider
Where are you headed and where have you gone
How can you know how to catch the dawn?

The mystery of it all continued to tease my mind as I shoved the map back into my pocket. I gazed at the clock on the wall opposite me. It was way past midnight now. I glanced apprehensively at the weirdos, camera toting tourists, and the darkness, through the glass doors, and stepped up to the counter to ask the clerk when my connecting bus would be boarding.

The downtown San Diego skyline jutted into the hazy, blue

Pacific sky as we rolled into town, and the Greyhound pulled into the station. My pack would be riding down on another bus and hadn't arrived yet and probably wouldn't until later in the day. I was dirty and irritable because I'd been separated from my toothbrush for days and my jeans had been glued to me for days. I scanned the Yellow Pages for a hotel and chose the Pickwick for a cheap room but still a luxury for me. I stepped straight into the shower and washed my hair with a bar of soap. Then clean and in a better mood, I put my clothes back on–it was becoming a road habit now–and fell asleep on top of the bed, jacket spread over me.

Later, my pack was waiting for me at the terminal, and I could relax. My next goal was to find a crash pad within my means. After scanning the Yellow Pages again, I came across a place I thought might be a hostel of some sort. I phoned them up and they said, "Yeah, come on down. We'll give you a place to stay for a few days. My name's Frank."

Finding the place wasn't difficult. He'd given me clear directions, and the San Diego streets were well laid out in an organized fashion, numbered, and everything was ultra-modern and clean. I took an instant liking to San Diego. I walked up the main street, turned a few corners, and there it was–a big, old, white house with a fierce looking German Shepherd tied up on the front veranda. Edging my way gingerly past the barking dog, I walked into the lobby and up to the front desk, asking, "Hey, where can I meet Frank?"

A couple of men looked up from the color TV they were watching, and one of them told me that Frank had just stepped out and would be back in a while. I flopped down on a shabby but comfortable looking couch and gazed around. That was odd, not another girl in sight!

"Hi!" I attempted some friendly conversation, but the guys kept their eyes glued to the TV and slugged down cold beers. Geez, I was hot, and nobody offered me one. I sat down beside a Mexican with middle-aged spread, and in between sips he asked me where I'd come from.

"Came in from San Francisco this morning," I replied.

"San Francisco, eh?" He looked thoughtful. "I used to live there a long time ago. We had the bohemians then–Jack Kerouac and his gang, writing poetry, and sitting around in music dives. I used to know him."

"No kiddin'! I've read *On the Road*–it's fantastic," I said enthusiastically.

He went on. "Then you had the beatniks, and after that came the hippies. Something's always happening in San Francisco!"

"That's for sure," I agreed. "I'll return someday, but for now, I'm heading down Mexico way."

A few minutes later, Frank, a tall, lean, "been there, done it all" dude, early thirties maybe, with what seemed like "save the world eyes," strode into the lobby and smiled at me, extending his hand.

"Hello, Miss...?"

"Kellar," I said, accepting the handshake.

"Now, Miss Kellar," he asked, with a hint of curiosity in his eyes, "when did you get out?"

I stood there, my mouth open, and all I could manage was a dumb, "Hunh, get out of where?"

A ripple of laughter floated around the lobby, and I felt my face getting redder than the heat would have provoked.

"Get out of jail, of course," Frank replied, questioning me. "You did just get out of jail, didn't you? This is a halfway house for male ex-cons."

Now I felt really stupid. "Um, ah, I wasn't in jail, if that's what you mean." I stammered, "I just need a place to sleep for the night, if you have space. Just passing through, you know?"

"Oh," Frank pulled on his beard thoughtfully, "well, I guess that we can put you on a mattress upstairs in the room where my wife and I sleep, if you don't mind. The dog usually sleeps there, but it'll be safe."

"Oh, no," I replied hastily. "I don't mind dogs, so long as they don't bite."

I filled in the form, and Frank hoisted my pack. "That's kinda heavy for a little girl like you, isn't it?" he asked, surprised.

"Aw, heck, no," I replied. "Everybody asks me that. Course, I wouldn't want to have to carry it too far in this kind of weather."

I followed Frank up a narrow stairway to a Spartan looking bedroom with two mattresses on the floor, and Frank set my pack on the one by the window. He turned to me and whispered, "Don't want the guys to know, but just to celebrate your visit here, Nicki, we'll take you out on the town tonight. Do you like live plays?"

"Wow! Don't think I've ever seen one," I admitted.

"Then you're in for a treat," Frank smiled.

I was getting a really good impression of San Diego by now. It seems that every city you pass through has a soul. Almost like the people you know, some are good, some are bad, some are friendly and want to be generous toward you while others turn their backs on you and walk the other way. Every place has a subtle influence on you, whether you are aware of it or not, so why not choose the place that's good for you? I'd felt good vibes in San Francisco and not so much in Monterey or Los Angeles, but then, I'd only seen L.A. at night. Maybe it was different by day.

I went downtown to see about getting a tourist visa to enter Mexico and was glad to discover that it was free! I browsed around in shops and lingered in a bookstore that sold the largest assortment of astrology books I'd ever seen, and wouldn't you know? I didn't have the cash to buy any. Even if I could, I wouldn't have been able to carry them with me. So I sighed and made a mental note that San Diego had the books that I wanted, and maybe someday I'd be back this way again to pick them up.

I ate at a health food store. Not that I was a fanatic or anything, but I did take my vitamins and usually drank bottled water. It was dusk when I caught a bus back up the same street to the halfway house, and the guys were *still* lounging around watching TV!

Wandering back out onto the front porch, I talked with one of the ex-cons leaning against the railing. He was either stoned or from another heavy scene, judging from the way he talked. "Hey, man," he asked, "where are you goin'–like?"

"Whatcha mean?"

"I mean, what's your gig like?"

"Headin' down to Mexico to see what's happening down there," I answered, not sure whether to stay and talk with this man or run away from him.

"Oh cool, cool, yeah." He paused a moment, lost in thought, then continued, "I can dig it man, that's groovy. Like, what are you goin' down there for?"

Well, I thought I just told you, I thought impatiently. "Oh, to check out the scene, look around, and travel–you know?"

"Well, what is your scene?" I asked him.

"Oh, um," the guy nodded, as if he was strung out on heroin, and maybe he was. "I met these two chicks, um, you know, an' was living with them. One of the fuckers–well, you know the heat was watching them anyway, and when I moved in, they knew I was pushing, so they crashed it and busted us all."

"For what?" I asked.

"Just grass, man. Just fuckin' grass," he replied angrily.

"Well, that's too bad, man," I sympathized.

"So now I'm on parole for a few years. I'm just hangin' in there. Mexico, you say? Cool, cool. Like to go there myself," he rambled on.

We rapped on about drugs and the unjust laws of San Diego and how you'd better watch your back here because the cops in San Diego were the absolute worst.

"Like they got this neat little community here, and they don't like people like us corrupting it, you know?"

Later that evening, Frank pulled up in an old pickup truck, and a few of us, including Frank's Mexican wife, jumped on for the ride to the theater downtown. Frank had lined me up with a tall, lanky, goony looking ex-con over six feet, who towered over me, hardly said a word, and smiled like an idiot all evening.

"And who else is going to help these guys out?" Frank shrugged. "Hell, the city don't want them, and after getting out of jail, they just wander the streets, looking for trouble that lands them right back in jail where they came from."

Frank was as groovy a manager as you could get. After the show, he smuggled a joint and a bottle of vodka and ginger ale "to celebrate my visit" past the ex-cons still sitting around the lobby. Upstairs in his bedroom, his wife, my date, and I proceeded to get zonked. "Lanky" kept edging closer and closer to me, trying to put his arms around me. Frank stripped naked and crawled in beside his wife. I wasn't in the mood for any bullshit. I'd been on the road for three days without a decent night's sleep. "Lanky" lay down beside me. I rolled away. He rolled closer until he just about pushed me off the side of the mattress.

"Come and get under the sheets," he whispered.

"Hell, no–I just sleep in my clothes on top, like this," I replied. "Can you give me my jacket, please? I don't feel right without it covering me while I sleep."

"Oh, c'mon, baby." He grinned that silly grin again. "You don't need that. You've got me."

"I think I'd rather have my jacket."

But there was no persuading "Lanky." He placed his long, ape-like arms around me, and I struggled to get away. This went on for hours. I was underneath the window on the floor now, having been pushed completely off the mattress, and the magic of the eternal train whistle blowing in the distance, once again, infallibly mesmerized me. For a brief moment, I stopped struggling and listened.

"Man," I whispered, "you know what it's like to wanna go and keep going? To follow your heart and let life show you the way? Man, I love that sound!"

"Yeah," mused Lanky, "I used to be a truck driver once. It gets in your blood–traveling all the time."

He paused a moment. "You say you're goin' to Mexico?"

"Yeah," I replied, "might catch a ship out of Veracruz to Jamaica."

Lanky was impressed. "Whew, Mexico alone? Gotta route map?"

I rummaged around in my pack and pulled out the page that Kate had given me, with the route drawn from San Francisco to the Caribbean and back up to New York. Lanky examined it, and an odd look crossed his face. "Did you know that that's a drug runner's route? Starts in California, crosses the border into Mexico, circles S.A. and the Caribbean and ends in New York. I know because I used to do it."

I was stunned. "No kiddin'? Somebody gave this to me. It's supposed to be a band tour route."

"Well, maybe your musician pushed drugs in between gigs," Lanky suggested, a look of knowingness crossing his face, and he glanced at me again, grinning.

The impact of Lanky's words hit me like a sledgehammer. Had I somehow been duped? My mind was suddenly filled with questions. What the hell was I doing, following a drug runner's route? I had already resisted the temptation in San Francisco to take hard drugs, but where was the journey leading me in terms of resolving more of Nick's karma? Why hadn't I been told about this map in the trance sessions? Why was I being pulled farther and farther south into Mexico if the purpose wasn't entirely musical? Would I confront Nick the drug runner as well as Nick the musician on this journey? Would there be more encounters with musicians and other opportunities to perform? *"He touched the coast with his music."* There was a nagging urgency inside me that ignited my restlessness even further, and I knew there was no turning back now, regardless.

"More than one reason for travelin' I guess." I tried to shrug it off. I knew that Nick had been a user, but I had never thought of him as a pusher. Maybe music didn't always pay the bills for him, or else it was the only way he could get a cheap fix. The thought disturbed me–that I could have been an international drug pusher–that he could have brought hell into the lives of others, for the sake of his own addiction.

Lanky continued, "You can love the road too much, but I ain't got much choice these days. I'm stuck here on parole for two years anyway, so come to bed, darlin'." He pulled me closer, and groped under my shirt. I pushed him away, rolled over, and turned my back on him. Frank and his wife were snoring away on the other side of the room, and in a moment of panic I thought, *They couldn't help me if this guy jumped me. It'd be over with before they woke up.*

Sitting on the mattress, my back to Lanky, I gazed out the window and the words to one of Nick's songs sprung into my mind. I tuned him out until all I could hear was the sound of the train clacking through the night.

Oh, train whistle, in my mind, oh, train whistle, till I die.
I'll be ridin' the rods chokin' on dust, ridin' the rods '
cause I know I must, ridin' the rods, baby, in my dreams,
even if all I ever eat is beans, 'cause
I'm the Billy Bo supreme!

I didn't get any sleep that night again, either. The struggle continued in the dark until dawn when Lanky began swearing and throwing vulgar remarks my way–"little bitch, cock teaser" and assorted others. Frank's wife woke up and got ready for work. Lanky finally gave up the battle, after throwing a few more insulting remarks my way and left. Frank's wife witnessed what was going on and nudged Frank, who came out of dreamland. He apologized for Lanky's behavior and, after his wife had gone, invited me to sleep beside him. Her side of the bed was still warm, and I accepted gratefully, finding some measure of security in the fact that Frank, after all, was in charge here and could do no wrong. I managed to catch a few hours of sleep until a voice shouted up the stairs, "Hey, Frank, when the hell are you gonna get up?"

Frank yawned and got dressed, and I packed it in and got the hell out of that house. I beat it back down to the Greyhound Terminal and caught the next bus to Tijuana.

Mexico

Oh, Mexico
Tijuana, rusty shack homes
Buckets full of muddy water
Tiny, old women and children
Gazing at me with eyes of lost dogs
I came to see your fiestas
And saw your poverty instead
There were beggars underfoot
And a scorching sun overhead
Crying children and pregnant women
Adios, Mexico
I'll not be back again.

Chapter Twelve

Train to Guadalajara

On the morning of February 16, I caught a bus to Tijuana and stepped off the bus with my pack and two Canadian girls from Vancouver, also bound for Mexico, and the three of us walked across the Mexican-American border.

The border inspectors looked me over and asked the usual questions, inspecting my passport and tourist visa–Where was I going and for how long? What was my purpose in traveling? Again, I played the role of student on vacation. I was in a great mood and had nothing to hide, and I guess they must have sensed it for they passed me right through, along with one of the other girls from Vancouver, but the other girl wasn't so lucky.

She was taken aside by a female border official and searched, possibly because she looked guilty, but her guilt was only nervousness, and they eventually passed her through. I don't know how thoroughly she was searched, but she returned blushing and didn't say a word for the next half-hour.

Finally, we all passed through and walked onto the streets of Tijuana. The first whiff of it turned my stomach, and I fought the urge to puke. The Third World poverty hit me like a ton of bricks when I saw a brown, mongrel dog defecating in the muddy river beside us, while a child lowered a bucket into the same garbage strewn, muddy water a few feet away.

Rusty, dirty, ramshackle shacks scattered along the river's edge. Strings of laundry flapped in the breeze. Barefoot children in dirty clothes shouted gleefully as they played, ducking under the lines. Trying to reason with my stomach, I followed the girls down to the bus station, and I bought a ticket for Mexicali in the Baja California while my two new friends decided they were going to Ensenada.

On the route map of Nick's journey, there were several key circled areas beginning with the San Francisco to San Diego route, which I'd just completed, then another, heading southeast along the Arizona/Texas/Mexican border jumping off from the Monterey, Mexico area/Brownsville, Texas port. Here he had boarded a ship across the Gulf of Mexico stopping at Cabo Catoche in the Yucatan, before making another stop at Jamaica, thereby bypassing most of Mexico, but I had chosen to travel through Mexico to the Yucatan with the goal of reuniting with his stop at Cabo Catoche, and travelling onward to the Caribbean. So maybe I was exploring new territory that even Nick hadn't visited. I wasn't so sure about going deeper south into South America; the other circled locations *"He just touched the tip of South America with his music"* had been the towns of Maracaibo, Venezuela and Cumana, and Buenos Aires as well as Trinidad, Tobago, Puerto Rico and Miami, Florida *"before heading back to New York"* the New York/Cleveland, Ohio area.

And so we parted, and I was alone, on the road in Mexico, an innocent babe, bewildered by the passing signs in Spanish. We rolled along the countryside, barren except for the occasional "house," lots of barbed wire, and scrawny looking cattle grazing by the sides of the highway. It was warmer now. I leaned back against the seat as the unfamiliar odors continued to rock my stomach. We arrived in Mexicali, and I took a cab down to the train station stopping to change some American money into Mexican. At that time, it seemed as though I'd been cheated.

"Peso, what's a peso? How much? *Cuanto?*" I asked, consulting my Spanish phrase book. The clerk jabbered something back in Spanish and handed me over what I thought might be enough, but I wasn't sure. I took the money and ran.

At the train station, I met three American girls, Nancy, Sue, and Kathy from a commune up near San Francisco on their way to Guadalajara with a French Canadian by the name of Renard, who was born under the sign of Cancer the Crab.

I counted out the centavos, which looked like pennies. There were cinco centavos, and twenty centavos coins, which looked like brown quarters and pesos as well as coins, which came in fives, tens, twenties, fifties, hundreds and so on. I was starting to get the hang of it and purchased my first "*cerveza,*" Mexican beer. Beer had never tasted so good before in the heat of the day.

We all boarded the train for Guadalajara as the sun began to fade in the west. Our tickets were second class, and the train was a slow-moving relic from the distant past; the Sonora Baja California/Pacific Railway. Nick could have ridden this one, I was sure. I couldn't see any sleeping berths. It was filthy. There was no food service, and the filthy, cubby hole bathrooms, with toilets that dumped to the tracks below, had no lights in them, so I had to carry a flashlight and hold my nose at the same time when I needed to go pee. No way was I going to sit down, so I braced myself, crouched down, and aimed for the hole as best I could.

The first few days, I walked into the men's bathroom because I couldn't read ladies in Spanish yet. Then I started to study my Spanish phrase book more carefully and learned some basic phrases–how to buy things and not get cheated.

We all slept upright in our seats, which were too narrow to lie in lengthwise across, even for little me. It was crowded, nevertheless, and we moved along slowly through the Mexican countryside stopping at every little town and settlement during the day and night: Puerto Penasco, Sonora, Caborca, Benjamin Hill, Hermosillo, Empalme and Guaymas, Ciudad Obregon, Navojoa, Culiacan, Mazatlán and Tepic.

At each stop, the Mexican men, women, and children would crowd against the waiting train shouting, *"Tacos! Tortas!"* and not stopping at that, they would board the train parading down the aisle aggressively pushing their wares–food, blankets, leather goods and homemade liquor.

February 16th and 17th, and still we were rolling along the Mexican countryside, which was changing now from flat, stubby plains to a semi-jungle with mountains and deep valleys. The nights were cold, and I sat covered in blankets, shivering, and thought it would never end. I hadn't brushed my teeth since San Diego, and my clothes were dirty. I was dirty and hungry, and still we rolled along. It was an exercise in endurance, but we were all in it together.

The girls from California, Nancy, Sue, and Kathy, were welcome company during the boring daylight hours, sharing oranges and organic food with me. I bought some food from the locals, sampling tortas and tortillas, picking out the pieces of pork because someone had told me it had worms. I hoped that I wouldn't get the *tourista*, but I did anyway. The lyrics and melody to one of Nick's songs played with my mind:

Travelin' Blues

I hear that ole train whistle blow
A comin' down the track
Gonna take me back
I've heard that whistle many times before
But tho it's a different train

It's only one train more
Seems I only get home, then I have to hit the road again
Chorus:
  Wheels, rollin' down beneath my head
  You know it's always been my bed
  And I don't wanna change it now
  Wheels, rollin' down beneath my head
  You know it's always been my bed
  And I don't wanna change it now.

Now while I shivered through the cold nights, I clutched my aching belly, swallowing Aspirin and cursing the day I ever decided to cross that border and venture into the midst of these horrors. How could Nick ever have "ridden the rods" when I couldn't even manage riding a passenger train in Mexico? Shame, shame!

I woke up in the night. The train had just lurched to a stop at another little village station, high up in the mountains, and in a daze, my head-on Renard's shoulder, I blinked semi-consciously, sensing the lack of motion beneath us, hearing the shuffling movements of passengers coming and going and unfamiliar shouts in the darkness, and was confused. Drugged with sleep, I slipped back into the dreamless void.

Renard and I talked about drugs. It seems that he had tried just about everything there was, including heroin, and that he almost died from it. It was in Montreal that it had happened, and he told me the story.

"I am with my friends, you know, *mes amis*, and am drinking maybe a little much booze, when they ask, 'Renard, you want to try some heroin?' And I say, sure, so they tie me up, put the needle in, and I lie down on the couch and start to choke. I turn purple and fall asleep, still choking. They panic! A friend of theirs has died of this before this way, so they fill me full of downers, and I come to, and I am all right."

I gazed at him, a question in my eyes. "Are you going to try it again someday?"

"Someday, yes, and in Guadalajara, I hope to pick up some grass and maybe the magic mushroom–the *peyote*. What about you? Do you use drugs?"

Drugs again! I hesitated a moment. All of a sudden, there was a sinking feeling in the pit of my stomach. What if "going with the flow" meant riding a tide to destruction? I shook off the thought. Of course, I'd be fine–God was with me, and my guardian angel was on the watch. Hadn't Kate reassured me?

I smiled sheepishly, "Oh, just a little grass and hash. I tried LSD a few years ago and nearly flipped out..."

And here it was again..."Oh, you must try heroin. Now there's something! You haven't seen much yet. Do you drink at all?"

"Oh, just a little, from time to time. I'm not really into it. Why, are you?"

Renard smiled apologetically. "Well, I was once what you call an alcoholic, but since then I have been off booze and I can control it, you see, but I still love it."

And we continued talking on and on about drugs and about life and Mexico. Renard had been here before and knew a little Spanish. Nancy spoke it fluently because she'd lived in Mexico when she was a little girl.

Renard continued, "I know this girl, back in Montreal, and she is a–what you would call a junkie–and she supports her family by prostitution, but she is a wonderful friend of mine." Renard sprang to her defense. "You might think that it is bad, but she is a good person, and there is nothing wrong with what she does. I stay with her once in a while."

And still we rolled along on our way to Guadalajara. I'd decided that I would get off with the rest of them, instead of continuing on to Mexico City alone. Besides, I couldn't stand riding that train much longer.

Through Los Mochis, Mazatlán, and Tepic, we passed families camping out in wooden boxcar homes, desert, and uninhabited wilderness, and one day the train hit a cow that was on the track and threw her over the bank, dead instantly. I cried out against this accidental act of cruelty in anger, but Renard only smiled and said, "I hope someone comes back for the meat."

The train chugged along steadily, making progress despite the local stops. I watched with curiosity, the armed guards who rode along with us carrying their rifles and pistols in plain view, observing them as they stood watch over the village folk pushing their wares.

Finally, on February 18th, we arrived in Guadalajara. Civilization again, only this was a different kind of civilization than the one that I was used to: beggars on street corners, children selling chicklets, and a bustling, huge marketplace, where they sold everything from food to clothing and hardware.

At night, the Mexican mariachis serenaded us and the Mexican men clamored for our attention, buying us beers and chattering away in Spanish, while Sue, Kathy, and I struggled to understand, and Nancy intervened and translated for us. Eating at the marketplace! For the first time, I sampled the best of Mexican cuisine; homemade tortillas dipped in exquisite hot sauces, and suddenly overcome with a craving for chocolate, running from vendor to vendor asking for el chocolate, pronounced *el chok-o-lat-e*.

I followed the girls faithfully, terrified of getting lost and forgetting our address, not wanting to repeat my San Francisco predicament. We had rented a room at a cheap, student hostel for only nine pesos each per night and shoved the two double beds together and put Renard against the wall, flanked by myself, then Sue, Kathy, and Nancy, all in a row across. I wasn't very happy about having to sleep beside Renard, but beggars can't be choosers, and I wasn't about to argue with Nancy, who was running the show.

Following Nancy, Sue and Kathy through the marketplace in Guadalajara, Mexico in March 1973.

I discovered, to my dismay, that I couldn't deposit used toilet paper into the toilet. Instead, it would have to go in a little basket of its own beside the toilet. That didn't seem very sanitary to me! The shower had no enclosure or curtain, just a bare shower head sticking out of the wall, which sprayed cold water all over the whole bathroom: over the toilet, over the basket of soiled toilet paper, and over my towel.

At night, I rolled up in my sleeping bag and tried to ignore Renard while he pleaded his case, "How can I sleep here tonight with such a *jolie fille* beside me, keeping me awake?

By day, we watched American movies subtitled in Spanish, and I made the acquaintance of a conga-bongo player by the name of Sol, who was a Yaqui Indian. He spoke a little English and claimed to be a substitute drummer for my favorite rock band, Santana! He also claimed to be a close friend of Carlos Santana himself, who lived not far from Guadalajara, and professed to be in love with a dancer in San Francisco. Small world! Maybe the stripper who had harassed me the day I jammed with Point Blank?

But I was overwhelmed by being in such proximity to one who knew the famous Carlos Santana personally and fascinated by his conversation about the *peyote*, the magic mushroom, which he produced, from his pocket, wrapped in foil. When he opened it, I gazed upon something forbidding, an ugly, grayish pulp with dark seeds scattered throughout it.

Taking my bongos between his knees, Sol said, "If you want to play the bongo, you must *feel* it! If you want to feel it, you must take drugs and become a part of the band that you are playing with." I couldn't believe I was hearing about "Stone Free" again, down here in Mexico, of all places. Again, I was being pressured to take drugs.

Sol, showing me "how the bongos should be played" while Renard and I observe in Guadalajara, Mexico in March 1973

"Come with me to Lake Chapala tomorrow, you and Renard, Sue, Kathy and Nancy. We will take the magic mushroom and really *feel* life. It will make you experience things you have never seen before. You will bring your bongos, and I will sit with you and teach you how to play them as they should be played." It was tempting, but I knew that I couldn't accept his offer. I had to distance myself as much as I could for my own safety. I'd heard about peyote. It was the "key to another world," but how could I handle another world right now when I was having difficulty maneuvering in this one?

"Then come into my room, and I will show you how to play the bongos anyway," suggested Sol, embracing me with a deep kiss. Maybe I was playing groupie because of his association with Santana, or maybe I had finally admitted I was lonely, but as the invisible lyrics to "Black Magic Woman" swirled in my memory, I dropped my jeans, and the hunting knife on the leather belt that I'd been wearing around my waist slid to the floor in a temporary surrender. We made love beside my drums, his dark skin against mine in the heat of the day. I vowed that it would be the first and last time on this journey that I would succumb to my human weakness, lest I betray its spiritual purpose. The next day, he left to search for his girlfriend up in San Francisco. It would be the last time I'd ever see Sol again.

We stayed in Guadalajara about a week, and then one day, Nancy, Sue, and Kathy met an old friend at the marketplace and made plans to leave the next day for San Blas. There wouldn't be enough room in the car for me, so I had to face the fact that I was on my own again, without a translator, in alien territory. The thought terrified me.

I explained the situation to Renard, telling him that he could come with me if he wanted to, but I wouldn't sleep with him. We could share expenses. This only angered him more, knowing that I'd just slept with Sol. "No, that won't work," he said, shaking his head. And so that same morning, Nancy hugged me goodbye and scribbled her home address in California on a piece of paper so I could look her up someday. And I said my goodbyes to Renard too, shouldered my pack, and headed for the bus station to buy a ticket for Mexico City.

I found myself riding in a luxuriously air-conditioned bus, sleek and clean, but generic, speeding down the highway. It seems that when you suffer through the tortures of primitive conditions and meet circumstances that test and often irritate you, you have to admit, when it's all over, that you wouldn't have had it any other way. Anyone can be a tourist, but not just anyone can be a traveler and merge with another culture the way that I had.

Chapter Thirteen

Mexico City

When I stepped off that bus from Guadalajara, it was nigh on to midnight, and as I went around to the side of the bus to pick up my pack, I fell into conversation with a middle-aged man from Toronto, who was on holidays in Mexico. He invited me to dinner, and I accepted, and we continued our conversation over dinner in the bus terminal restaurant. He seemed protective in a fatherly way and paid for my meal. Together we scanned a map of Mexico and the guidebook that he'd brought with him, one of those helpful but touristy books that every intelligent traveler must remember to bring with him. We looked for a cheap hotel while he shared his complaints with me about the rising prices of food, accommodation, and entertainment in this city that he had been visiting for many years. Must have been a Virgo!

Afterwards, I caught a taxi downtown to a cheap hotel and paid for my single room while he paid for his separately–no problems there! Once inside the room, I stripped down and stepped into the shower, enjoying every minute of it, studied a book about Mexico while my hair dried, put on a nightgown and, for the first time in ages, had a good night's sleep.

The morning brought hot sunshine, and I walked around alone, exploring the city while Mexican men eyed me royally. I wandered through Chapultepec Park and several museums and shops, returning to the hotel hungry. Across from the hotel was a food stand, so I ordered something Mexican to eat, and while I was devouring it, two Mexican men sat down beside me and tried to make conversation in English.

First, I looked at them, dressed in business suits–*square*! Then I attempted to finish my dinner, but they persisted.

"What your name? Where you from? Why you alone? Where you stay and for how long?"

I answered their questions in between bites of tortilla and thought they'd get discouraged, but they didn't, so I finally accepted a date with the one called Ernesto, who had buck teeth but a kind face, later that evening. This seemed to satisfy them, and they stopped bugging me. I went back to the hotel to write a few letters and send postcards.

Later that evening, Ernesto arrived with his companion, Javier. They were still dressed in suit and ties, although I was in blue jeans and runners, not having packed much in the way of fancy dress for special occasions.

We drove around Mexico City, finally ending up at an outdoor café where they served beer. Over beers, they prodded me into conversation again, but I wasn't in the mood to be sociable. They took it the wrong way.

"Why you so sad?"

"I'm not sad, really, just thoughtful, I guess."

"You always gazing off into space–like this," and Ernesto imitated my "tune-out." "You look right past us like we aren't here. Is strange, no?"

I looked dumbfounded. "I don't know."

How could I explain to them that I was feeling down, that I had the blues? I smiled and then tried to concentrate on the present, although I seemed to be drifting off onto a cloud of thought as I am often apt to do. Maybe I was missing San Francisco or even Point Blank. More than that, I longed to play the keyboards again, but I tried to be the lady who they expected me to be.

"Let's look for that jazz joint," I suggested, "the one in the tourist guide that's supposed to play American music."

We found it in the cellar of a building, and I could have sworn I was back in The Pub in Kingston, where I used to listen to country music. A noisy rock group was belting out the Rolling Stones in Spanish.

I thought, C'mon, man, where's those old, authentic blues? Where do they play them as I hear them in my mind? Dark, basement joints with hip people sitting around rapping with one another while a black sax player plays his heart out...Then the party gets a bit wilder and the bottles go round–wine, liquor, and tea–and the band comes to life. The crowds LISTENS as they dig those real, authentic jazz blues. Man, everybody sways with the rhythm of the drums and laughs excitedly as a Latin-American combo pounds through the brains of the people and the crowd digging Saturday night somewhere in my subconscious past–but it's not here.

I was still experiencing it in my mind, and I know that there was such a place, but this ain't it, baby, so Ernesto paid for the drinks, and we walked back out onto the streets of Mexico City. Then somehow, Ernesto and I were walking alone through Chapultepec Park, studying statues and inscriptions in Spanish. I was getting sleepy, but we held hands, and still he persisted in examining statues. Finally, I had to give him the hint that I was tired, and maybe we'd better go home. I reminded him that I hadn't gotten much sleep the night before.

"Oh, I am sorry because you are not having a good time. Maybe you will have better fun tomorrow?"

"Yeah, maybe, after I get a good night's sleep and wrap

myself up in a gorgeous dream and slip out of this world into the next, which is more real than this one anyway. Yes, Ernesto, it's time to go back to the hotel." It was one o'clock in the morning. Ernesto couldn't know how much I valued my dream world.

View of Acupulco as seen from the
rented villa in March 1973.

The next morning, Ernesto offered to take me to a friend's home, where I could stay for as long as I wanted, free of charge. Toward afternoon, we hopped buses around town and arrived at the home of Ernesto's friend where there were already several American girls staying. It was a happy scene, a lovely apartment. The girls had just showered, and a maid was coming in to make dinner and do the household chores.

I had brought a cassette tape of some of my songs with me, and they had a cassette tape player, so we put my songs on, and I talked with the American girls. The plan was that we were all going to go to Acapulco the next day. Halfway through our conversation, the tape player started chewing up my songs. I freaked out, but Ernesto reassured me that he would fix it when we got back from our little holiday in Acapulco.

Chapter Fourteen

Acapulco

We left Mexico, the six of us crammed into Javier's tiny Volkswagen, with a few joints and a bottle of Mexican liquor. Jubilant and carefree, a few drags of Mexican grass and a few swigs of Mexican liquor, and we were all stoned except for the driver, who seemed to keep up with the passage of time, even if we could not. Somewhere in between Mexico and Acapulco, we drove from a dry coolness into tropical humidity that wouldn't quit. My speech seemed frozen in animation while my mind raced madly. Listening to them talk, jabbering back and forth, I became paranoid. Were they discussing me? Each laugh became a laugh directed at me, a subtle ridicule of my clothes, my habits, and appearance. But how could I tell?

In the middle of the night, we bumped along a deserted dirt road to a trailer park in the middle of nowhere and damn near knocked the bumper off. We pulled up in front of a PEMEX gas station, and maybe it was the combination of liquor and grass, but I thought I saw a horse wander up from out of nowhere, drink thirstily from a water trough, then wander off again while some of the guys relieved themselves by the side of the road. We drove on, suspended between the beginning of time and a preconceived ending that eluded us.

Cramped and irritable–three in the back and three in the front– Ernesto casually offered his shoulder to lean my head on. The two American girls were singing at the top of their lungs, in the front.

Silently, I swore, "Oh, Ernesto, damn you. Will you leave me alone?"

Ernesto pleaded, "I think you are angry maybe?"

"No! Will you quit putting your arm around me? And, no, I don't want any more dope. Will someone please take that Carole King cassette out or I'll smash the damn thing." The thoughts didn't translate into words. They were too hostile. That Mexican grass was too powerful. It had turned my mind the wrong way, and I wasn't sure I could handle it, but the thoughts continued to race through my mind.

"Stop treating me like a helpless female." It was the Mexican way. Some women would have appreciated it.

We continued our journey speeding along the lonely night highway until the intense heat pressurized our stoned heads at 3 A.M. We darted about the deserted streets looking for a hotel, any place, to sleep off the dope and find water to quench our thirst, some food to relieve the hunger pangs, and most of all–a bathroom, to relieve our swollen bladders.

And they didn't seem to have a clue what they were doing, knocking on doors, asking for prices of rooms–obviously, the plans hadn't included making reservations. Eventually, we were rescued by such a proprietor who lies in wait for drunken, stoned, and stupid tourists such as us, who are searching for a room at three in the morning.

We found a veritable palace in the hills, from where we could practically glimpse Acapulco Bay, and it was only twenty-five pesos a night each, which included a shower and toilet (oh, luxury), two bedrooms with two single beds and an outdoor patio type kitchen, with stove and sink.

Without hesitation, I marched in and threw my gear down on the first single bed nearest the door. If Ernesto had any ideas about sleeping with me, he was going to be sadly mistaken. I kicked off my shoes and promptly fell asleep. Ernesto took the other bed, without complaint, and the two other Mexicans doubled up with the American girls in the other bedroom. They didn't seem to mind, in the least.

Morning came, and on the floor of the shower stall, a little pale worm was wiggling blindly. I tried not to step on it while I had my shower. Sleep had improved my disposition somewhat, and I watched a lizard outside on the patio skitter up a wall. *Buenos dias!* The shower was busy now.

"Where are we going today, Ernesto?"

He answered grumpily, probably put off by the lack of attention the night before.

"Ah, we go to the beach to swim 'an maybe buy some grass."

The girls were ready now, and we grabbed our purses and packed into the car again. It was a beautiful day, sunny and hot. Javier maneuvered the vehicle through the traffic down town, and we got a bit to eat at a Mexican version of a McDonald's.

The tourist elite of Acapulco! Skyscraper hotels, and everything Mexican, cater to your service man! *Cuanto es!* Double priced food, outrageous commercialism. Oh, Acapulco, I love your humid, heavy air, like breathing fumes of condensed warmth, and your miles of pristine beaches–Americanized Acapulco. Pot-bellied, middle-aged couples strolled hand in hand down hot sandy beaches in search of rejuvenation while the beautiful youth perfected the myth of an honest to goodness Acapulco tan!

Mexico, you have suppressed my ambition, belittled my intelligence, and reduced my romantic ideals to a skeptic's suspicion of everyone and everything. No harm implied, but it's simply this–that I am a protégé of middle-class Canada, who has been injected into the mainstream of a still struggling and backward Mexico. So I am lying on warm Acapulco sand, and somehow it doesn't matter that all the Mexican men seem to care about is what is between my legs.

We are insane, Mexico! The warmth, the embryonic ocean represents security, and I run impulsively into the waves, which toss me off my feet. I arise, spitting salty water and laughing in delight. Glorious life! Let me battle those waves! I'll conquer them, and I'll dive through another one in triumph. Finally, exhausted, we return to the flat, warm sand, smearing oil all over our wet bodies, and of course, the oil slides off, but I continue to smear it on, nevertheless.

Hot sand underfoot, I stand at the edge of the water and forget time altogether while I watch the shiny particles of sand slip into the ocean. I stand so long gazing at the water, I fear that people are staring at me, or is this drug induced paranoia on my part? I am momentarily lost and wander around searching for my companions. Wherever they are, my security truly rests. They wouldn't have left me, would they? And, suddenly, as if from a million miles away, a hand waves me over. With a sigh of relief, I deposit my burned feet under the shade of a palm tree shaded table. Now ravenously hungry, I wander over to a nearby Mexican vendor and buy some candy, something coconut, resembling the American version of unbaked cookie dough, rolled into a cylinder shape. And then, I don't want it because it is melting sticky, all over me. The thought pops into my mind.

You don't want this. It'll make you sick, for sure. Throw it away! Ugh, the sticky candy and the sticky salt water are blending together, and the humidity is pressing down upon us again. Time doesn't seem to register. Maybe we will never catch up to it!

Ernesto pulled me aside and asked me to accompany him to

make a purchase of Mexican weed on the beach, somewhere. We found the guy, a dark-skinned Afro-Mexican, waiting by an overturned boat, and Ernesto bargained with him in Spanish, but as the money was handed to him, a large package of Acapulco Gold was slipped into my purse–a sizable deal, but why was I being made a carrier? I hadn't volunteered. Ernesto pushed me along through the crowd. So, we continued along the beach carrying the precious bundle and met the others in the car, waiting for us, down by the beach.

Javier drove madly, as erratically as the tempo of our thoughts. We headed out of town and up along a winding road in the mountains of Acapulco overlooking the Bay. The view was fantastic! A joint was rolled and passed around, and after a few puffs of this stuff, whatever it was, we were off on a really heavy body stone for about the next five hours.

Vague remnants of feelings, sensations of excruciatingly hot pavement under bare feet, register as I follow the group from the parking lot to a supermarket. It wouldn't have been so bad if it wasn't for my purse. I was scared that I'd forget it–leave it somewhere and lose my ID, my money, and passport! I clutched the bag and held onto it tightly. I followed the girls into the air-conditioned supermarket looking for bananas. It seemed like all I'd eaten since arriving in Mexico had been bananas, but then, we bought more bananas–and it was so cool in there. Popped open a Coke and chugalugged the sweet nectar down. And what did Javier buy? Some oranges–some *pan*, some fruit, and beer. We returned to the car and unloaded the groceries, but they weren't finished.

The group wandered off again to buy more food, and I was on the verge of flipping out. I sat down on the pavement and grabbed one of the car tires with both hands and hugged it for dear life. I was sitting on the sidewalk, melded to the tire, which wasn't going anywhere, because it was attached to the parked car, while people walked by staring at me. The sky was spinning, the pavement was on fire, but I was securely grounded to a tire. I heaved a sigh of relief while my mind tripped on.

Maybe they have gone off and forgotten me, but they won't go anywhere without the car, so I guess I'm okay. I'm flying high just like Nick used to sing about. Got my purse? Got my bananas? Anybody want a banana? I don't know if I'm coming or going.

But they all return laughing, or are they laughing at me? I must look pretty silly, hugging a tire. Ernesto squats down, arm around my shoulders to reassure me, a look of concern on his face.

"Why are they always laughing? I'm not laughing."

And then we're home again, and Ernesto gets to work dividing the package into separate shares, one for each of us.

It was night now and still humid. Perspiration flowed down my body constantly, and I showered to obtain relief, but it didn't seem to bother me. What really bothered me was being badly sunburned and aching and Carole and her Mexican lover are thumping around in the room next door, and Ernesto might get ideas, and hey, I'm only human too, but hell! Isn't this what gives the Mexican men the idea that all foreign girls are promiscuous? Since my own loose episode in Guadalajara, I'd managed to regain a firm grip on my own desires and intended to keep it there.

In Mexico, as Ernesto explained to me, "There are two types of women, the good ones who get married and have a family, and the bad ones who inhabit the bars and sleep around."

I guess I seemed like the first kind to him, or else he had come to that conclusion. I wanted to pack it in and leave that night. If I could only free my soul and soar above the clouds like Nick used to do.

"I'm sailin' on a Puffy White Cloud. Don't bring me down, Mama." I like it up here where it's sunny and free. Don't bother me. Time enough to be lookin' round, time enough to be comin' down, and I wasn't high enough to be that high.

The next morning, we all hobbled onto the patio, sore and aching from the previous day's sunburn. Everyone wanted to visit the beach again, but this time I opted out. Ernesto tried to persuade me to come, but I insisted that I wasn't up to it. So, the group left me alone with my thoughts, and I rested on the patio and read for a while.

About noon, I wandered off in search of a Coke and something to eat. Someone directed me to a little Mexican household where the lady of the house offered me a sample of her rice and sauce concoction, smearing some of it on her hand and holding it out to me.

"Es bueno?" "Si, es bueno," but I don't want any–"No quiero, gracias."

She gave me some bread and a Coke. When I returned, I met the landlady of the premises sitting on the steps with her little dog and, finding that she could speak English, decided to have a conversation with her. She told me that she had come from New York originally and had lived in Acapulco for several years now, with her dentist husband. After putting up with the high prices and the extremely hot and humid climate, she was now considering returning to the U.S.A. She warned me about the evils of Mexico, the poverty, the sickness which ranged from worms to dysentery and worse.

"Did you know, the other day, I saw them dragging a block of ice down the street, and without cleaning it, chop it up to put into the drinks that tourists buy? Whatever you do, don't drink that stuff!"

And I told her about my travels and ultimate desire to reach South America and to perform my songs. She fixed me some dinner and a few of her friends dropped by for a while. I sat there, trying to understand the conversation, which was in Spanish. Basically, I understood that they were talking about a black dog and her puppies. Then it was *"Buenas tardes!"* and they left, leaving me with the landlady. We continued our conversation in English, and afterward, I thanked her for the dinner and went back to the patio of the little villa.

Soon after, the gang returned with some fresh fruit, and we packed our stuff in preparation for the trip home. We gave our keys back, said our goodbyes, and dusk was falling as we drove away from the little house in the mountains, back down the mountain into the main streets of Acapulco, past the fancy, tourist deluxe hotels to drop off the two American girls at a budget hotel where they were staying–not too many bugs and even a washroom! Kisses and hugs were exchanged, and the boys and I were on our way back to Mexico City.

The trip back was better because it was less crowded, and by now Ernesto had stopped bugging me, and my sunburn was healing. We returned from the dusty heat of Acapulco to the coolness of Mexico City, back to the apartment, where Ernesto and I crashed and fell asleep.

In the morning, Javier's brother, whose apartment we were staying in, told me that I could stay as long as I wanted, free of charge, and not to worry about money or anything like that. The very next day, I took my damaged cassette tape around the corner to a stereo store, a few blocks away. They all spoke Spanish, but somehow, I got the idea across that I needed help to fix it and left it there. When I returned the day after, it still hadn't been fixed, but a clerk who spoke a bit of English and I got together, pried off the top, and unwound the tape. It was twisted and chewed up in places, but we smoothed it out and test played it until it was perfect. I was overjoyed, supremely happy; it had meant that much to me, to have Nick's songs ready to go again.

Altogether, I stayed two nights at that pad and went out with Javier's brother to a disco (my first) and to dinner. He kept asking me why I seemed sad, and I honestly couldn't explain why. Besides not being your ordinary kind of chick, how could I explain my fascination for the road and the comforting feel of a backpack as I walked down the road bound for the unknown? Why didn't dining and dancing appeal to me? I didn't know. Why did I enjoy sleeping alone in dingy hotel rooms? Couldn't explain that either. The poor fellow was puzzled and confused by my behavior, but he might have understood me better if he'd heard the words to "Cocomo Road."

I tried to explain to Ernesto. "Ernesto, I love to travel. That is what makes me happy. It's in my blood. I must move on. Do you understand that?"

He didn't, but he made an effort to, anyway. Mexico gentleman that he was, he brought me down to the bus station, even making connections for me to travel south on an evening bus to Veracruz. Then, shyly, for the first time, he kissed me goodbye, and I wondered to myself, are all Mexican men as romantic as this one? I had to admit that he'd been good to me, and I should be grateful for that.

Thanking Ernesto for his hospitality, I was soon on the road again, heading into the unknown as shadows of evening settled over the land. The question was, what karma had Nick left behind in Mexico, South America, and the Caribbean? I seemed to have vague memories of trips, not for music, and my thoughts turned to the route map again and Lanky's suggestion that it was a drug runner's route. It certainly seemed to be turning out that way. I'd chucked the package of dope from Acapulco somewhere along the way. I wasn't about to let my search for a past life as Nick jeopardize the life I was living now. I was sure that once I'd been bilingual; Spanish as a second language seemed possible. I was drawn to both the language and the culture, but then Nick's father had been Mexican, and most likely he'd been raised bilingually. I don't think I realized how completely Nick had overwhelmed my whole reason for living at this point. It was almost as if Maureen, the middle-class chick from Ontario, Canada, had ceased to exist for a space of time as I was drawn further and further into the mysteries that the road had waiting for me to solve.

Jamaica Is Calling Me

In Mexico 1973
In mango country by a coconut tree
Across the Gulf of Mexico
Jamaica, I drempt of thee
When I was a frisky, hippie girl
You were my seductive pearl
And though the years spin by
I still sing this song
In "Rasta land" I know I belong.

Chapter Fifteen

On the Road in Mexico

It was a long bus ride, sitting beside a plump, Mexican woman holding her even plumper Mexican baby, so I became sleepy and tried to relax with my head against the hard window, bumping and rolling along without a care in the world except to reach some given destination, sometime.

I lay back and enjoyed the sound of the motor purring underneath me and the motion of the bus and miles of highway closing behind us in black, never to be visited again miles, strange miles, foreign miles and foreign people and me among them—ME, grinning inside at being so foolishly carefree and so glad to be leaving Mexico City.

The night was salty-sea humid as we rolled along toward the seaport town of Veracruz where that boat just might be waiting to take me to Jamaica. Oh, crazy dreams, how they vanish when awakening to reality. Pulling into the bus station, I was shaken down from a cloud nine of imaginings and faced with the urgency of doing something about it all.

And because it was only about three o'clock in the morning, and I was tired and irritable, I swung my pack to my back, with my precious bongos still perched on top, and set off down the deserted, dark back alleys to find a hotel room to spend the remainder of the night.

The first hotel I walked into revealed a night clerk sleeping down behind the counter. When I woke him up, he glared at me with the eyes of "Whatever you want, I don't have it." This didn't dissuade me in the least.

"*Un cuarto para una persona, por favor,*" I explained simply, but he made it clear through gestures and Spanish jabber that there weren't any rooms, not for me, anyway.

It was too late to argue. Infuriated, I strode out of the lobby of that hotel, right down the street to another, more expensive hotel, and inquired again. This time I was in luck, although I had to pay about three dollars Canadian for the luxury of a room with double bed and shower. It was nice, though, with clean sheets and suited me just fine, so immediately after putting down my pack, I flung body onto bed, pulling my sleeping bag around me for comfort, and sank into a deep coma of sleep.

I awoke to daylight, the shrill voice of a maid outside my door, and urgent pounding on my door. I pretended that I didn't hear her and fell back asleep again. After all, I'd paid well for my lodging, and even if I slept past check-out time, they weren't going to drag me out, were they?

But she persisted, chattering excitedly in Spanish too fast for me to catch. Was there something wrong? Was the place on fire? I glanced at the list of rules on the wall opposite the bed. It was written in Spanish, and if I'd broken one, I wouldn't have known anyway. Half-asleep and still groggy, I couldn't read English, much less Spanish in the heat of the moment. After pounding on the door for a space of a time, she finally gave up and walked away, muttering to herself.

I felt a bit confused at that point, disorganized, and scared because I didn't know what was going on, so I gathered up my things and left, hiking through the back alleys once more, past Mexican saloon bars with noise and laughter drifting into the streets, thinking again what Ernesto had told me about the bad girls of Mexico, wondering if there were any hanging around in there. And I was curious enough to come close and peek inside the dark interior, but that's as far as I went.

The ships in the harbor looked intimidating, and my plan of jumping a cargo ship went out the window. I didn't want to take the time to hang around, asking questions. It would be easier to bus it to Acayucan, where I could secure a ticket to Merida, and then I'd be in the Yucatan, right across from Jamaica. I bought another bus ticket from a rude and curt Mexican clerk, who became impatient with my bad Spanish, and this pissed me off even more, but I settled back into my seat, on a journey that took us through outlying little villages, stopping at every one.

On that bus, I was probably the only English-speaking person. The Mexican people seemed friendly enough, yet I got the impression that they regarded me as some sort of odd curiosity. The village streets were filled with plenty of children who seemed to be thriving amidst the noise, dirt, and squalor. As we pulled into each little town, they rushed out, children and adults alike, selling everything from chicklets to homemade candy, cakes, fruit and bread.

"*Pan, tacos,*" was the call, "*Tacos, senorita?*" And they would march right up the aisle of the bus boldly, displaying and selling their merchandise, hustling a buck, every way they could. In fact, I was afraid of most of the stuff, fearing that it might bring back a reoccurrance of the *tourista* but settled for a bag of homemade potato chips.

By the time, we reached Acayucan, it was evening again, and I discovered that the next bus leaving for Merida wouldn't be available until the next morning. Weary and impatient, tired of arguing with bus station clerks, I checked into another cheap hotel for the night, shutting the door, locking out the hostility and confusion. I threw my pack down and stretched out on the bed, discouraged. The urgency that was driving me toward Merida was relentless, like a monkey on my back that I couldn't reason with, and I was lonely for the first time in a long time. I broke down in tears and allowed myself a moment of weakness. Then, spent and subdued, I pulled out my maps and travel books and studied the route. How much farther did I have to go? It wasn't far, considering the distance that I'd already traveled, almost the whole length of the country of Mexico, but at the rate that I was going, it would take forever to reach Merida. Why should I care? There was no time limit on this, was there?

I tossed the map down and peered out of the window at the villagers milling around the marketplace below. This was the smallest Mexican town I'd stayed in so far, and curiosity lured me out of my sanctuary to explore my surroundings.

I found a fairly modern supermarket where I bought some food and chocolate, then continued up the street past an open park. I sat down in a not-too-dirty Mexican restaurant and ordered a meal. As usual, a Mexican man came over and tried to start a conversation. I smiled and indicated that I couldn't speak Spanish very well, only *pocolito.* I told him and the waitress that I was from Canada, and they were delightedly excited. When I had finished my soup, bread, and coffee, I felt better and decided to wander around some more.

I came across a church where a Roman Catholic mass was being conducted. The doors were open wide, so I ambled in shyly and stood watching the priest conduct the sermon in Spanish, studying a nativity arrangement, set up against one wall. Then I felt, for the first time in a long time, some sense of peace and contentment, and wondered if he would mind if I sat down, but I didn't, standing there at the door, ready to flee at moment's notice.

Lift up thine eyes to the Lord, from whence cometh your help, oh bewildered and weary people of the earth! In God shall I find the peace and truth that I am seeking.

"God, would you mind very much if I knelt down right here in the doorway of this fine and beautiful house of Yours and prayed? I want so much to find You." And I prayed silently, standing there, my special prayer, The Lord's Prayer in Latin, that I'd memorized for moments like this.

Pater noster, qui es in caelis
Sanctificatur nomen tuum
Adveniat regnum tuum
Fiat, voluntas tua sicut in caelo et in terra

I love you, pure goodness and truth. Everywhere I go, I feel Your presence and am reassured. Do I have to wander this life as well as the last one, seeking You, or shall peace of mind come to me and calm my frustrated travels? I sought You in LSD at Strawberry Fields, and I see You here in this little Spanish town. Maybe I've been seeking You for as long as my soul can remember? From all my wretched lives spent upon this wretched earth, I appeal to You to help me find You. Help me find the truth and in doing so, enlighten others with my illuminated wisdom, so that they might feel this intense bliss that sometimes wells up in me, whenever I think of You and all of Your miracles. My life is a miracle, surely, and my life is certainly in Your hands, whomever You might be. I can't see You, but I can feel that You are near and won't desert me. Forgive me for being so weak, but I am only one who needs You. We ALL need you. When shall we see Your face? It was my voice and Nick's simultaneously repeating the words:

"Our Father who Art in Heaven! Hallowed be Thy name."

I prayed silently and as the moment prompted, just as Nick used to do, guided by his mama in the Deep South, who believed that God could answer every prayer, if you only had the faith, but not as my own mother had taught me, or certainly not my Canadian father who had scoffed at religion.

And I wished that the Roman Catholic priest might invite me to stay here overnight instead of that noisy, Mexican flophouse where it was so lonely. I didn't really know what I was doing, standing in the doorway of this church in Acayucan because I wasn't even Roman Catholic, just a weary wanderer who had a case of the blues.

But when eyes began to turn my way curiously, and the priest lifted his gaze to behold this solitary ghost of a Canadian girl, far from home, I retreated self-consciously back onto the dusty street and returned to my room, for it was getting dark.

In the morning, I managed to get on a bus heading for Campeche, which stopped at the next nearest town of Villahermosa and finally arrived in Campeche at about one o'clock in the afternoon. There, I was told that I would have to wait until midnight to catch the one and only bus to Merida, and I resigned myself to Mexico's ways, pulled out some cigarettes, and wandered down a back street to pass some time. Pestered by the inevitable male attention, I moved myself and my pack farther away from the bus station to a nearby park, where, in the heat of the day, a group of Mexican school children accosted me, laughing and talking and pointing to their English language textbooks. I smiled agreeably and attempted to carry on a conversation with them in English for a while. Either they didn't understand or I was such a novelty that they didn't want to leave, but I had to finally bid them, *"Adios, adios.* See you tomorrow."

This they seemed to think was hilarious and giggled and pointed and continued to crowd around, making no indication that they were going to leave, so I shouldered my pack once more and headed back down the street to the station, leaving them chattering excitedly among themselves.

Back to the bus station for a meal and some conversation with strangers who spoke English. We all ordered the same thing, and I was beginning to gain weight on Mexican food, especially *arroz con pollo* and *plátano con leche*. My companions were women, one of whom was from California, on holiday. The minutes tick-tocked by, and still it was several hours away from midnight. I went on a search for a clean bathroom with real toilet paper in it, and an office worker, who was just getting off late, ushered me into hers. I thanked her profusely. An old man who spoke excellent English in the bus station gave me the name of a cheap hotel in Merida and told me to call him if I needed help when I got there. In a gesture of friendliness that reinforced my faith in humanity, he offered to guard my pack while I wandered about. I sat down on the sidewalk and wrote lyrics to a new song that had just come into my head, rolled a Mexican cigarette, and watched the people coming and going, as I smoked it.

My spirits began to pick up until a Mexican appeared out of the shadows and indicated that he wanted to sell me some dope or smoke with him, but we would have to find the cache that was hidden somewhere down the road. I told him that I didn't have the time and ducked back into the terminal trying to avoid him. Luckily for me, the bus pulled into the station at that moment. I stepped up to the front desk to buy a ticket and bumped into two Americans buying their tickets, who indicated they were going my way.

Into Merida

A bus ride by night in Mexico land
Along a paved road I lie sleeping
Semi-consciously between midnight and dawn
Morning wakes me to view in passing
A white, square adobe window
Mexican lying in his hammock watching TV
South by southwest past mango trees
Swamps and jungle
Past the hidden pyramids of the Yucatan
Progresso beach shaded by coconut trees
On the Gulf of Mexico stout Indian peasant women
In chattering groups wave
As we roll on into Merida.

Chapter Sixteen

Sagittarius Mind, Sagittarius Heart

We boarded the bus together, and en route, I told them I was a bongo player traveling down to South America, and they informed me that they had just come in from Frisco and, before that, Canada. They were really groovy people who spoke my kind of language like, "Man, that's cool, baby, and honey, you are going to Merida too? Hang in there and come along with us. We're going to Jamaica!"

And the cool cat with the American girl gave me the distinct vibes of a Sagittarius, and she gave out very friendly vibes herself. Later, I did discover that Jason was indeed a Sagittarius, and Tinkerbelle was so named because she had bells on her luggage that tinkled when she walked. She was also Scorpio born, only one-week younger than myself!

Jason smiled at me, flirting openly with his eyes, and I flirted back. Although we were only strangers, we were soul brothers of the road, riding through the night on that bus bound for Merida, Mexico.

We rolled through the night, talking from time to time, back and forth across the aisle, cat napping, semi-jerking to a stop at obscure places in between. We ran out and bought food and drinks while Jason helped us along with his fluent Spanish and breezy, optimistic manner.

Heavy-eyed and head-achey from lack of sleep, we pulled into Merida the next morning and caught a taxi downtown to a hotel that Jason and Tink had stayed in before.

At this point, there was something weird and confusing going on with Tink dressing up and hurrying out to get some papers downtown and whispering to Jason something about money and Jason locking himself in the bathroom, and he was there for about fifteen minutes.

When he came out, carrying a needle, some pills, and a spoon, I jumped to conclusions. "Oh, Nicki, you've finally come up against it. You've met up with a needle freak, don't it figure, man?"

But Jason only smiled casually, packed it away, and told me he was using antibiotics to cure an infection. Mexico was the best, man, because you could get almost any drug over the counter that you wanted down here, without a prescription. We got into a heavy mind-soul rap about the mystical and my mission to "Go back, Jack" and do it again, reincarnation, astrology and I Ching.

Being a Sagittarius, he understood instantly what I had been trying to get across to others since I'd been enlightened, but he warned, "Don't tell this heavy stuff to just anybody, baby, because they don't care, and they don't understand. Some might even abuse you for it, and the others will call you crazy, but I've known about this all along. That's why Tink and I are on our way to Jamaica. Jamaica is The Promised Land, one of which will still be left standing when the earthquakes come to destroy California and the East Coast of the U.S.A. Tink and I have bought some land in Jamaica and are planning to set up a commune there and live in peace and simplicity by the Laws of God. Do you want to join us?"

"I don't know," I replied. "I don't know if I want to settle down yet. How old are you?"

"Me? I'm thirty-five, baby. I come from San Francisco. That's my hometown, but I've been on the road a long time. You ever heard of Neal Cassady?"

"Oh yeah. He was Jack Kerouac's closest friend, who was mentioned as Dean Moriarity, in his book *On the Road* and later became involved with the acid psychedelic scene in San Francisco with Ken Kesey and the hippies. In Tom Wolfe's book *The Electric Kool-Aid Acid Test*, he was the fellow who drove the Magic Bus through the United States on the Acid Test Initiations. Why?"

"Well, he was a buddy of mine!"

"You're kidding, man!" I was astonished.

"No, man. I'm not putting you on. I learned how to drive from him. Man, I was on that bus."

"Didn't he die somewhere in the wilderness of Mexico?"

"Yeah, he died, but I'm still in contact with him."

My astonishment knew no boundaries. "Oh, that's so cool! You talk to spirits too?"

"Yeah, I speak to him through a Ouija board. He told me all about Red Radio and Cosmic Unity and Universal Mind Flow."

Jason leaned closer and whispered, "Baby, one night this message comes through on the board. Go out for a walk and you will meet someone, so I do what I'm told, and out in the darkness I come across this crazy stranger, who seems to have been expecting me. And he starts rapping off about Red Radio too!"

Jason shook his head warning, "Red Radio is bad, baby. They try to block Bobby from me."

I was puzzled. "Bobby who?" I asked.

"Bobby Jordan, baby."

Jason grinned and flashed a sparkle of "I dig you" flirtation from the depths of his steel blue eyes like an elusive butterfly darting about in the sunshine but never completely disappearing. Red-haired, quicksilver, mysterious weirder than thou. I was fascinated.

Jason continued, "Baby, you see, in the beginning, we were all a part of a special group of people. Vibes attract vibes–right?"

"Yeah."

"See–you can dig me, and I can dig you, and we have come together for a reason. The world is in the last stages of collapse. Everybody knows about the earthquakes that will destroy San Francisco, L.A., and New York."

"They know if they've read Edgar Cayce," I admitted.

"That is why we're going to Jamaica. Jamaica is The Promised Land. Atlantis will rise from the depths of the ocean again, and we will be there to see it! Many people will die, but we shall exist forever because we are the chosen ones! We will live in Jamaica, and there, baby, everybody smokes the weed, grandmothers and children alike. Man, there the vibes are so heavy, you wouldn't believe it. I've been all over, but Jamaica is the only place where I can relax. It's magic, baby."

I was concerned. "But, Jason, what about the rest of the people who will die? We've got to save them! Get the message to them before it's too late! God is not so cruel that He would let thousands of innocent people die, the good along with the bad."

"No, they don't deserve to be saved, baby. They're happy in their materialistic ignorance. Truth is there for those who seek it. Remember Sodom and Gomorrah. God destroys the wicked."

"Yes, but for the sake of ten good people, He promised to save the city of Sodom when Abraham appealed to Him."

"But were there ten good people?"

"No, man, but where there is some good, there is hope for mankind. I believe in people. They can change for the better–always."

"I once thought so too, baby, but I threw all the notes and

messages that I received away, and I suggest that you do the same. If people want to find the truth, let them seek it, just as we have."

We were interrupted by Tink, returning. She produced a document, smiling triumphantly.

"Yeah, Jason, honey, I got it all right—no hassle and the money too. Just played the middle-class tourist, and they were very friendly. Now what?"

"Well, we can't go to Jamaica because you don't have further identification since you lost your purse."

Tink frowned. "Yeah, everything, my birth certificate, driver's license—money."

"Well, that's life, babe," Jason said philosophically. "Can't do anything about it now. You're lucky you were able to get a new tourist visa."

Tink was dismayed. "But what good is it, Jason? Without my other ID, I can't go anywhere."

Meanwhile, I was trying to sort all this out, thinking why didn't she phone home and get her family to send her new ID through the American Embassy? No doubt she could have. I'd heard Jason mention that her daddy owned a successful nightclub in the States. She came from money.

"Me and Jason are in a hurry to get to Jamaica, honey. You see, that's our home. We have land there, and we are gonna settle down, and I'm gonna have lots of babies! We've been on the road for a year now, and I'm just sick of it. We want to go now. We've been waiting for this so long."

I interrupted, "What about money? I thought you said you lost your money."

Jason turned to me and half smiled a secretive grin. "Traveler's checks, baby."

I was confused. "Do you mean that you have a stash of traveler's checks?"

"Not exactly," Jason replied. Then glancing at Tink, for the go-ahead, he continued. "We didn't lose the checks. We still had them, but we thought we'd like to see if we could get more, so we did what these other chicks down in Campeche did. You retain your original checks and go to them saying that you've lost them. They will refund your money, of course, with a new batch of traveler's checks, and then you take out the batch of old ones, spend them and the new ones, and you have doubled your money."

"Fine, I replied, "but they have a record of the serial numbers on the ones that have supposedly been lost, so when you cash them in, they're hot on your trail. It might take a while for them to realize that they've been double-crossed, but eventually, they'll catch up to you."

Jason humored me. "We realize all that," he said, "but if you keep moving from town to town, cash in your checks in one coast of Mexico and head for the other side of Mexico, you can stay clear for a little while, anyway, and by that time, you've left the country. Only, we can't leave until Tink gets more ID, and we might soon run into problems with that illegal money deal behind us, so we have to get out of Mexico soon, you dig?"

Okay, so now I was clued in. I was bunking in with a pair of criminals on the run from the heat across Mexico.

"Yeah, I dig it all right." And I didn't like it one bit.

Jason brushed away my worries. "C'mon baby, let's go get something to eat." Before I had time to ponder the mess I'd gotten myself into, Jason whisked Tink and I away to a restaurant down the street and ordered us each a full course dinner.

And here he was, smiling and chatting away in Spanish to all the waiters, who seemed to know him, as if he were a local popular figure.

Over the meal, I continued to worry, whispering to Jason, "I don't know, man. I dig your situation, but why did you do that bad money deal? It's contrary to a Sagittarian nature to be dishonest."

"I wouldn't do it, ordinarily," admitted Jason, "but we were in a kind of a bind. We sold my car a few months ago, and she worked for a while in restaurants waitressing, but we still didn't make the kind of bread we needed. I usually deal in grass, but I only had enough to put through one shipment from Jamaica, up the East Coast of the U.S.A. It costs two grand to move a shipment of the best Jamaican grass you've ever smoked, baby. Wanna get in on the action?"

A mouthful of tortilla halted in mid-air as an image of the route map flashed into my mind. What the hell was going on here, pushing dope up the Coast. Was that what Nicki had done? Was I coming face to face with more of his karma and was this another test?

"I don't think so, man. I've never had $2000 in my whole life at one time. Where would I get that kind of money?"

"Oh, there's ways," Jason smiled indulgently, "but the main thing for you to remember is that you believe that you're in this because you realize that Jamaican grass is a way to God, and by encouraging the distribution of the drug in the U.S.A., you are working in the ways of the Lord."

I couldn't dig that, but I kept silent. We returned to the hotel room, and Jason got out some grass, and we passed the joint around, which quelled my fears for the time being. It was good stuff, and then something weird happened. I unbuckled my leather belt and hunting knife, pulled open the drawer in the bedside table and shoved it in and I *knew* I'd done this before. I'd been here before, quite possibly in this same hotel room. But how could that be possible? As I moved from bed to table, I experienced what is called déjà vu.

"Nick?" I asked myself, and turned to Jason. "Man, have you ever done something that you could have sworn you'd done before but hadn't? I could have sworn that sometime, in the past, I'd been lying in that same bed, walked over to that same table, reaching for that same drawer, but I've never been in this room in my life, or at least, in this life."

Jason only smiled mysteriously and replied, "Now you're beginning to dig the context of past, present, and future, baby. What is has always been and always will be, and the grass will reveal itself to you." He paused a moment, "But why the knife, Nicki?"

"Just in case I get jumped, ya know," I replied, casually.

"Haven't you heard the old saying, 'Those who live by the sword, die by the sword?'" Jason asked.

"Whoever said that I lived by the sword?" I replied, a bit flippantly. Jason and I always had these amazingly profound conversations that I loved totally, which didn't interest Tink in the least. She took off her clothes and spread her naked body across the bed while Jason and I smoked the last of the dope.

Tink was sleeping now, and Jason read out of his battered and falling apart *I Ching*, an ancient Chinese science of divination that I'd heard about. Asking question after question, he threw three American coins down on the bed, six times. After each series of throws, he calculated the results and translated them, to produce either a broken or unbroken line, and this gave the answers to the questions that he was asking. I was fascinated.

The hot sun blazed down on the town outside, and the huge

fan on the ceiling spun around and around. In Mexico, everything slows down at noon and everyone takes a siesta. It's the only sensible thing to do.

Jason slipped into the bathroom again. Tink woke up and demanded to know where he was.

"He's in the bathroom," I said, so she strode over to the door, still stark naked, and banged on it. Jason opened the door a crack and swore at her.

"Fuck you, Tink, will you leave me alone? You always do this!"

Tink's was crying now. "C'mon, Jason, don't do that. You know it makes me unhappy."

Jason gave her a glance of annoyance, "Tink, for Pete's sakes, you know the agreement we made! Let's not start this again." And they continued to swear at each other, and Tink would not stop banging on the door. Jason was getting severely peeved. He was in the final stages of tying up his arm, so he could shoot penicillin that would help to cure the mosquito bites that he had scratched and infected all over his body, or was that just a story? Why would she have been so upset over penicillin? Maybe it was heroin. God forbid that I should meet Nick's karma in Jason. This was the first time I'd come this uncomfortably close to a needle.

I made a fast exit and sat down in the hotel hallway, in the lotus posture, trying to meditate and rise above it. The fighting brought back bad memories of the fights that my married lover and I used to have, back in Ontario. So, if Jason wanted to shoot drugs into his body, it was his body, and Tink had no right to stop him, but I couldn't stand the sight of the needle myself. It had taken me three weeks to get up the courage to get my shots before leaving for Frisco, I was that needle shy.

All this I meditated on as I sat there in that sweltering Mexican hallway and eventually Jason left too, slamming the door behind him. He sat beside me and apologized. "Tink gets carried away, sometimes."

I sympathized. "I know. I used to yell at my boyfriend pretty fierce not so long ago, but I got to the point where I realized that I'd rather be alone than fight all the time. It's not worth it."

Jason continued to reassure me. "She isn't always like this. I love her, you know, and we've been through a lot together."

I turned a woeful face toward Jason. "Do you think she's maybe a little jealous of me too? Like, it isn't very private with the three of us in one hotel room, even if it helps to pay the bills."

"Oh, she might be a little jealous, but she'll get over it. She'll have to. We're going to be a family, living on a commune in Jamaica."

"She's like some Italian mama, isn't she, Jason?" I grinned. "Maternal as hell."

"Yeah." Jason stood up and grabbed my hand. "C'mon, let's get Tink and all of us will go see a movie. Do you like movies?"

"Sure thing," I smiled enthusiastically, "so let's go!"

Tink wouldn't go, so Jason and I went to see another one of those American movies subtitled in Spanish. Halfway through, he slipped out and went back to check on Tink. I slipped out and searched the lobby looking for him but was distracted by a stray cat, which I followed down the street.

"Kitty, kitty, c'mon kitty, what are you doing all alone here?" The cat looked at me suspiciously and ducked under a vendor's curtain.

I was down on my hands and knees and had my head stuck under the curtain calling the cat when Jason reappeared. He'd been standing there, watching me, an amused smile on his face. I stood up, brushing the dust off my pants apologetically.

"You like cats?" Jason asked.

"Yeah," I admitted, "these Mexican cats are pretty skinny, aren't they?"

"Well, they don't feed them very well down here, and they kick them around," Jason said.

"Oh..." Of course. We weren't back in Canada now where cats and dogs were pampered. It was a battle for survival for pets in Mexico. People had a hard time themselves, making it.

"I went back to check on Tink," Jason explained.

"I know."

"Let's go back to the hotel," Jason suggested and took my hand. We went back to the room, and Tink and Jason made up and went to sleep, and I fell asleep too.

The next morning, we decided to go to Campeche for a few days. Tink and Jason had plans brewing, and they included me. We took a bus back to Campeche and checked into a hotel room that had a private shower. Some of the places I'd stayed at had communal bathrooms and showers, so this was a touch of luxury.

The hotel included a restaurant with little saloon type swinging doors, and it was comfortably cool in there with two beds and an overhead fan. I settled down then and read the biography of Neal Cassady, which Jason had with him, and he and Tink had a siesta.

Later in the evening, we went for a walk, out into the marketplace, where a celebration was going on and took in a movie in an ancient old theater of a place that was dusty and falling apart with ghosts of the past drifting through empty balconies. Tink confided in me about her desire to have a baby, her former old man, and how she used to be all for women's liberation but now believed that the pill opposed God's Law.

"Do you realize," she said, "that by taking the pill, you are preventing babies from being born and reincarnating souls from returning to earth to work out their karma?"

"Maybe," I admitted, "but the way I look at it, those souls can reincarnate elsewhere until I'm ready–if I'm EVER ready. I love my freedom way too much to be tied down with kids so early in life."

Tink sniffed, "Pshaw! You can travel with kids."

"It's a hell of a lot harder and more expensive," I argued.

Jason stood on the sidelines watching us, that amused little smile on his face, and didn't intervene to break up the argument. He only commented, "Everybody has free choice over their own body."

Apparently, he had deserted a wife and child somewhere back in the U.S.A., and he didn't seem too eager to be taking on new responsibilities, it seemed to me, regardless of Tink's enthusiasm for a family.

Halfway through the movie, which was about a woman having an abortion, I'd had enough and escaped out the front door. Upon impulse, I jumped on the back of a motorcycle parked in front and sped off with a cute Mexican guy for a tour of the city. We explored a picturesque castle on a hill together and had a great time. On the way back, however, he took me down a side road, put his arms around me, and started kissing me. I threatened to walk back to town if he didn't stop, so he reluctantly took me back to the movie theater where Jason and Tink had hardly noticed that I'd been missing.

*****

That night we had a séance. Jason pulled out a Ouija board and placed it on a rough, wooden table in the hotel room and shot speed into his arm in preparation for the long session. It took about two hours to get the board set out and marked exactly to his specifications because his hands were doing weird things and his mind seemed to be totally fucked up. Tink and I sat back yawning with boredom and hoped that it wouldn't take up too much of our precious sleeping time.

Finally, Jason was ready to go and we placed our fingertips on the planchette, which started to move almost immediately around the board, spelling out nonsense words.

"C'mon, Bobby," urged Jason, "we want to talk to you, man. Let us know that you're here."

The planchette started to move across the board and slowly spelled out–STOP H!

"Okay, Bobby," said Jason hastily, "no more H. Now what do you want us to do?"

"I have stopped it," insisted Jason. "Is Neal there?"

The board replied, "cool, man."

Tink and I giggled, and Jason grinned. "Now that's Neal all right."

"I want to ask the board a question," I said. "Is it okay to go ahead?"

"Sure," replied Jason, "go ahead."

"I want to know what these spirits think about the spirits that were guiding me back in Canada, through my sister Kate, and if they know about my mission."

The board replied–"OTHER SPIRITS CONFUSING YOU WITH TOO MANY DETAILS."

"Good spirits," I asked.

"Yes," the board replied, "GOOD SPIRITS," and the board continued, "NICKI, LIVE. FOR DUTY TO GOD. MAKE A PLACE. BLACK-WHITE, SAME ONE. OLD LIFE PAST. START NEW PART OF US ALL. FROM HERE, GO HOME. YOU ARE

ALIVE. TAKE TIME FOR MIND, PRISTY. NOTHING ELSE MATTERS NOW. ASK, LISTEN WITH FAITH."

"Well," commented Jason, "they've given you a new name–Pristy. I kinda like it, don't you, Tink?"

"Yeah," agreed Tink, "I've always liked the name Pristy."

I was disgusted. "Well, I hate it! Ask them if I can use Nicki instead."

Jason explained patiently, "The board named us Jason and Tinkerbelle, and we didn't object."

Jason paused the session. Tink and I stopped to rest, and Jason reinforced his drugs. Then he, place a half tab in each of our mouths and instructed us to swallow.

"Aw, what the hell?" I thought, and obediently swallowed the pill. I didn't have the faintest idea what it was, although Jason had told us it was speed.

It didn't seem to do anything to me although Tink claimed she was speeding.

We went back to the board, and although it was well past midnight, Jason insisted that Tink and I keep at the bloody board. The messages continued, "GO NOW TO JAMAICA. PEOPLE NEED JASON. STOP H. GIVE PAPERS TO TINK. SEND MAUREEN TO NEW YORK. FOLLOW LATER. PRISTY NEEDS LOVE. PRISTY NEEDS A MAN."

Jason looked surprised at the last two lines of the message and so was I, but he just replied, "Well, everyone needs love."

Through all of this, Tink was silent, and I had no doubt that she was moving the planchette and dictating the messages. What was this, some sort of con to trick me into cooperating? I wasn't that stupid, but I went along with it, just for fun.

I asked, "How is everybody at home?"

It replied, "EVERYBODY FINE. YOUR SISTER MISSES YOU."

My thoughts turned to home and how much I missed Kate, my mother, and my cats, yet I felt that I was still bound to them, although I was far away. A pang of homesickness besieged me.

The board continued, "GIVE ID PAPERS TO TINK, SO SHE CAN GO TO JAMAICA."

What the hell! What kind of bullshit was this! "Who did they think they were fooling?" I thought. I needed my own papers. I was starting to get alarmed, and Jason noticed my agitation.

"Let's get some sleep," he suggested hastily, and dropped the topic. He put away the board, and I fell into a restless sleep plagued with nightmares.

But my money was running low, and now I depended upon my companions to share the bills or I wouldn't be eating, so it seemed as if I didn't have any choice in the situation I'd gotten myself into.

The nights that we all slept together and Tink would make affectionate gestures toward Jason, he turned his back and ignored her. He was obviously so hung up on the needle that he didn't have time for sex. I felt sorry for Tink, tied to a man like that.

He talked about God and man's purpose while neglecting the people around him. Although he was outgoing and won many friends, it was a superficial alliance, and wherever we went, it was easy come, easy go–Hi, man, bye, man, and that's it, man!

Was this Angela's way of showing me Nick? Inwardly, I thought so, and it wasn't hard to see the similarity between the two. True, Jason wasn't an H addict now, or so he said, but he had admitted that he'd been one years ago. And they say, once an addict, always an addict. At any rate, he hadn't lost his interest in the needle, and that, in itself, was a bad sign, showing that the man was still dependent upon drugs to function in his daily life.

I thought about this as I lay in my bed, down in Campeche, Mexico, watching the fan spin around and around above me. I thought mostly because there wasn't anything else to do there except wander around in the marketplace and write letters home. Every day was like the next.

Jason continued to pressure me to hand over my tourist visa and birth certificate to Tink, so she could leave on a plane for Jamaica as soon as possible, and I could reapply and tell them I'd lost mine. Just like the traveler check scheme. How could that work? Could two people with the same ID cross the border? I didn't think so. The axe would fall on me, but I didn't know enough about Mexican law and how it worked. I was getting nervous, I was almost out of money, and the plan of jumping ship to Jamaica and finding work aboard hadn't materialized. The problem was, I wasn't streetwise enough to be living the life I was. I didn't know how to survive. My middle-class background was catching up with me.

We finally left Campeche and caught a bus back to Merida, back to the hotel that we'd stayed in before, and checked in for the night. I knew that I was going to make a run for it, using the last of my money to buy a plane ticket to Miami. Jamaica would have to wait. I went to sleep that night planning to escape the next morning.

But the next morning, I awoke to an empty hotel room. I'd slept with my money belt on, so I still had my passport and the last of my traveler's checks, but in a panic, I noticed that my driver's license, tourist visa, and birth certificate were gone! Jason had shot the last of the downers, but he must have missed and blood was spattered all over the clean, white sheets. On the bedside table was a note.

Dear Nicki,

Our dream has come true, honey! We are finally on our way back home to Jamaica. Here are the names and addresses of people in New York who will give you money, put you up, and help you make arrangements to meet us in Jamaica at our commune in Ocho Rios where we will all live in peace and harmony forever.

Hugs and kisses–Peace and Love
Jason and Tinkerbelle

In a fit of fear and anger, I grabbed the bloody sheets and pillows and threw them in a rumpled heap on the floor uncovering Jason's syringe, on the bed. It still had a small amount of his blood drawn up in it. I stared at it curiously, reached forward, and picked it up. I'd never handled one before. A few tablets had been left scattered on the bedside table. It would be so simple to clean up the set, take the remainder of those tablets, crush them with a Coke bottle and mix them with water. Was that how he did it? Inject this into my vein–no more worries, no more cares, no more blues, just lie back and follow Jason's example, just as Nick had done thirty years before–inject the dope and drift off on a puffy, white cloud. I could forget my loneliness and my continually frustrated search for God and my reason for living.

But I heard Kate/Jessup's voice echoing in my mind, "Go back, Jack, do it again, and get it right this time!"

Do unto others as you would have them do unto you, baby, and don't harm yourself either because harm inflicted upon self is as great a sin as harm inflicted upon others. Damage your mind and body with drugs, and you come back with a load of problems. The problems you thought you escaped from are still there, remaining to be solved. Only you return with the impression of that beautiful escape–needle yourself out of the earth plane and tread the path of merry-go-round. But wait! Step off that merry-go-round and stand still for a minute until your head clears. Do you feel a little better now? Oh, yeah, the dizziness is gone, and you feel a little funny standing there while the merry-go-round continues to spin and your head is reeling, and while you still haven't quite got it together, you feel a little bit more confident. Hey, girl, this is earth that you are standing on, and you DO have to live on it. From the earth, God composed man, and to the earth we all will return, mind, soul and emotion filling the void.

So, this is what happened to me, Nicki/Maureen, and well do I remember as a little girl spinning around and around because it was fun to get dizzy and fun to swing as high as I could, so much so that it almost toppled over, so frantic I was to get away.

That was the beginning, yet only the beginning of a subconscious desire to escape. Nick, still in the mind of the now toddler Maureen's body, swallowing a whole bottle of baby Aspirins and in that six-year-old child, was rolling down the lawn and spinning around and around.

Twelve years later, still trying to escape, you walked amid the burning smoke fires of Strawberry Fields Rock Festival with other generation seekers devoted to delving into the inner mind and consciousness, perhaps abusing drugs in the sincere effort to expand awareness, one year after Woodstock and not yet eighteen.

There, with thousands of others, your head zonked completely with illusions of sparkling dust particles that jumped away from your fingers, oh so delicately, and images of an Alice in Wonderland Red Cross tent, so real, with all those dazed and immobile people lying on stretchers on the ground, also zonked out of their minds, coming down from crazy land to buy more magic pills. Come on up again, man, where we are all so zonked that we don't know if we are coming or going. Just like that crazy forest illusion-delusion you kept seeing flicker in and out of reality, that pool of water deep in the woods with those laughing and naked male-female young people, splashing and swimming naked before your very eyes. When you reached out to touch them, they were gone, and you were alone in that forest glade, so sad and weird, just there, are you all alone, lost in eternity on LSD and still Nicki/Maureen, trying to kill-escape herself out of reality, and baby, you almost did it that time; if it hadn't have been for that helping hand, reaching into the midst of your confusion and talking you down and trying to seduce you at the same time.

Then, suddenly being pitched into a sea of darkness, blind, utterly blind, yet with eyes still open, such a panicky feeling, screaming, "*God, where are you?*" In a hallucination, you watched yourself run out onto the motorcycle racetrack to be struck by a motorcycle, and you saw your body lying smashed and bloody in the dust of the heat and screamed because you didn't really want to die, only to find God, but you saw no gentle Christ-like figure descend from the sky to reassure you with words of pure truth. You only felt another human hand upon yours and someone giving you a cool drink of water and saying gently, "It's okay. Just settle down. You're not dead. You're right here with me. It's not for real. It's all in your head."

So, gradually, you began to relax, and it was true, you were still alive. The darkness began to recede before your very eyes, the strangest feeling, and then you could see your arm, move your hand, your fingers, legs and finally, looking up into the clear, you saw the blue eyes of a young, blond-haired hippie with a peace sign hung on a leather necklace around his neck, completely naked and very real. And he was holding you in embrace, a gesture of love.

Suddenly, you were all business and all Scorpio and all sensible, as you struggled out of his embrace and tried to walk, like a toddler taking a first step, out into the blinding sunshine, wondering what year you had just been born into. But he answered curtly, "Don't you remember, baby? This is the Mosport Rock Festival and it is August 1970."

A three-year old flashback and now Mexico! Was it all a dream or could life really be this incredible? Was this an LSD illusion too? Baby, I don't know, but I know that it happened.

Perhaps this is what saved me from repeating the same mistake. Because I truly believed that you reap what you sow, and because now I knew that karma was real, I gathered up the dope and the needle and points and threw everything in the garbage in a final gesture of triumph, a belated attempt to correct the mistakes of the past. I moved my bongos and my pack upstairs, to another room, where I could get away from this scene, sleep, think, and wake up in the morning, knowing exactly what to do.

Chapter Seventeen

In Trouble

A nd so I had the keys to both rooms, and I still hadn't removed all of the traces of Jason's addictions from the room. I resolved to do something about it in the afternoon because I knew the maid wouldn't get around to cleaning the rooms before then. I decided that I would go down to la estacion de policia to report my missing tourist visa and try to obtain another one.

I was walking down the streets of Merida with an eager-on-the-make Mexican lad who spoke enough English to be helpful, showing me which bus to catch and translating for me. I finally found the office, made my request, and sat down out of the smothering noon-day heat waiting for my new visa, which, I was sure, would come immediately.

But there were problems. First of all, I had to retrace my steps and tell them when exactly I had crossed the border at Tijuana to Mexico, so they could check up and confirm and reaffirm and all that jazz, but I didn't remember and wasn't sure, because in one day, I had been in San Diego, Tijuana, and Mexicali, heading on a southwest train to Guadalajara.

This made matters more complicated, so they had to make a phone call to Tijuana and the line was busy. When they finally did get through, Tijuana said that they didn't remember me either but could I have crossed the border on February 17th?

They told me, "Come back tomorrow, and we will get this all

straightened out. Don't worry, this happens all the time, losing visas, and it will only cost you a few dollars to replace it." I walked out, very pissed off, and glared at my Mexican sidekick, who was still trotting faithfully by my side, while I occasionally swore at him in English. Even this did not discourage him from following me.

I got back to the hotel and walked back across the open courtyard to the room where the blood-spattered sheets still lay crumpled on the floor and the needle and points, tin-foil package of drugs, lay in the garbage can, waiting to be carried away. My sidekick followed me into the room, muttered something in Spanish, and looked very disturbed. He then mentioned something about going to the beach in Progresso, to swim in the warm, ocean waters of the Gulf of Mexico and this was not far from Nick's jumping off spot of Cape Catoche, Mexico.

Because I was in a worried, anxious state of mind, I agreed to get away and have some fun for a while. On the way down to the bus terminal, we ran into another traveler who was from California. He was alone and looked a little lost, so I invited him to join us. He agreed, and we were on our way.

We left Merida for the little seaport town of Progresso, just a short distance away. As we left, I could smell the sea breezes floating toward us from the ocean. We made a transfer down on a primitive local bus with wooden bench seats. It took us right to the highway alongside the beach of the beautiful Gulf of Mexico.

It was absolutely deserted in the mid-afternoon sunshine. I stripped down to the bikini that I was wearing underneath my clothes and ran into the waves. Laughing, ducking under the waves, I came up smiling at the sun, gazing at the beautiful, white, deserted beach and the two men standing on the shore watching me–one short, plumpish Mexican and the other tall, skinny Californian. I waved them over, and they followed me into the ocean.

We swam a little, and the Californian wandered off to examine sea shells lying scattered on the sands, and soon I joined him, gathering up some to take with me back to Canada. My Mexican companion nonchalantly broke the silence. "What do you theeenk of sex?"

I replied sternly, "Oh, *no es bueno.*" His face fell, and I giggled to myself.

"No bueno? Sex is fun, is not?"

I shook my head. *"No, no bueno,"* I teased him. I was having royal fun with him. Shame, shame. He'd been so good to me.

He changed the subject, and we discussed the elaborate beach houses on the shore, mansion-like castles, some very impressive–probably owned by rich Mexicans or Americans–and then he gave me a lesson on how to climb a coconut tree. This was funny because every time he tried to shinny up the trunk, he got only a third of the way up and could get no farther and had to slide back down. He looked like a fat, Canadian porcupine, the ones that I used to come across in the backwoods near Slide Lake.

Then I attempted to reach the coconuts and skinned the inside of my knees and palms and slid down laughing.

Another Mexican, who had been watching us from the front porch of one of the beach houses, now showed us the correct way to climb a coconut tree, using a walking technique. I watched in awe as he walked up the trunk effortlessly and picked two coconuts, just for me. He then took his knife and cut off the top half, giving one to me and another to my friend. I drank the still warm milk and bit into the soft, bitter coconut, but it was a refreshing treat on that hot afternoon.

It seems that the coconut tree climber was the caretaker of

several of these houses, and he took the time to show us through. The first was commonplace enough, with the usual bathroom, kitchen, and bedrooms, but the second, ah! The second was huge and palatial, luxurious, with a winding staircase, chandeliers, and a huge dance floor lobby. The kitchen and living rooms were large and airy, although sparsely furnished with antique furniture and old photographs from the turn of the century. I was transported back in time by a young, curly black-haired, American girl, all dressed up in a frilly, white dress, staring at me from pictures that lined the wall and dresser, and wondered who she was. Did she haunt these elegant rooms? What traces of her life had she left still drifting through these rooms? I descended slowly, down the winding staircase, savoring the mystery of it all.

After hours of just sitting on the front porch looking out to sea and rapping with my new friends in both English and Spanish, I decided it was time to say goodbye and head back into Merida. It was getting on toward evening, and the mosquitoes were starting to buzz around. Maybe they carried malaria. The salt water had matted our hair, and I was dreaming of a shower, a comfortable bed, and a meal. As we left that mysterious, deserted beach cottage to wait for our bus, I worried and swatted mosquitoes, and scratching, thinking that I didn't have protection against malaria, hadn't taken shots for it, until the bus finally found us, in the casual Mexican bide-your-time way, and we were soon heading back to the city.

In Merida once more, the heat and the noise descended upon us. This was another world. As I left to return to the hotel, the Californian asked me if there were any hooks in my room that he could hang a hammock, so we could split the expense. I went up and checked, and it DID have hooks, but this night I needed to be alone, instead of dealing with an unknown roommate. I had to prepare myself for the trip back to *la estacion de policia*.

The next day I found my way there alone. My Mexican sidekick was nowhere to be seen. I wasn't prepared for the holocaust that erupted there that afternoon.

I thought I recognized it, but I refused to believe that it was my old tourist visa lying there on the desk, along with my other ID but the *Agente de policia mexicano* confronted me, saying, "We took these off a girl and her boyfriend who were trying to leave the country illegally. I believe they're yours. Is this true?" The blood drained from my face, and I felt suddenly unsteady.

"They must have been stolen," I stammered and I swore inside and cursed my stupidity, cursed Mexico, cursed my karma and cursed just because I was scared and in a fix. I picked up the visa and ID and examined them. My eyes met his, and I admitted, "Yes, they're mine. What happened to my friends?"

"Oh, they were caught at the airport, arrested, and thrown into jail, where they have been for two days" he answered casually."

He looked puzzled. "How long were you travelling with these people and why? They are criminals, wanted for cashing in illegal traveler's checks and you were in their company."

I couldn't think. "Oh, about a week, I guess." I stammered, "We were sharing expenses. I didn't have much money."

"And the rest of the time?" His eyes drilled me and I felt uncomfortable.

"I traveled alone or with other young people from time to time."

He scratched his head thoughtfully. "You said nothing about your identification being stolen when you first came to us for a new tourist visa."

"I didn't know if I'd lost them or if they'd been stolen. I had no proof.

"Well, we will have to phone Mexico City to check your record, but, in the meantime, come with us."

He showed me into a room, empty except for a long, wooden table, a few chairs, and a fan in the ceiling spinning around. Motioning me to sit down, he closed the door, leaving me alone, head propped up from elbows in a woe is me, what have I gotten myself into pose.

Well, wasn't it just like Nicki to get into trouble? Indeed, this journey was turning into more of a mission of karma than I'd bargained for. I remembered asking Kate, "Do I have to undertake this journey?" and her reply, "unless Nick might rather come back in another way in punishment." Punishment indeed! I shouldn't have expected a joy ride.

Several hours later, I was still sitting alone at that table in the sweltering heat of the day when an office worker took pity on me and brought me a bottle of pop and some crackers and cheese to nibble on.

Finally, the official returned and placed before me a typewritten page with places to sign, and he asked, "Mexico City said your record is clean. Can you read Spanish?" I shook my head.

"You'll have to translate it for me."

He picked up the paper and read it aloud. The gist of it was a declaration that my statement was true, and it specified that I had only a certain amount of time that I could remain in Mexico. I wasn't being deported–exactly, only pushed out gently. Would I agree to those terms?

I agreed and signed the dotted line, hoping this was the end of it.

Following him back into his office, I sat down while he discussed my case with another Mexican, in Spanish. While I was sitting there, two American guys with backpacks were ushered in. One of them dug into his pack and pulled out what appeared to be a bag of marijuana, then another, and another! What was coming off? They didn't seem worried but smiled all the while. Maybe they'd made a deal. I'd heard about Mexican bribes and corruption before.

I sent them a quick, "Well, boys, you're in trouble too glance," out of the corner of my eyes and received an understanding grin, but what the hell! They turned and left, leaving me still sitting there.

The official returned with another typewritten page, which he gave to me and explained, "This is to replace the paper that was stolen from you. It will entitle you to leave the country within five days, but after five days you will have difficulty leaving. Do you understand? So, I would advise you to leave as soon as possible. You mentioned Saturday? Do not worry. You will not have difficulty entering Mexico again, and you are not being deported, but I hope that you have learned not to mingle with these types of people again."

I nodded, silently in relief, and with that, he handed over the visa, and my ID and I was free. I fairly flew back to the hotel room, packed my things together, and got down on my knees and thanked God once more, for watching over me.

March 8th, 1973

Kate:

I'm coming home from Merida, Mexico. Will give details later. Trip to Jamaica is out, but I'm satisfied enough with my trip, even if I didn't make it to South America. Should be home by March 15th. I'm reconciled to believe in Nick but realize Maureen as well.

Nicki/Maureen

Liberty

They say that girls can't wander
But I proved them wrong
I did everything that I wanted to
I had so much that I had to do
Life set me forward, life set me free
All I ask of you
Is that you give me liberty
It is true that the wanderlust
Is really a neutral soul
Who strikes the heart of all
Who stop to heed his call
I can't express the way I feel
But I can tell you where I've been
I can tell you tales of wanderings
And describe the sights I've seen
Male or female, set me free, the only life of my soul is me
And the road is where I'd rather be.

Chapter Eighteen

Down in Miami

I was never so glad to leave a place as I was the Mexican police station on that swelteringly hot March Day in Merida, Mexico. I made fast tracks for the Pan American Airlines office downtown and, with almost the remainder of my money, bought an airline ticket home that would transfer from Miami to Chicago to Toronto.

I was left with ten dollars, enough to pay my hotel, buy a few meals, and maybe enough, if I was lucky, to catch a bus home from Toronto. The plane would be leaving on Saturday, and I should arrive home by Monday morning, March 12th.

That afternoon, I returned to my hotel room and, in a thirsty moment, gulped down a bottle of milk that wasn't homogenized and probably not pasteurized, and lay down on the bed with a headache which got increasingly worse. Soon nausea took over, and I knelt before the toilet and vomited. Within the hour, I vomited again, until there was nothing left in my stomach, took a few Aspirin, and went to sleep. Strange, I hadn't vomited during my entire journey until now, but this was the second time I'd been sick in Mexico, the first being the *tourista* en route to Guadalajara.

When I woke in the morning, I was still weak and dizzy but concluded it must have been the milk. I spent the day at the hotel, transferring to a smaller and cheaper room, without either a bathroom or a fan, for the night. That night I climbed up onto the window ledge above my bed and blew harmonica blues as I watched the sun set hazy red streaks of sunset through the window, praying for the nightmare to be over soon.

The next morning, I paid my bill and caught a bus to the airport with enthusiasm for the trip home, making the acquaintance of a fellow Canadian. He told me he'd come all the way from Belleville, Ontario, on just a hundred and fifty dollars by hitchhiking and camping out on the beaches of Mexico, with a party of scientists involved in the space program. Well, who was I not to believe that story?

When I got to the airport, I headed straight for the baggage counter to get my pack checked. I was early, so I spent some time talking to a group of Mexicans who spoke good English, watching arrivals and departures. The plane headed for Miami full of tanned tourist types and businessmen. And I sat back, made the sign of the cross, and uttered a "Thank you, Lord," once more as we flew over the Gulf of Mexico.

After a brief stop at Tampa, Florida, we touched down in Miami, and I passed through American Customs, without a hitch. They didn't even search my pack as I'd thought they would. Soon I was walking into the lobby of Miami International Airport in Coral Gables. I discovered that my connecting flight would be delayed, so I settled down to wait for it. It was good to be among English speaking people again, regular bathrooms, clean surroundings and comfort. I'd been in Mexico almost a month.

I was so relieved at the smooth flow of events, excited, and spaced out in the parking lot taking a cigarette break, that I watched the wind rip my plane ticket out of my hands and blow it away. Frantically rushing around, I vainly searched the ground, but it was nowhere to be found! I didn't want to worry the family. They would say, "I told you so! Losing her plane ticket! Hanging around with criminals, barely avoiding a

Mexican jail! It's something that Minnie would do." I still had my pride, and I'd get home on my own steam.

In trouble again, ten dollars in my pocket and no place to go, I curled up on a bench in Miami International airport at one o'clock in the morning and prayed for God to come to my rescue. I had enough trust to believe this would happen, and I reasoned that my faith had surely been tested many times during the journey, and He'd never let me down. A feeling of peace fell over me as I placed myself in His hands. I was completely down and out, with only ten bucks to my name. He could do with me what He willed. I drifted off into an uncomfortable sleep.

I struggled out of a head-achey rest to someone politely clearing his throat and standing over me. He was an airline pilot, still dressed in uniform, on his way home from a flight, kind of a paunchy, Clark Gableish type, not my type, more my mother's. But he had kind eyes and was probably about thirty, I guessed.

"Why are you sleeping here, girl?" he wanted to know.

Over coffee and an English muffin, I informed him of my plight.

"So why don't you come and stay with my brother and I for a few days, until you get on your feet and decide what you're going to do?" he suggested. "We live in my sailboat, but there's a bunk for you, if you want it."

I figured that this was part of God's plan for me right now, and I'd better go with the flow, so I said yes and loaded my pack into his sports car convertible with the top down. We roared off into the hot, humid Coral Gables night, warm breezes off the ocean, blowing back my tangled hair.

We arrived at a pyramid shaped, wooden building that housed his sailboat, anchored in water. This was interesting. Just let me spread my sleeping bag over the deck, and I'll sleep beautifully, thank you. But we ended up drinking rum and Coke on the grass outside instead, and it must have been nearly three o'clock in the morning, listening to Carole King, then retreated to the bunk below. He followed me.

Inevitably, he started laying the seduction act on me, but tonight I wasn't in the mood for any foolishness. I cut him short and went into my lotus posture, the one I'd used in San Diego at Frank's halfway house with Lanky, while he, now naked and rolled up in blankets, rolled his eyes and, "Let's go to bed!"

But I climbed out of the bunk and back up onto the deck of the boat, spread my sleeping bag, and fell asleep in an instant.

That was a good night's sleep, and in the morning, Mr. Pilot had cooled off somewhat and acted almost like a guilty little boy. I forgave him, seeing how he was a Taurus, and Taurus men just can't help being sensuous. Now he turned protective and took me out to dinner. While we ate, he offered some common-sense advice.

"Have you got enough money to buy a ticket home?"

"Nope, I've only got, ten dollars left."

"Can you wire home for more?"

I didn't really want to bother my family. Here again, it was a case of, "Oh, it's Minnie, getting into trouble again." Wouldn't you know it, rub it in my face, why don't you? And yet, I knew, I was probably going to have to, anyway.

"Well," said Taurus, "you could get a job somewhere close by and work for a week or two until you earned enough money to get home."

"Wow!" I replied, "would you put me up that long?"

"Sure thing," he replied.

"But I don't have a working permit," I lamented. "Remember, I'm a Canadian citizen."

"That wouldn't matter if it was just for a few weeks," he assured me.

What about hitchhiking up the East Coast of the U.S.A.? Would I be able to hack it? Maybe, but I'd have to leave my bongos behind. I couldn't walk for miles with the extra weight. Maybe I could hitch a ride on a freight train. That was something I'd always wanted to do. The worst they could do would be to catch me and throw me in jail, and at least the American jails were cleaner than the Mexican ones.

Leave it to Taurus to bring me back down to earth and keep me there. He got me a job in a motel within walking distance, fed me well every night, wined and dined me and almost treated me like a little sister. It was great, and I discovered that I wasn't all that anxious about getting back to Canada anyway. It would probably still be knee deep in snow and sub-zero temperatures, but here, in Florida, the weather was absolutely beautiful. So I played my bongos and my cassette tape of my songs, walked a lot, exploring the area, and then I went to work.

It was hard work. I made beds, lugged cleaning carts, mopped toilets, sweated, drank a lot of pop and practiced my high-school French on the French Canadians working alongside me. Two of the chambermaids were Mexican, so I got my *Buenos dias* and my *s'il vous plait* mixed up with my *por favor*. Still, I persisted, until the second day, when I returned to work from lunch ten minutes late and was fired.

I was twenty dollars the richer, however, when I left that motel, but still had to swallow my pride, phone home, and ask for plane fare. The money came quickly, and it looked like I was going to be able to get home on time, anyway.

Taurus and I had serious conversations about his hopes and dreams for the future. He envisioned sailing around the

Caribbean Islands naked, lying outside on the deck, getting a good suntan, making love by moonlight with a lady friend and living the good life.

As far as roommates went, we argued a lot, and he told me that with all of my crazy ideas, I'd never be able to fit into normal society and live a decent life. Why, they wouldn't even let me into stewardess training with my weird beliefs and love of bohemia supreme! I might have been a female Jack Kerouac, but I wasn't a nut. That hit home. My dad had already branded me a kook.

I thought about all the people I had known, lived, and worked with and came to the conclusion that while I might be called eccentric, I was no more of a lunatic than the next guy. Maybe I was a wild chick, but heck, I was only twenty and still learning!

All journeys do eventually come to an end, and as I sat back on the plane to Toronto, I wondered about the future: inevitably a job, and a chance to save more money, then perhaps, I would get to Jamaica at last. Hell, maybe not.

I wondered about Tink and Jason stuck in that Mexican jail. Probably her wealthy father who owned a nightclub, would pull some strings and bail them out. Surely they would be waiting there for me in Jamaica when they got out of that Mexican jail, so maybe I was safer in Canada, after all!

The Prophet

Elusive butterfly truth
My people hunger for you
Soul bound mystic sleeps not
Nor lives as a person ought
Prophet born to illuminate
Miles in my dreams
Chasing moonbeams
Many more awake
Just for truth's sake
I've lived a miracle or two
Just to bring them to you.

Chapter Nineteen

Home Again

It seems as though jets spoil all the fun in traveling. This is partially because they are efficient and get you there on time for whatever you are in such a hurry to be there for. However, I was in no hurry to arrive back home in mid-March, Canada. I started shivering as soon as I saw the gray, cloudy skies and passed through Customs and Immigration without any trouble. They took my pack apart, however, wanting me to declare the hiking boots from San Francisco, the Mexican shirt that Ernesto had given me, and almost even the sea shells from the beaches of Progresso.

I changed currency and picked up my heavy pack once more, and my bongos, amazingly still tied on top, and hopped on the wrong bus. It took me a while to figure that out, but I finally found the right one that took me downtown to the subway station. Riding the subway brought back memories for me of a time when I lived for a month in Toronto, with my married lover two years previously. Then, I used to ride the subways, simply for the sheer joy of experiencing them. Now, it was to get down to the Toronto bus station where a bus would be taking me farther east to Kingston.

In the bus terminal, I made the acquaintance of a musician who was a personal friend of the musicians Murry McLaughlin and Bruce Cockburn. It was the bongos, of course, that drew him to me. He was on a series of night gigs, all the way down through the U.S.A. and even down into Mexico, where I'd just come from. He was in that grinning and adventurous frame of mind that I knew all too well and even invited me to come along, but I'd told the family I was on my way home, and they'd be expecting me.

The bus pulled into Kingston way past midnight, but I hadn't arranged to be picked up. As usual, I wanted to get there on my own steam, so I didn't have a plan. After pulling my gear off the bus, I stood outside shivering for a time, trying to adjust to the winter weather. It was a disappointment, same cold, crusty, snow-covered grass and roads, bare winter trees, still mid-winter, spring around the corner I knew, but already I missed the heat, tantalizing smells of steaks on the barbecue, and the sea breezes of Florida.

Half deciding to hitchhike home, I shouldered my pack and turned toward the highway, when, from out of the shadows, a taxi driver who must have been watching me approached.

"You weren't thinking of hitchhiking home at this hour, were you?" he asked gently.

"As a matter of fact," I replied, "I was."

He shook his head disapprovingly. "You're taking too much of a chance at this hour of the night. Where are you going?"

I scuffed a dirty boot in the wet snow and replied, "Heading about a half-hour east out of Kingston to Perth Road. I don't have any money left."

"Can't you call your family, someone?" he asked, concerned.

"They're all sleeping," I shrugged. "Don't want to bother them."

He paused thoughtfully. "I can take you there."

"I can't pay you," I replied, doubt in my eyes.

"That's okay. I'll take you home anyway," he offered.

This was strange, and for a moment, I wondered if there

might be a catch to it, but sincerity shone from his eyes, and I was tired and didn't want to argue with him.

"Sure," I replied, as he put my pack in the trunk, and I hopped in.

It was a lonely, dark ride that way, hardly any cars on the road. I would have been stranded if I'd tried to hitch it, cold, hungry and stranded, as a matter of fact. Was this a gift from God? I wondered. It seemed too much of a coincidence to be logical.

We talked about my wanderings and adventures through the U.S.A. and Mexico, and he seemed impressed.

"Well, I've got to hand it to you. You sure have a lot of courage," he exclaimed.

Was it courage or was it just plain fool hardiness? But I smiled at the compliment. It was just something I had vowed to do, and I'd done it to the best of my ability.

It seemed like, in no time at all, the taxi found its way through Perth Road, past pasture and farm land, iced-over swamps and ponds and rocky hills, then up the snowy, deserted, rural road to our house, lights out, windows darkened, everyone in sleepy land. I felt as though I'd just stepped out of a dream and that Point Blank and Guadalajara and Acapulco and Coral Gables had never happened. It had all been part of an amazing technicolored dream, and except for my suntanned face and body, I would have believed that.

The taxi driver took my pack out of the trunk and set it carefully on the ground. I turned around to gaze at the big house, sleeping in the shadows, not a sound over the countryside, blanketed in snow, a clear black sky, moon and stars shining vividly. For some reason, I felt sad. I hadn't realized how addicted I was to the thrill of the road, and now it was over.

I turned around to thank the driver, and both he and the car had disappeared! Had they even been there at all or was this also part of the dream? "Maybe he was an angel," I wondered. I unzipped my coat a little and searched. Yes, the cross was still there, and I suddenly felt a rush of happiness knowing that God and Angela had been with me, even to the very end of it.

I tiptoed into the kitchen, through an unlocked side door and turned on the light, rummaged around in the cupboard for cereal, a bowl and spoon, in the fridge for milk and sat down to eat. I was ravenous.

Moments later, I looked to see Mother standing in the doorway, wearing a robe and slippers and smiling.

"Maureen, you're home! Why didn't you phone us and ask us to pick you up at the bus station?"

"At this hour? I just got a taxi instead. I didn't want to bother you."

Then she shocked me as she began to relate the odd experiences that she'd had after I'd left for San Francisco.

"I did automatic handwriting," she blurted out, looking a bit unsure.

My spoon halted in mid-air, as I turned to ask her what this was all about.

"Well," she continued, with a slightly puzzled look in her eyes, "after you left, I was really worried, and I knew you were in danger, although I couldn't explain it, so I sat down and wrote you a letter that didn't sound like me at all! I sent it to San Francisco, to Aquarius House, hoping that you'd get it. Did you?"

"No," I replied. "I'll contact them right away and have them send the letter back here. I'd love to read it. It might be important."

Then I knew why I'd felt a little uneasy about leaving San Francisco prematurely. My timing had been off. A letter had been on its way to me, and I'd missed it.

Home Mother noticed the cross, still hanging on the necklace around my neck, and smiled. "The Lord took good care of you, Minnie."

My mother, my faithful friend.
Taken at home in Perth Road, Ontario
approximately 1998 holding her kitty

I returned her smile. "He always does, Mom. He always does." I felt oddly out of place. Half of me was still down in Mexico, waiting for a plane to Jamaica. Yet, the madness couldn't have continued. In running from city to city, searching for Nick, I'd become Nick again, but I wasn't sure I wanted to be Maureen either.

My cats were there, welcoming me back to my bedroom. I gazed out the window at the Canadian winterscape, somewhat softened now in March, with the oncoming of spring, over the rocky hills, the garage, where Father's jeep and tools were housed, the barn, where the horses took shelter, over the snow and ice-covered lake beyond, pulled off my road weary blue jeans and fell into a dreamless sleep in my own bed.

Much to my surprise, Kate hardly took notice of my arrival and more or less ignored me! The very one who'd sent me off on such a wild goose chase that I'd risked my life for! My father looked pissed off, probably because I'd had to ask for money for the plane ticket home. It wasn't exactly a warm-hearted welcome that I walked into, but I took consolation in the fact that Mother was happy. However, the whole feeling that settled over me was one of major let-down.

Several weeks later, the letter Mother had written and sent to Aquarius House returned in the mail and it read:

February 1973

Maureen:

For a while after you left, I had a very depressed feeling. When I thought of you it was bad vibrations. Maybe E.S.P? Anyway, I seemed to feel you were in danger, drugs involved and black people. I had very strong visions of you surrounded by blacks, and they were urging you to take hard drugs. I was very upset for quite a few days. I was even thinking of getting in touch with the San Francisco police. You know, I don't usu- ally use my E.S.P. but this came unbidden and it was very frightening. I tried to warn you against being used by these

*people, but I knew your need for music was strong and I had a
bad time of it. Were you in danger? I'm curious to know, because I don't understand my own feelings.*

*I'm feeling easier now but am getting a feeling of indecision
about you. You are still searching. I have a strong feeling that
you are a good person and that people may want to corrupt and
discourage your faith in the good in people. You must be prepared to recognize the evil in some people as well as the good
for your own sake, be more cautious about people.*

*There is a funny thing about this, religious vibrations in
you. I get a picture of you as a missionary working for and surrounded by children. Isn't that strange! Especially here, but
you are <u>GOOD</u>. I don't think you realize it yet, but I think you
will be of service to mankind somehow. Perhaps your involvement with the psychic is just a cover up for your search for
God. Isn't it funny that I should think this but it's almost as if
I am writing automatically so maybe it's not my thoughts at
all!*

*Go to the missions and churches and perhaps you will feel
something inside. I will wait to hear from you and get an address to get in touch. Meanwhile, I'll try to keep in contact by
using my E.S.P. as it comes to me, go with God.*

*That's what it is, you're seeking out the misfits. It must be
that you sense their confusion and know that they are lost.
There's something about you, you don't know it yet, but you
are going to find out perhaps not right away, but it's there, a
closeness to God and good. Why didn't I realize it? It's just a
feeling that I have received lately and I feel so much better
knowing you are protected by your goodness and faith.*

*I always thought your cross was a decoration, now I sense a
deeper meaning to it and your love of Latin. You will use your*

*music to make people happy to bring them to a spiritual awak-
ening. I write this under compulsion–maybe it's not me at all,
it certainly doesn't sound like me.*

*Now I see why you have not much interest in material
things, why you went through the period with Chris, you were
trying to help him. It wasn't physical as much as a longing to
help him out of his troubles, your compassion for him. There is
a reason for all of this. It's so clear to me now. You will find a
way to be of service to men, keep your spirits up. God is with
you and He will reveal it to you in time.*

*Keep your mind clear and listen and be prepared to experi-
ence this awakening. It will come. I feel it and then you will be
at peace and know what you are going to do.*

*Maureen: Am going to mail this as is. In reading it over, I
still don't understand it but perhaps you will. Hope you have
not moved on.*

Mother

I put the letter down, amazed, and turned to Mother, asking,
"How did you know I was in trouble with black people in San
Francisco? How did you know that I went into a church in
Mexico to pray?"

Mother only smiled mysteriously. "Maybe I have psychic
abilities too!"

This was stranger than strange; the "influence" had apparently
extended to other members of my family besides Kate. It was a
whole new side of Mother that I'd never seen before...but Father
was a different story.

"Do you think Dad will mind that I'm back home again?"

"He's glad, Minnie, even though he won't admit it. He's had
a lot on his mind lately, and you too...He goes to court next week

to fight the expropriation case. He locks himself in the library all day, poring over legal papers. I'm worried about him."

I nodded. "Can't beat the government, but you sure can try." I sighed.

One afternoon, I popped into the library, and Kate was there, in the old familiar brown leather sofa, studying for an exam.

"How're ya doin', Kate? Heard you had another operation."

Kate waved it off. "I've lost count. Hey, Min, is it good to be back home again?"

"Better than a Mexican jail," I grinned, "but I didn't get to Jamaica. Ran out of money and got into some trouble down there."

"Yeah, I heard," yawned Kate, in a disinterested gesture. "Maybe Jamaica will find you."

"I don't see how," I replied. "And I didn't get the diary."

Kate replied impatiently, "Does it matter? Did you go back, Jack, and do it again?"

"Yeah," I exclaimed. "It was amazing." My expression changed to regret. "But, Kate, I was told by an ex con in San Diego, that the map you gave me, was a drug runner's route! So Nick must have been pushing drugs from South America up the East Coast of the U.S.A. to New York. He wasn't just a musician."

Kate smirked. "Is any musician, just a musician? They all do it. You didn't run drugs or do heroin did you?"

"No, of course not Kate."

"Then you resisted temptation. You passed the tests. You've got nothing to worry about."

I'm not finished. Nick's death is still on my shoulders. He was responsible for not only causing his own death but also bringing hardship to others.

"What do you mean?" asked Kate puzzled.

"God forgives but karma is Law. It's written in the stars.

Kate laughed. "Min, you're obsessed about this. Why don't you get out and have some fun? Mike's been calling for you. Wants to go out Saturday night to the 401 Inn in Kingston."

"I'll give him a call. Maybe I can forget this, just for a while."

Mike and I had a great reunion, and I filled him in on all of my adventures in California and Mexico while he listened eagerly. "I wish I'd been there!"

Yeah, I could imagine Mike in Mexico all right. He would never have returned. The dope would have done him in.

The club was packed as Mike and two of his friends and I shared our adventures over rum and Cokes, and Mike didn't hesitate to fill them in on our escapades at Strawberry Fields, several years before.

"Man, if you want to try some powerful shit, do Sunshine or Purple Micro Dot!" Mike whispered, a glazed look in his eyes. "It's something you'll never forget."

His friends, boys from the backwoods of Perth Road, cow pasture country, sat, their mouths hanging open, in absolute awe, taking it all in. "Geez, wish I'd gone," one of them lamented.

Daniel Lanois and his band were up that night. He was truly a master of entertainment–not only music, but he also played the part of a comedic puppet, hanging his arms limply and making funny faces, getting a roar from the audience. Afterwards, I invited him to sit down at our table, and I bought him a drink. I judged him to be about the same age as our group.

"I liked your act, Dan. Are you touring right now?"

"I'm not on the road all of the time," Dan replied. "I have a recording studio in Ancaster in the basement of my mother's house."

"Ancaster! No kiddin'..." I gasped. "I spent my childhood

there. My father owned Kellar's Steeplejacks Ltd. Hey," the thought struck me. "I've got some songs that need to be recorded..."

"Well, why don't you come to Ancaster?" Dan replied. "I'd be happy to record them for you. It'll be a homecoming for you too."

"Wow. I'd love that," I exclaimed." Dan gave me his address and telephone number and returned to the stage to finish the show.

Later that night, I tiptoed into Kate's bedroom and nudged her.

"Hey, Kate! Guess what! I met a musician at the 401 Inn tonight, and his name is Daniel Lanois. He's got a recording studio in Ancaster and has invited me down to record my songs.

Kate mumbled sleepily, "That's nice Minnie." She turned over and went back to sleep, but I was too excited to get much sleep that night.

The next day as I sat in front of Grandma's old piano organizing and rehearsing Nick's songs that I would record at Dan's studio, a wave of religious devotion swept over me. Flicking on the tape recorder three songs spontaneously poured through me. Although I sang the lyrics and played the chords, the songs weren't mine. Could they have come from the angels? I decided to call them

"The Angel Music."

Brothers join hands all those who wish to free
the Universal Spirit from you and me
He whispered in my ear just the other day and
He told me, He told me, a wonderful thing!
He said, I'm waiting for all of my long lost
children and now musician I would have you sing.

Chapter Twenty
Recording with Daniel Lanois

The bus ride down from Kingston to Toronto and Toronto to Hamilton took the better part of the day, but Dan was waiting for me, as we'd previously arranged, and he gave me a ride over to Ancaster from downtown Hamilton. It had been over ten years since my father had moved us to "the sticks," as we called it, and we passed right by our old house on Wilson Avenue, bringing back a flood of memories for me.

He took me on a little tour through his mother's cute, little bungalow, introduced me to his mother and his sister Jocelyn, and ushered me downstairs to his homemade music studio where there was a grand piano waiting.

"Nice house, Dan," I commented admiringly.

"We like it," he smiled.

Soon the tape reels were turning as Dan sat in the recording booth behind the sound table. I'd just finished "Jamaica Way," vocals and piano.

"Great song, Maureen," remarked Dan. "When were you in Jamaica?"

"Well, I haven't been there yet. Someday..."

How could I explain?

"No kiddin'," Dan puzzled. "Sounds like you've spent half of your life there."

"Yeah, it does, doesn't it? You know, I can almost see the mountains, the ocean, hear the reggae, feel the sand under my feet..." I was daydreaming again.

"I don't very often get musicians in here who sing about places they've never been to. You're a real mystery." Dan scratched his head, thoughtfully.

"Well, that's nicer than being called a kook!"

"Who calls you a kook?"

"Oh, my dad," I remarked ruefully. "He doesn't understand me."

"Well, he's mistaken," Dan smiled. "You're a real black magic woman."

I laughed, delighted at the comment.

Dan eyed me curiously and then glanced up at the clock on the studio wall. It was late.

"So, Maureen, why don't you stay here tonight? It's too late to go back to Kingston.

You say you've got a brother in Hamilton?"

"Haven't seen him in years," I replied.

"Well then, you don't want to bother him at this late hour. You can sleep here."

"Where?" I asked, looking around.

"Right here, in the studio," Dan replied and left the room, and returned, pulling a roll-away cot. He set it up next to the wall, beside the piano, blankets, pillows.

I felt awkward. "Thanks, Dan, for all you've done for me. I'm sorry that I can't pay you." I sat down on the cot.

"Don't think you have to," Dan replied softly.

"I'd like to..." I whispered, and his eyes met mine. Dan sat down beside me and drew me to him with an embrace and a passionate kiss. I shifted, making room for him on the cot. Here I was, falling for another musician again. Dan unbuttoned my shirt, and it fell to the floor. He turned off the light. I melted into him and cast my fate to the wind.

The next morning, Dan drove me back to the bus station, and we stood, holding hands, beside the Greyhound Bus. The morning after is always awkward, but by the way I was feeling, I was sure that I wanted this to be more than just a one-night stand. I'd never met anyone quite like Dan Lanois before. There was something about him that garnered awe, kind of like speaking to the prime minister even, that rendered me shy, intimidated, almost wordless but adoring. Even then, I sensed that his ambition would carry him far. It was love. Maybe it was hero worship in its infantile stage, but I knew I'd never wanted a man more than this.

"If I can't find work in Kingston," I told Dan, "I might move back here. I could stay with my brother." I glanced anxiously at Dan, looking for approval. He must have known, of course, that I meant that I wanted to be near him.

"Give me a call, when you settle in," Dan replied, but it wasn't exactly the kind of reaction that I'd hoped for. It was more of a friendly reply, "I'll do what I can to help you, just like I'd help any friend, manner of speaking." A little on the cold side, but maybe I misinterpreted it. I think I expected more–a warm embrace, a kiss, a "What a great idea. Can't wait till you get here" reaction.

But then we hadn't known each other very long. Even if I believed in love at first sight, it didn't mean that he did.

"Dan, about last night..." I began awkwardly, fumbling for words.

He smiled warmly, a little more human and squeezed my hand.

"I'll be in touch. We'll record more songs." And with that, I boarded the bus home, threw him a kiss at the window, and gave away my heart.

The next day, Kate wandered into the library den, and I was curled up in the favorite, brown leather chair, staring out the window.

"Hey, Min, how did your trip to Hamilton go?" she asked with the curiosity that only teenagers looking for gossip radiate.

"Well," I replied thoughtfully, "I went to Ancaster, and just like he said he would, Dan Lanois recorded my songs...and..."

Kate grinned knowingly.

"You're chasing him! Minnie's in love. Be careful, Min. Remember, love's a two-way street. I don't want to see my big sister getting hurt again, like you were with Chris."

There was just no way to fool Kate. I replied, "Thanks, Kate, for caring," and gave her a big hug.

A month later, I was pounding the pavements of Hamilton, looking for work. Passing by the new City Hall, I paused, scanning the shiny building and the manicured grounds, the fountain spouting water, the people coming and going, and clutching my satchel of resume papers, headed for the main entrance.

Approaching the clerk behind the counter in Human Resources, I inquired expectantly, "Hi. Are you accepting applications?"

She smiled and pulled one out, along with a pen. "Here," she said, "fill this out, please."

A few days later, I was all settled. I had a room in an old boarding house on Mary Street, across from The Colonial bar in downtown Hamilton, within walking distance of City Hall and a new job in the Building Department. It was a flophouse to be sure, cheap rent and questionable company, but it was all I could afford, and I was on Dan's turf now. I reached for the phone a little nervously and dialed his number.

Dan picked up the phone. "Hello?"

My heart melted again. "Dan, it's Maureen. Remember me?"

"Hey, Maureen, where are you at?" Dan asked.

"Here. I'm right here in Hamilton. I got a job at City Hall and a room in a boarding house downtown, and I'm all settled in."

"That's great," Dan replied without much enthusiasm.

My excitement faded. What was with him? I paused.

"So...hey, maybe we could get together now, do some recording, have dinner together..."

Dan interrupted, "Look, Maureen. I'm in the middle of something here..."

I babbled on, "You said to call if I moved back. I thought..."

Dan hummed and hawed. "Yeah, I know. But I'm swamped here at the studio, and I'm going on tour soon, and I've got rehearsals, and you know the music business..."

"But what about my songs? I've got some contracts from BMI here that I don't understand. Maybe we could get together, and you could go through them with me."

Dan hesitated, attempting to be tactful. "Sorry, Maureen, I've got my own music to think about. I'll help you if I can."

"Well, what about us, a relationship?"

Dan replied slowly, "Look, we can be friends. I don't have time for a relationship. Come by the studio sometime when I get back, okay?"

Slowly, my dreams of realizing an ideal relationship of soul mates, both dedicated to music, dissolved in front of my eyes. I'd been certain that this knight in shining armor would sweep in, rescue this lonely soul, and set her on the proper path with love and support. Wasn't I worth as much? I'd taken a gamble and moved away from the security of my family's home to Hamilton, sure that Dan was the one–"love at first sight." And I was ready to make sacrifices for him. I'd already proved this. It was without a doubt meant to be. God had picked him out for me. I was certain of that. We were the same age, even came from the same neighborhood. If my father hadn't moved us away from Wilson Avenue when I was 10, I'd probably even have met Dan and gone to the same high school as him. Was I somehow the victim of a thwarted destiny that I could only blame my father for? But apparently, Dan didn't want someone like me who had thrown herself at him so willingly. I'd made a big mistake in the scheme of male/female relationships. Perhaps the lure of the chase would have been more tantalizing for him, but I didn't want to play games. I wanted security in a relationship that I could build my life around. I was young and I was ready.

Hey, I was a pretty good keyboard player! I could be a real asset in any band. Maybe Dan needed a keyboard player. I was tired of being lonely, tired of trying to survive on next to nothing, tired of losers and one night stands, yearning for that eligible someone who never arrived and fighting off the undesirables at the same time. Nick might have been able to catch his love on the run but it was no life for a woman. Heck, didn't I deserve a husband and children? At the rate I was going, I'd self-destruct just as Nick had, and worst of all...nobody cared!

I dropped the phone to the floor as tears and self-pity flooded my eyes, uncontrollably. Throwing myself on my bed, I wept, curled up, alone. A sharp knocking on the door went unanswered. Betty, a roomie from Newfoundland, poked her head in.

"Maureen, why don't you join us downstairs? We're having a drink."

She paused in the doorway, watching me sobbing into the pillow, and remarked softly. "When you're up to it," and tiptoed away.

Chapter Twenty-One
Down Jamaica Way

Jamaica Way

Way down, down Jamaica way
I went lookin' for Montego Bay
Left my home, just to follow the sun
But you know, it's not for everyone
Oh, man, on Montego Bay
You can swim and rest your cares away
Come all to Jamaican shores
You won't have to look
Won't have to look no more.

Slowly, as the days sped by, I resigned myself to the fact that Dan *didn't care*. If he'd visited me at 60 Mary Street and seen the conditions that I lived under, he would have been shocked. The house was filled with transients who partied day and night. Drunks stumbled in the hallways and vomited on the floors, all manner of drugs were being dealt, and random sex in the numerous bedrooms was ongoing. It was like living in a whorehouse, but it was cheap rent, a convenient location, and I didn't have any money yet for anything better. Even when I got my first paycheck from City Hall, it was barely enough to cover the rent and buy food. Still, I managed to put some down on a Fender Rhodes electric piano and amp, just like the one that the band Point Blank had had, so I could continue to practice in my spare time. And I hoped for the call from Dan that never came.

Then, discouraged, I threw my fate to the wind and joined in with the wrong crowd. I chugalugged wine and beer, smoked pot, and danced the night away. We had been overrun with Newfoundlanders who had the same lackadaisical philosophy– Betty, Terry, Lystra (a young woman from Trinidad), assorted oddballs and streetwise others who dropped in at all hours of the day and night. No, I hadn't left the road. The road had found me again, and it continued on, under the guise of another name.

Terry and the Jamaicans

One evening, there was a knock on the door and, just like that, two Jamaican men were standing there, waiting to be invited in. Apparently, our girl from Trinidad, Lystra, knew them and introduced Ossie and Rashi to us. Holy smoke! And all of a sudden, I dropped into the world of the Jamaica that I'd heard so much about but hadn't succeeded in reaching.

"Minnie, Terry, Betty, meet my friends Ossie and Rashi. Minnie, I thought you'd be interested in meeting Rashi. He's in a Jamaican band called Peace Train–reggae music!"

"Wow! Jamaica! I'd sure be interested in hearing your band, Rashi. I play the bongos myself." I couldn't believe what was happening, another coincidence that was a synchronicity. I blurted out, "I was on my way to Jamaica, not too long ago, but never made it, ran into some trouble."

Rashi smiled warmly, "You missed a good place, Minnie. Jamaica is the best place in de whole world. Come with me to a Jamaican party gig. Bring your drums, but we'll have congas there."

"Where?" I asked, breathless.

"In T.O., this weekend. Wanna come? I can pick you up in de truck. Lystra's coming."

"Sure," I replied enthusiastically. "Count me in!"

Evening in T.O., in a dark club, darker than any I'd ever been in, Lystra and I took seats up close to the band, giggling nervously in anticipation and absorbing the exotic Caribbean atmosphere. It was exclusive to Jamaicans, and only a few Caucasian girls sat shyly on the perimeter, taking the chance on venturing into its forbidden midst. It smelled of spices, beautiful white beaches, the fragrance of poinsettia floating in the air, Rastafari, *ganga* and dreadlocks, but it somehow felt strangely familiar to me.

Rashi and his band were up on stage, playing. I sat at a table with Lystra, eating curry goat meat and rice, drinking rum and Coke, and watching couples swaying to Bob Marley and Burning Spear. The rhythm swept through the room, inviting one and all to take a chance and try de dance. In a hazy, alcohol fueled dream I bolted from the table and slipped behind the stage congas.

Time slipped the track, and then I wasn't Maureen anymore. I was Nick sitting behind a big set of congas on a Jamaican stage, filling the background. Whoops! Cheers! The crowd swayed in front of him like heat waves on a hot, paved road on a stifling day in August. They loved him. He was on fire, and the others had all they could do to back him.

Rashi's eyes were transfixed on me. He put his guitar down and motioned to the others to keep the rhythm going. He grabbed my arm and guided me to the dance floor.

"Dis is how we do it in Jamaica," he smiled, moving his legs, his hips. And I copied him, completely into it.

The night drifted away, and Lystra, Rashi, and I returned to Hamilton in the wee morning hours. Lystra thanked Rashi and slipped away into the house while I remained, searching for my bongos in the dark.

"Man, I had a blast, tonight. I really got off on the music, the drums, the dance..."

Rashi's arms slipped around me. He leaned over and kissed me hard on the lips. I pulled away from him. "Let me go, Rashi. It's just the music. Remember that."

"Dat hard fe remembra when me with you." Rashi gasped, turning reluctantly away. He called out as I hopped out of the van, "Comin' by to take you to practice tomorrow night. Another gig in two weeks. We need a bongo player!"

I turned and paused. "Okay. See you tomorrow then."

Rashi sat in the van watching, for a few minutes, probably hoping I'd invite him in, but I wouldn't get in too deep with Rashi. I couldn't fall for every musician who played guitar! He pulled away from the curb, tires squealing.

Night after night, rice and peas, mango juice, beef patties, Jamaican weed, rum and Coke, reggae. They would come and get me in the middle of the night when I was sleeping, sneaking up the back-fire escape, knocking on my window, and steal me away to smoke the ganga and party the night away. Then I'd drag myself to work the next day, sleepy eyed and hung over. My secret world consisted of clubs by the name of Gord's Place in St. Catharines and the Club Afrique and The Cockador in Toronto.

January 7th, 1975

Dear Mother,

I spent New Year's Eve in Hamilton with Lystra at the Club Afrique and spent some time with a member of Rashi's band, "Peace Train"—this young man from Trinidad called Lenton who I am now seeing. I dropped Rashi after a week because he was living common law with someone else and because he wasn't really my type. Lenton seems better, especially since he is single and his guitar is a Fender!

When I first saw him, I liked him—maybe because he was dressed up like Jimi Hendrix in a black robe costume and black hat with a feather in it and I just couldn't resist the man.

I will keep in touch and hope you will too. I don't know when I'll be home next. I travel on impulse so I could be home when I feel the need.

Love,

Maureen

I ceased to exist in a Canadian world. "No Cry Woman" and patois filtered into my ears and coursed through my veins. Jamaican hospitality drew me to them, a home away from home, whole families dancing and celebrating life through the hot summers and cold winters that were Ontario. It didn't seem to matter anymore. I'd come to Jamaica, just as Kate had said I would, and now I understood the mystery and the magic that pervaded this culture, that fascinated me, like a cobra dancing in front of me, hypnotizing me, drawing me closer. Ossie taught me the lyrics to a Jamaican folksong. *"It's been a long time, I been away from my home, from my family—It's been a long time..."*

Money Go Round

Dig the materialistic merry-go-round
You swing with the penny pendulum
We are a clockwork candy bar
With timed washroom debuts
Distributing funky memos to
All the clockwork people
I am the tick-tock person
So wind me up and watch me work.

And, in my loneliness, I finally crossed the line and ended up in Lenton's bed in T.O. We made inter-racial love with his Fender guitar propped up against the side of the bed, and I let my imagination run wild and daydreamed that I was in bed with Jimi Hendrix. There is an old saying, *"Once black, you'll never go back,"* and I could understand why. Having been haunted by the ghost of Nick Jackson so long now, I was more black than white anyway, I reasoned so why not go all the way with it?

By day I worked at my dull office job, answering phones and filing for the Building Department, surrounded by conventional coworkers saving money for their houses and weddings and overweight, middle-class responsible types, paying mortgages, while at night I slipped the time track back into the world of the Jamaicans. I ran around town, collecting reggae songs, and Lystra and I always had a big pot of rice on the back of the stove at the boarding house. My coworkers looked at me strangely and kept their distance. I must have reeked of *ganga* and curry.

My roommates in the wild house on Mary Street watched me sink deeper and deeper into the Jamaican culture, and the friendly but concerned Newfie Betty Brown pulled me into her bedroom long into the night for heart-to-hearts about her love life and questions about where I was headed. She sympathized. Of course, Newfie Screech was Jamaican Rum, and she could relate.

Terry Miller, another young Newfie, was on a self-destructive trip of his own. Raised in a dysfunctional home, Father beating Mother up, eight children crowded into two rooms, he had left home in his early teens, illiterate, already a confirmed alcoholic, and had only his friendship to offer.

One evening, as I sat on the couch in the main room littered with dirty ashtrays, empty beer cans, beside a greasy looking, cross-eyed, buck toothed, sad loser, looking out the window across the street at The Colonial, he came staggering in, carrying a half-opened bottle of Screech.

"What's up, Terry?" I asked.

"What's a life with a wife, and what's a life without one? Ever heard the saying, she's seen more cock ends than weekends?"

I laughed uproariously. Terry was the only one who could make me laugh.

"I hope you didn't mean me, Terry. You're a riot!"

Terry winked, took a big swig of the bottle, and offered it to me. I shook my head. Terry was a real actor. He could make the whole world his stage, and I was always part of the attentive audience. Either you were repulsed or you were amused. I chose to be fascinated.

Terry grabbed his crotch and proceeded to prance around the room.

"Scuze me, darlin'. I gots to piss so bad, the crabs are runnin' for lifeboats!"

And he dashed for the bathroom, through the kitchen. After a few minutes, he returned and sat down beside me and the loser. Leaning toward me, he pushed his whisky breath toward me and whispered, "Girl, I gots ta tell ya somethin'."

"What?" I asked, moving a few inches away.

"Well, you might not like what I'm sayin', but you don't know what you're doin' with those Jamaicans. Listen." And his eyes took on a more serious expression.

"I may not have much education, but I got my education from the streets, if you know what I mean."

"I don't understand," I replied, puzzled.

"I heard it through the grapevine that Rashi wants you, and he ain't gonna take no for an answer. You don't wanna mix with those people. They're not your kind."

"Well, are *you* my kind?" I asked, angrily, flashing him a look.

Terry tried to placate. "Listen, girl, I'm tryin' to help 'ya. You made him mad when you wouldn't let him jump ya. You're a tease, not a sleaze, but you can't befriend a Jamaican and not go along with him."

"So, you're my bodyguard," I retorted.

"Well, you ain't got nobody else lookin' out for ya, have ya, girl?" he questioned, and I had to admit that he was right about that.

"There's been rumors that he was gonna corner ya some night

and shoot ya full of heroin so he could have his way with ya. That's what I heard from the grapevine," Terry whispered urgently. "Just wanted to let ya know. I'm here if ya needs me. I'll call some of my buddies up, and we'll give 'im a good shitkickin'."

I didn't know what to think. Terry wasn't known to be a liar, an alcoholic for sure, a dramatic showman, a hard worker, who busted his ass in a scrap yard daily, but not a liar.

He took another swig of the bottle, stood up and almost fell over. I grabbed his arm and steadied him, helped him back to the couch, and settled his head on the pillow. He focused on me with glazed, grateful eyes.

"Thanks, beautiful." And then he passed out.

What Terry had said worried me, but I was in too deep to get out, it seemed. The Jamaicans now regarded me as one of their own. I was lost now, every bit as addicted to them as Terry was to alcohol. And I knew that Nick's karma was leading me down an uncertain road.

I'd continued in my studies of astrology, making side trips to Toronto to buy astrology textbooks in stores that stocked them there. I hustled up a part-time evening job teaching it at the local YWCA in Hamilton, and *The Hamilton Spectator* even sent out a photographer and wrote an article in the newspaper about Hamilton's own "Stargazer." In Kingston, Ontario, I went on a radio talk show with Floyd Patterson, enjoying my little bit of local fame.

I delighted in having the knowledge of how astrology works so I could help other people understand the influence that the planets had on their lives. Through the astrology chart, I could see the past life karma that a person had been born with, both good and bad, or in biblical terms, how they were reaping what they had previously sown in lifetimes they could no longer remember.

Hamilton Spectator newspaper photo - Taken in 1974 when I was known as "Stargazer" who worked in the Building Department at City Hall by day and taught astrology at the local YWCA in the evenings.

I felt truly blessed by being given the facts of my previous life in order to know how it had affected my life as Maureen. I often wondered where this talent for astrology had come from, finally concluding that I must also have had a lifetime in India learning and practicing this talent previously, another lifetime that had left its distinct mark upon me.

As a teenager, I had sometimes spent days alone in the wilderness camping on the shores of Slide Lake in solitary meditation like the holy men of India did. In fact, prayer and meditation had been a daily habit of mine that had nothing to do with my Canadian, Christian upbringing. It was in meditation one summer afternoon that I experienced a flash of complete 360-degree vision and saw, through the back of my head, a water snake crawling up behind me, whirled around, and lo and behold, it was true. The miracles of India had always fascinated me, and now I had truly experienced one!

Professionally, I could have had it made, had I put my nose to the grindstone, with a lifetime union job at City Hall and rising fame in the occult world, but I didn't want to be a clerk or fortune teller; I wanted to play the blues!

I had finally looked up my brother, Bob, who was living in Hamilton and driving buses for the Hamilton Street Railway, and he had invited me to visit. He was living with his live-in girlfriend, Susan, and her son Mark, from her first marriage, in a two-bedroom apartment on the outskirts of town, in Stoney Creek. He seemed happy enough, surrounded by his expensive, white leather furniture, looking through huge penthouse windows, mega stories up, in what Jimi Hendrix would have called "a cage." Still, he seemed happier here in Hamilton than he'd ever been in the Godforsaken backwoods of Perth Road.

I hadn't been able to get my musical career off the ground in

Hamilton, despite joining the Musicians Union and auditioning for a rock band in the area. My keyboard boogie-woogie just didn't suit "Takin' Care of Business." Without Daniel's direct "hands on guidance and involvement," I felt frustrated in my efforts to "get into the scene." It was so much harder here than it had been in San Francisco, and if you've ever had to pack up and drag a Fender Rhodes piano to auditions and gigs, man, you'll never forget the backbreaking labor of it. I couldn't afford a vehicle and had to rely on the help of friends to get me around.

At night, I went home to my flophouse and reached out, one more time, to him. In the interim, I'd entered a song-writing contest with BMI in Toronto, hosted by Mr. Lehman Engle, Dean of Broadway Musicals. And one of Nick's songs, "New York," had won me a place in the songwriter's workshop classes, training to be a writer of Broadway musicals. I'd attended one workshop in Toronto, but I wasn't really interested in becoming a writer of Broadway musicals. In fact, I'd never even seen one, in all of my life. Still, it was a major victory for me musically, and I wanted Dan to know about it. Up in my bedroom, I dialed the number to Dan's recording studio.

Daniel's brother, Bob, manning the studio behind the sound booth, picked up the phone.

"Hi, Daniel," I inquired, hopefully.

"No, it's Bob, his brother. Dan's on tour with his band. Can I take a message?"

"No," I replied, disappointed, "just tell him that one of the songs that we recorded won in a contest hosted by Mr. Lehman Engle, Dean of Broadway Musicals, in New York City."

"Wow. Congratulations. I'll let him know," Bob kindly replied.

"Any chance that I might be able to see Dan sometime soon?" I asked, still hopeful.

"Probably not for a while," Bob said. "He's pretty busy on the road, but I'll let him know you called."

Setting the phone back in its cradle, I slumped into a chair and burst into tears.

Not too much later, I got a letter from Daniel, and it was very businesslike.

Dear Maureen,

Sorry I didn't write you sooner, but I was away for a while. If you still plan on visiting, give me a call and make arrangements. I am always home on Sundays, and the rates are cheap. The group is working regularly, and things are working out just fine.

I have been doing a lot of writing, and I am happy to say, two of our jingles are presently being played over local AM radio. This is a tremendous breakthrough for us. It means more contracts and good money. I am not the greatest of letter writers, so don't get discouraged if my replies are a little late. Keep up your work on the piano and the percussion. I enjoy hearing from you.

Love,

Daniel Lanois

I suppose there was some consolation to be had in his proposed effort to be friends, I thought sadly, and he did end the letter with "Love," but it didn't warm my bed, didn't ease the loneliness in my soul, and it didn't repair the damage to my still wounded heart. Dan had made it obvious that he was married to him music and didn't need a wife. I couldn't wait for him forever and I needed to get off the path I was on before it destroyed me. I tucked the letter away for safekeeping. I would keep it forever and, decades later, read it again and cry.

Chapter Twenty-Two

The Turning Point

Streetwise Boy

Streetwise, blue-nosed boy
From Newfoundland
Worshipped me from afar
Watched me, a freedom junkie
Getting into the wrong car, and said
"Girl, I'm the one with tattoos on my arm
And I wasn't raised on a farm
But what your daddy doesn't know
Might kill you
So we drank whisky and rum
Smoked a little grass
I couldn't see the knife at my back
And I didn't even ask
But I, a lonely girl running wild,
Took refuge in his bed
"What are you doing with my kind of
breed?" he asked
"Better you than dead?" I said.

I was twenty-two. I'd given up hope that my soul mate would ever come to rescue me and even given up hope that I'd someday get back into music and satisfy my heart's desire or was it Nick's?. I was tired of jobs that stifled my creativity and didn't pay a living wage. I was tired of the nagging loneliness and the risk of casual sex that had driven my generation. Women's Lib had opened up the door to a Pandora's Box. You could attempt to live like a man, but your female instincts still could not be denied. Tink was right about that, at least. Jamaica had indeed come to me, and whatever purpose this had served in dispelling Nick's karma, I wasn't sure. Despite the insinuated threats on my life, I was still alive, but it might not be for too much longer, at the rate I was going. It was time to jump off the parallel time track and escape from both Nick and Jamaica.

However, I continued to search for information about Nick, consulting an American psychic by the name of Betty Riley, who had written the book *A Veil Too Thin*, about her own reincarnation experience. She sent me a letter:

Dear Maureen,

As I held your picture in my hands, attempting to pick up vibrations that would be helpful to you, a song keeps running through my head "Just Molly and me and baby makes three— happy in my Blue Heaven." It doesn't make any sense to me but maybe it will to you.

With all that you have told me in your letter, I hope the impressions I received (which isn't much) is not being influenced by this. I cannot be sure, but I shall give you my impressions as they come to me.

Young, black boy, the period is the early twenties. I'm focusing in on the year 1923, the location is in Kentucky, large family, working on some type of farm, seem to be sharecroppers or something like that. Seems to be eight children in the family, the mother and father are very docile people outwardly and do not allow the "white folks" to know their true feelings. Very proud people, believe in working hard and not making trouble.

The family is not mistreated by the white landowners, but each child that comes into the family is expected to "pull their own load" as soon as they are able to.

The one I am picking up is number 6 of the 8 children. He is small for his age and a bit frail. He is a difficult child, rebellious actually, he has a keen mind, creative and quick. He is not like the rest, more of a dreamer, always thinking of faraway places, always thinking of different ways to make money that will not require hard work. He has music in his head that won't go away. He is regarded as a troublemaker. I pick up a name of Jud for Judadia. He has an attunement to music, and sings and dances for the "white folks." They pitch pennies at him. He is always underfoot where he shouldn't be. The people who own the land are unhappy with his "bothering folks." His mother and father "don't want no trouble."

Moving to a period when he is about 15 and he leaves home—his family is tired of his making trouble for them. He is restless, the music is still in his head. He goes north to "make his fortune." Hiding away in trains, stealing food, hiding and running and singing and dancing for pennies, whenever he has the chance. I pick up the New York area. I see him shining shoes, working in really bad sections of town. He has a horn in his hands, he is older. I don't know where it came from (the horn). He knows how to play it and makes music in the streets and people throw money. He's got all this music in his head and it comes out through the horn and through his mouth and the restlessness in him, the searching for something shining shoes, doing odd jobs to stay alive, but he can't stay in one place very long, the restlessness in him makes him move on. He doesn't trust people. I do see a woman with him. I get the name Camilla, a very pretty lady, well dressed. Also, I am getting a big man, well over six feet and almost three hundred pounds. He looks like he has a lot of money. Camilla has something to do with this man. She is within his aura. There is a connection, but I can't tell what. The big man is very angry because Camilla, feeling sorry for Jud, tries to help him somehow. I feel compassion around Camilla and Jud and fear around Camilla and I feel a lot of people fear him. He has a lot of influence over many people. He has a bad reputation for hurting people. I see him very clearly. He wears a dark colored hat with huge red and yellow feathers, a dark suit with wide stripes. He has two gold teeth and diamonds on his fingers. He carries a cane with a carved handle. At times, he wears a fur coat. He and Camilla are both black.

Judadia dies of knife wounds and is buried in New York Harbor. He never made it to his 21st birthday. He never made his fortune, never got all the restlessness out of his body, never got all the music out of his head.

It's taking its toll on your life, Maureen. It is overshadowing who you really are in this lifetime. It has made and continues to make relationships difficult. His restlessness has become your searching...to find out who he was, to be his own person, to find peace...it has become your search. You also have a keen mind as he did, a natural creative flow and a natural rhythm. I feel that what you need, if you have not already done so, is to be regressed. To ask the questions of why and how, so you can put it to rest at last. If you have been regressed, then I suggest that you try it again and again, until you have all the pieces of the puzzle put together. For you are overshadowed by that which you were. It has great influence over your life and you must get on with it and put it to rest. Until you do, it will forever be there. I think, at times, even you do not fully understand why

*you react to certain situations and people as you do...it is this
influence, my friend.*

　Love, Peace and Light,
　Betty Riley

Despite the discrepancies between what I thought I had been
told about Nick and what Betty had told me about Jud, there was
a paragraph in this letter that tied both of them together and that
was the referral to "the horn" that Betty spoke of. In automatic
handwriting, a song had appeared in 1973 about "Belle's Bugle"
that I hadn't understood.

Belle's Bugle

*Back in New York, when times were frugal
My ole friend Luke went and stole Belle's Bugle
By the time she gets around to realizin' the lack
She'll have to come to Frisco to get it back
Chorus:*

　*So we're rollin' along
　On our way to SF
　We got holes in our pants
　And I got 50 cents left
　Well, ole Belle loved that bugle like a baby
　So I kinda think she'll follow us, justa maybe
　But you know that Luke an' me done it all in fun
　Oh, whoops! Here comes ole Belle, on the run!*

Well, that seemed to solve the mystery that Betty referred to,
about the horn, in his hand. "I don't know where it came from."
Apparently, he and "Luke" had stolen it from a woman called
"Belle."

I wasn't sure about the name change from Nick to Jud or

about the location of Kentucky as a childhood home because the type of dialect that Jessup had spoken in the trance conversations was typical of the St. Bernard Parish area outside New Orleans, according to research. I couldn't find the name Judadia in any of the baby names I researched. Both Betty and I agreed that he had "ridden' the rods" and was a street musician. Both of us felt that he was restless, and that restlessness that she talked about was exactly what I had felt when I was on the road in Mexico–"the searching for something that won't go away." The family problems and the labeling as a "troublemaker" paralleled my own childhood. She didn't talk about why he was murdered and his body thrown in the New York Harbor, but Camilla and the "big man" were no doubt involved in gangster type activities, which had somehow involved him, so I assumed that the death was drug related.

Betty's version of Nick's death was different than mine. My information stated that he had died of a drug overdose in New York, and Betty claimed that he had been stabbed to death. Both of us felt that he had died in his early twenties.

All in all, her psychic information was very helpful to me. Perhaps she was right; maybe the answers would only be known in regression. The problem was, I couldn't find one who would do it.

✶✶✶✶✶

In my nagging loneliness, I'd begun to spend time with Terry, drinking, smoking, hanging out with the only one who seemed to have any real interest in me, touched by his sincerity and loyal devotion. Although our backgrounds were totally opposite, I found some comfort in the genuine friendliness and concern that all Newfoundlanders seem to have, or maybe it was the similarity between Nick and Terry and their poverty stricken and traumatic backgrounds that drew me to him.

The hospitality, the "devil may care attitude," the desire to jump right in and explore life, opened up a door of stifling restriction that my middle-class background had nailed shut. It melted the coldness, the indifference, the arrogance and the isolation. The conversation eventually turned to the idea of planning to have a child together. He had only turned twenty, but he wasn't exactly opposed to the idea. To us, in our youthful innocence, it was perfectly okay, although we weren't married, and as the old saying goes, "We didn't have a pot to piss in."

My sudden pregnancy was a total shock to everyone and caused a huge uproar in the family, who urged me to consider an abortion, even going so far as to arrange a doctor's appointment for me that I ignored. Despite them, I gave birth to a boy and called him Daniel James after the two musicians that I adored, Daniel Lanois and James (Jimi) Hendrix.

I continued to practice and teach astrology, even while pregnant, and although I left City Hall during my pregnancy, I was soon in and out of offices as a temp, all around the Hamilton area, a few weeks here, a few days there, enjoying the variety of it. Terry continued to slug away in the scrapyard until he got an even better job, cutting fish for the Finley Fish company, and never looked back.

Despite his addictions, he earned raise after raise. He was a hard-working fool, and an even harder drinking one, but no slacker. We even got a regular apartment of our own and moved to a nicer one later, and I was able to stay home and take care of Danny. We were a pretty good team, except for the alcohol, which turned the Dr. Jekyll and Mr. Hyde off and on in him, causing erratic episodes of mental and physical abuse directed at me. Indeed, I found myself in the position of "helping someone who was like I was" and fighting an addiction that I had no connection to, for in this life, I was addiction free. Despite this I had to endure chronic moments of despair when I would frantically search for him after midnight only to find "the Newf" lying passed out in a drunken stupor on the apartment stairwell landing. After one violent morning when he kicked me in the ribs with a steel toed boot because in a rush to work I hadn't cooked breakfast, I decided it was time to leave.

I become a mother in Hamilton, Ontario in February 1976. Here I am, holding little "Danny James", named after the two musicians I adored, Jimi (James) Hendrix and Daniel Lanois.

A cloud of uncertainty settled over me. I would sit, hour after hour, studying my astrology books, examining my chart and finally came to realize that several disastrous aspects I'd been born with–a Mars square Saturn and Neptune opposition Uranus, indicated the karma that I'd inherited from Nick. These bad stars that I'd been born under must have accounted for a lot of the trouble I'd experienced. Some of the karma, I'm sure, had been met, but as the hands on the clock moved closer toward the conjunction of transiting Saturn and Pluto over my natal Saturn squaring my Mars, I knew that my life was truly on the line, and the final debt that had been put on the shelf for all these years was finally coming due. I jumped from the frying pan into the fire and again, unable to control my loneliness, became involved with an unstable young man, an even a worse companion than Terry, who needed my help as much as I needed his.

Where can you hide when you know the storm is coming? What can you do when you know there's no salvation in running? Go home and lock the door, and it will be waiting for you, hiding in the basement, behind a closed door, on a dark street. Most people are unconscious of potential danger, unaware of what the future might bring. I was both aware and conscious, and there was more terror in knowing I was defenseless in the face of danger. Those who live by the sword will die by the sword. Hadn't it been written somewhere? But I didn't carry a knife anymore.

Nick hadn't made it out of his twenties. Maybe I wouldn't either, but I had faith that my guardian angels again were close around me. I knew it was time to pay back Nick's ultimate debt, his careless but deliberate path of self-destruction that had resulted in his own death. When the aspect in transit was exact, as predicted, it happened on a weekend when I'd left my son at home with my mother. I made a side trip back up to Hamilton attempting to make peace with the enemy, who had fled.

I was attacked by this unstable, young man, a practitioner of the black arts whom I'd been trying to turn back to God. Most likely insane and possessed in the moment, he turned on me. In a moment of terror, in an incredibly melodramatic moment, in front of a black alter and forced to either worship the devil or lose my life, I stood my ground, once more putting myself in God's hands and once more, God was with me. This son of Satan held a knife to my throat and and upon turning around to defend myself, my right baby finger was cut to the bone, right down the middle and my shoulder slashed.

In a slow-motion nightmare, that evening, I remember screaming and running down the steps of the old house, my blood spattering the walls and the floor under me, where I finally collapsed. But I was alive! The sirens of ambulances and police in the night were the last things I remembered before drifting into unconsciousness.

The police commented that it had been a miracle that I had survived. I was rushed to Hamilton General Hospital and into emergency surgery to stitch the stab wounds and slashed finger, and one thing I learned, when you have an accident such as this one, it's always afterwards that you feel the pain, not before.

Coming out of the haze of anesthesia, I sat before a doctor who was examining my stitched finger and asked him, "Will I be able to play the piano again?"

There was a slight look of doubt in his eyes, but he replied bravely, "Possibly. The plastic surgeon did an excellent job, Maureen. Do you have any family you can phone?"

The first one I called was my brother Bob, in Hamilton. When I described my situation, he was sympathetic and to the point,

"Sorry, Min. I can't risk upsetting my wife. She's about to have the baby any day."

So, I picked up the phone and called Mother. It was the only other alternative I had.

"Hello, Mother."

"Minnie, what happened? We haven't heard from you. Danny's wondering where his mother is."

Each forced word was torturous. "Mom, I've had an accident here in Hamilton. A crazy jumped me with a knife."

There was an audible gasp over the line. "Oh my God, no! Was it in the newspapers?"

"As a matter of fact, yes, it was–who cares? My arm is in a cast. I'm going to need help."

There was an awkward silence, then, "We'll send someone to come and pick you up."

"Sure, thanks." I hung up the phone, wearily, again being forced to accept the reluctant crumbs of charity thrown at me. I sank into the chair in the lobby and waited for the inevitable "I told you so's" and criticism. A friend arrived with a change of clothes, and a nurse assisted me in changing. When your arm is in a cast, it's an impossible task alone. Afterwards, I sank down into a lobby chair and dozed off until my ride arrived.

Hours later, we pulled into the driveway, and the front door swung open. Mother stood there, a horrified look in her eyes: my little son, Danny, wide-eyed and clinging to her fearfully. "My God, Minnie, what on earth happened?" She was stunned.

"I'll explain it to you someday," I replied wearily. "Can I come home?"

Mother hesitated reluctantly, but Father, who had been sitting in silence at the dining room table with a glass of homemade apple wine in his hand, spoke up with an aura of wisdom in his voice. "You know, Eileen, you can make some mistakes in life and get away with them. Others, you might not get away with. She just got lucky. Of course, she can come home. She's crippled, for God's sake. She's got a child to take care of."

Weariness was hanging over me. "Is it okay if I take the bedroom downstairs?

"Sure, Minnie," Father replied, sympathetically.

Gratefully, I headed for the downstairs bedroom and slipped into a dreamless sleep.

Weeks went by, and I had to have assistance with daily routines, eating, dressing and washing myself. My right arm in a sling and finger in a cast, I was forced to substitute with an uncooperative left. There were doctors' appointments, and the numbness in my finger lingered on. I made efforts to move it, but move it I must, and recover I would, if not for my own sake, but also for my son's. Gradually, the knife scars healed, but curiously enough, I wasn't concerned about my appearance. I felt as though I'd died and been reborn. In shedding the last of Nick's karma, a sense of peace and utter relief fell over me. At last I'd be able to move on and put him behind me.

One afternoon, I caught sight of my father, dressed for the bush and carrying two pails, and hurried after him. My finger was still in a cast, but the sling was off. He turned around.

"Are you sure you want to hike up to the Huckleberry Hills with me, Minnie? ...your hand and all?" His voice trailed off, and a look of pity flickered in his eyes.

"I thought, I thought I might be able to help you."

"Help? Well, maybe you could hold the pail for me while I pick blueberries."

"They're for the wine, aren't they?" I asked.

"Yeah, gotta stock the wine cellar. It's a long winter. The

neighbors will be over..." He chuckled to himself. We hiked along the bushy path, dodging overgrowth, stopping to catch a breath. I pondered a moment, then blurted out, "You know, Dad, I didn't always mean to be getting into trouble..."

He glanced curiously at me, considering this confession, coming out of thin air and replied, "I was only trying to protect you."

An awkward silence followed, and I cleared my throat.

"How's the court case coming along...the land, I mean?"

He sighed. "Lost again. Still fighting for a fair settlement... those damn crooked politicians. There was anger and frustration in his eyes. "They offered me a quarter of what the land was really worth. I would have got more if I'd gone along with the kickback."

He paused, a soul-searching expression in his eyes. "But at the end of the day, when you're standing in front of the mirror, looking at yourself, you've gotta like what you're lookin' at. There's some things that I just won't do."

This was a side of my father that I had never seen before, that he'd faced conflict and had to make a hard decision that tested his conscience. "I know where you're coming from...been there myself. You never told us anything about a kickback."

Disgusted, a looked of futility crossed his face. "Couldn't prove it. It was all verbal...under the apple tree on the front lawn. I tried to get publicity. They said I made it up."

Now the shoe was on the other foot. I felt compassion for him.

"That must have been hard...all those years."

He offered me one of the pails. I grasped it with my good hand, and we continued up the hiking path toward the Huckleberry Hills. Halfway up, I turned toward him.

"Dad, what do you think happens to us after we die? Do you think we return to live another life?"

He glanced at me and smiled, scratching his head, thoughtfully. "I think we get the answers after we pass from this Veil of Tears. I'm not so sure there is a plan. What about the expropriation of my property? What kind of plan was that?" His gaze swept over the valley bitterly, maple and oak woodlot, lush cow pasture, prime lake shore. "I lost a fortune," he whispered sadly.

I comforted him, a hand on his arm. "Maybe it's connected to karma from a past life. Everything happens for a reason."

He laughed scornfully. "Prove it, Minnie, and you'll be a millionaire someday."

I laughed. "Prove it? I think I've already been given that assignment already. Hey, by the way, I've applied to St. Lawrence College for the fall–The Early Childhood Education Program."

He replied, surprised, "What made you decide to do that?"

"Well," I replied pensively, "it's time to turn a new page–a clean life. "Working with children will do that for me...and I can still play guitar."

He smiled, reached over and took the bucket from my good hand, and we continued over the hill, out of sight.

With my finger still healing and the knife scars beginning to fade, I applied for student loans and grants for college. I was accepted into the program and, still living at home, began to plan with enthusiasm, for the fall. I decided to drive back and forth to school and leave Danny with Mother. He was now six and starting school. A school bus would pick him up from the front door and bring him back home again. This time I would succeed. I was sure of it.

One summer afternoon, I hiked into the bush, close to the house, and scrambled up a rocky, wooded hill in the old Maple Sugar Bush. There, surrounded by God and nature, I gazed up at a blue sky scudded with white clouds, listened to the breezes comforting the trees, and prayed.

"God, I've never been able to find a partner who was right for me, never been able to find someone who would make a real commitment to me. I've stumbled from one bad relationship to another like a blind person, making mistake after mistake. Please send me someone who will be good for my son and myself. Please send me a partner that I can love and trust and rely on. I can do my part, but I just can't make it on my own. The only one that I've ever been able to count on is You, from San Francisco to my life-and-death struggle in Hamilton." Tears were streaming down my cheeks because I knew it was true. And because I had faith, I knew that He had heard my prayer and would provide an answer.

Mystery Man

1983 rendezvous
With a mystery man, long overdue
Calgary bound by night
Christmas lights shining brightly
Across the land
I am adventure drawn
Eleven years since I last saw
A foothill's dawn
I picked his name out of thin air
He is here
He is there
He is everywhere.

I graduated proudly from St. Lawrence College with a Diploma in Early Childhood Education the first tangible goal that I'd ever been able to achieve. While there, I met a girl who introduced me to her brother Paul over the phone, by coincidence, another Newfoundlander, a heavy-duty bus mechanic, who was living and working in Calgary, Alberta–no, not a musician, just an honest, down to earth, simple, hard-working man with a good job, working at the Greyhound Bus Garage in Calgary. He had never been married before and had no children.

Success at last. I graduate from St. Lawrence College Saint Laurent in Kingston, Ontario in 1989 with a diploma in Early Childhood Education.

During the Christmas holidays, Danny and I took the train to Alberta where I met Paul for the first time. Intuition told me that this was the man that God had sent to Danny and I, and we would do well with him. The following year, my parents puzzled over my wedding plans to an invisible boyfriend whom they had never met, but I reassured them, it was meant to be. I would take another chance on love. Just concentrate on making the wine punch! Several days before the ceremony was to take place, at the Perth Road village church, he flew in with the ring, and we were married in a June ceremony. I was thirty-one and he was thirty-two. Danny was eight. We packed up all of our belongings in a U-Haul, which Paul drove across Canada to Calgary to begin a new life together.

Marrying the "Mystery Man", Paul Kirby, in
Perth Road, Ontario in June 1984.
Paul, Danny and I become a family.

I finally understood why my early childhood in the Kellar family had been so turbulent. I had been simply replaying Nick's own childhood conflict with Annie over again unconsciously, through my own family. The emotional damage between them had never been healed. She had turned her back on him, and he had turned his back on her, both of them totally ignoring the other. Nick had never returned home to New Orleans to make peace with her. There was no longer a reason to feel animosity toward my family for the suffering that I had endured for Nick's sake.

I was leaving all this and more of my karma behind as I traveled west with my new husband, to start a new life, and was glad to leave it all behind.

Chapter Twenty-Three
Moving to Calgary

I continued with my research, while I started working with children in daycare centers and school programs in Calgary. It became the city for me, where all of my dreams might finally be realized. It was a great playground, a booming metropolis, subsidized by the oil industry, sunny and rambling in the shadow of the Rockies, only an hour away from world famous camping and hiking. I dubbed it Little L.A. and never went anywhere without my sunglasses. It was far easier now, married, as a part of a team, to accomplish what I needed to do, without having to live the life of poverty that so often accompanies single motherhood, and I could now offer my son, Dan, things like camping holidays, musical equipment, nice clothes and expensive toys that I never could have drempt of providing him alone. Perhaps now, my dream of becoming a working musician might finally come true.

I immersed myself with enthusiasm into every avenue that offered an opportunity and discovered that this Leo city was like a child itself, in essence, proud, fond of showing off, the home of The Calgary Stampede, boasting fun and celebration, sporting, outdoorsy and uncomplicated, in direct contrast to the stuffy province of Ontario, where I'd come from.

My sister Kate, who had been so instrumental in launching my search for Nick, also overcame the trauma from her childhood head injury and graduated from Queen's University, with a Bachelor of Education, Bachelor of Music and eventually also a Masters of Education. She married, and moved to B.C. where she began a career working as an ESL teacher. My brother Bob eventually disappeared and his fate became a mystery.

Jamming with my sister Kate at White Rock, B.C. in 2014.

From the moment, I moved to Calgary in 1984, as inspiration swept over me, and I began playing a new Fender Rhodes piano that Paul had bought for me. Listening to The Doors, Buddy Holly, Creedence Clearwater Revival, and B. B. King, and cruising the music stores, searching posters for musicians wanted, I connected with local bands and went for auditions. The first band that accepted me was called Changes in 1985, and finally I was back where I wanted to be, in the world of music, this time, as a key player, not a "groupie."

This band was followed by several others, Tracker, a country western band; Jailhouse Rock and Roll Band, who were into Elvis Presley and '50s rock and roll; The Sundowners, who played everything from polkas to "Waltz Across Texas" for the seniors in the Legions around town; and finally, Dolly Dagger, who played The Doors and Jimi Hendrix at Panchos, a little café in Kensington. I considered all of these learning experiences, so even though I wasn't into polkas, or Anne Murray, I would perform to the best of my ability, knowing that it was only going to make me a better musician than I had been before. And this was the way that I would evolve from Nick without leaving him behind.

Playing keyboards in the band "Sundowners"
at the No. 1 Legion in Calgary, 1989

It was a fantastic learning experience, and although I always seemed to slip back into boogie-woogie, I could now even intro to the more recent rock music "Walk of Life" and understand where I'd gone wrong with the keyboard parts on "Taking Care of Business" back in the middle '70s. I graduated from a cumbersome Fender Rhodes electric piano to a Yamaha DX Synthesizer with loads of sounds and easier to move around and even used harmonica in a "Love Me Do" by the Beatles, for Changes. My bongos were also occasionally called for, and I picked up an acoustic guitar, and strange things started happening when several of Nick's songs flowed through without any previous instruction on guitar. I would tape the songs and ask other guitar players what chords I'd played, and how in the world did I know how to play the Delta blues??

My son, Danny James AKA DJ Kid V, following his destiny as a musician in Calgary, Alberta approximately 2012.

It seemed as though I was carrying Nick Jackson forward, using the best of the talents that he had given me, and expanding on them, improving my vocals, improving my keyboard techniques, even though I was a woman, and possibly the only white woman I knew at the time, who aspired to be a good blues keyboard player around Calgary at the time. I would sit, fascinated, mesmerized, soaking up every chord, every riff, absorbing the life-giving, soul-searing melodies, nursing a ginger ale and completely, helplessly, forever in love with the music that had stolen Nick's heart and mine. At the same time, my son, Dan, only a teenager, was already learning how to become a DJ and was immersing himself into the Calgary DJ scene. I was busy helping him to buy equipment and taking him to and from gigs and working on music myself.

So, instead of pulling away from Nick, I only drew closer, during the late 1980s and early 1990s. Frequenting the legendary King Edward Hotel Home of the Blues, I sat in with the best of the Chicago Blues Musicians, including Sam Lay, up from the U.S.A., Phillip Walker and B.B. Jones. One afternoon, when Buddy Guy took his guitar out into the streets and finished up with a club full of applause, I managed to sit down with him to talk about his old friend Jimi Hendrix, and I showed him a lead sheet of one of Nick's songs, "West 56th Street Blues." I was amazed when he scanned it and replied, "It's pretty good. I could use it, but I'd have to change the words around."

My old friends the Point-Blank band, in San Francisco, who were "hot" around the Bay area at the time that I had arrived in 1973, playing danceable jazz with some funk and soul mixed in, had been awarded a recording contract with Barry White Associates in L.A., performed with headliners such as Ike and Tina Turner, Al Wilson, the Stories (Brother Louie), Arthur Prysock, Sheila E and Escovedo.

Eric and Billy recorded and produced under the name Stratos-Billoon Enterprises, but conflict in the band split them up, and they had eventually gone their separate ways.

Billy Moon, who had lured me into bed and attempted to "buy my soul for the devil music," and who had jammed with the likes of Jimi Hendrix, Bob Dylan, and The Lovin' Spoonful, before they had been discovered, worked with Bill Haley and the Comets and toured with them across the country, was later inducted into The Rock and Roll Hall of Fame. He went on to found Gypsy Moon Music Recording Studios in Oregon and I was able to contact him and we laughed about the past.

I often wondered what had happened to Jason and Tinkerbelle, who had been caught with my ID trying to cross the border to Jamaica and had landed in a Mexican jail. Had Tink's father, who was well-off, stepped in to free them? I would never really know. And Charlie, who had led me to the band Point Blank when I first arrived in San Francisco would surely have passed on by now.

Chapter Twenty-Four

Exploring New York

I had traveled widely through the U.S.A. by now. In 1989, at the age of thirty-seven, with trepidation, I arrived in New York City on a Greyhound Bus, via an overnight stop in bustling "Sweet Home Chicago," remembering that I was supposed to have died in New York in 1943, either by a heroin overdose or perhaps by knife wounds, and maybe my bones were lying in the mud of the New York Harbor still undiscovered by time. Both endings were tragic at any rate. Most likely, no one would have ever really known what had become of me, and given my estrangement from family, they wouldn't have known either.

The Rose of Washington Square–Central Park–OD flophouse just off Madison Avenue–West 56th Street Blues–only New York has no charm. You feel like your gut is going down the drain and it's only two hours till sunrise when you can get it on the corner.

The stench of garbage and the aroma of a thousand cosmopolitan restaurants filled my nostrils as I exited the Port Authority Bus Terminal and wandered up the West 56th Street that I'd sung about but had never trod before, snapping photos for the album back home.

Now, I was truly walking down West 56th Street, forty-six years later, but not searching for a fix, just curiously exploring, and it was overwhelming to me, this dirty, famous city, deteriorated by time, probably once a magnificent and booming metropolis, now just a shadow of its once glorious past. I felt strangely anxious deep down in my soul, afraid of what might be lurking around the corner waiting, and I remembered the many hastily scribbled words that had described Nick's vision of this city.

Street busker in New York City photographed
curing my wandering through
Greenwich Village and Central Park in 1989

"Ding dang daddy from Washington Square–kick your legs up in de air." Could this be referring to the actual 1930 cover song by Louis Armstrong? Did "kick your legs up in de air" describe the dance moves of the day–the "swinging aerials" performed in the 1930s? What about *"soft shoe two"* and *"shuffle dance"*? These were the Afro American street dances of the time.

"Marlene, she's a Candy Time Doll. Marlene, she's my girl." Was this the "Candy Doll" sung by Ethel Waters? ...Then who was Marlene? "Yesterday tastes like paper in my mouth and tomorrow is a jewel of hope. I sail along on the applause of yesterday."

Past a seedy Washington Square with homeless people lying on benches or sprawled on the grass, police cars parked nearby. Uneasiness churning in the pit of my stomach, I marveled at the words to Nick's song, the one that Lehman Engel, Dean of Broadway Musicals, had chosen, summing it up well, even forty-six years late

New York

New York, big city
New York, it's a pity
New York, voices too loud
New York, got lost in a crowd
Millions of people, locked away from each other
Nobody seems to want to help his brother
New York.

New York paranoia pervaded the atmosphere. People walking by shifted their eyes from my gaze, and the only ones speaking were aimlessly wandering derelicts reeking of insanity or blind, old men playing guitars in dusty corners. Here is where history had been made, all the Bob Dylans, the Mamas and the Papas, the beatniks, Jack Kerouac, Allen Ginsberg influencing a whole generation and pushing them forward into the LSD inspired sixties.

This was a city of Broadway, of Wall Street, of hopes and dreams of a faceless crowd of immigrants who still flocked in daily to carve out lives for themselves. And it was here that Nick had also come, seeking fame and fortune, only to run the streets and die in anonymity. I finally engaged a taxi driver in menial conversation while we were on our way down through Greenwich Village, but hurried back to my hotel room before darkness after visiting Jimi Hendrix's Electric Ladyland Studios.

From my window, I could see the pushers and street people doing business in Times Square below, and the circus continued through the night in the city that never sleeps, a strangely compelling but repulsive scene that ticked off uneasy memories in the depths of my subconscious. I could not sleep but watched the dusk give way to dawn, streetlights to daylight in the shadows of my flophouse, hostel hotel room. I stayed away from the waterfront, although I was mysteriously drawn to it, wondering if Nick Jackson's bones were buried in the mud of the New York Harbor as Betty Riley had said or if the hotel "just off West 56th Street" where he'd supposedly overdosed was still standing. Was I in danger here? Was it possible to die twice in the same city? But I spent a day wandering through Central Park, feeling strangely out of place and eager to leave. After a few days, I got back on a Greyhound Bus headed for Montreal and hurried back to Calgary to play the blues.

Rock and Roll Mama

Smoky nightclubs populated by
Faceless crowds on a Saturday night
In the dim light, laughter and conversation
Float amiably across the room
Rum and Coca-Cola couples searching for a star
Regular faces greet old friends
Standing at the bar
I plug into the amp
Patch cord, keyboard
And the bass man smiles at me
There's nowhere in the world I know
That I would rather be
Kansas City in E
Intro in A
We swing into motion
Like the gears of a machine
Fitting perfectly together
The lead guitar gives me a nod to solo
Strangely enough
My fingers have a will of their own
As they race up and down the keys
I sit back in amazement and let them do what they please
This is a moment of joy
Stamped upon time
Nothing can destroy
For in these precious minutes
I've found my soul.

Playing keyboards in the band "Dolly Dagger" at
Panchos nightclub in Kensington, Calgary 1994

In the meantime, my old friend Daniel Lanois was on his way up the ladder of fame and fortune in the rock and roll world. A huge breakthrough via a friendship with Brian Eno brought Daniel opportunities to work with the band U2 in Ireland, and he never looked back. From time to time, I would read about him on the Entertainment Page of *The Calgary Herald* or flick the TV on and catch him in a press interview, finally on the Junos and then the Grammys, or find his CDs in the local music store. Strangely enough, my own son Danny went about ambitiously fulfilling the destiny of his name, Daniel James, (DJ) by becoming a local musical legend on the Calgary nightclub scene. These initials, DJ, representing both his chosen vocation and the musicians he was following in the footsteps of–Daniel Lanois and Jimi Hendrix.

At night in my dreams, I would rendezvous with Lanois, and we would have "heart-to-hearts." These dreams, which I recorded in my dream journals would continue for the rest of my life and I recorded them in journals, along with other psychic flashes and precognitive glimpses of the future.

Twist of Fate

Danny, do you remember me
Could you recall my name?
I've followed you for sixteen years
And watched you rise to fame
You're standing on a concert stage
Surrounded by dreams come true
Do you remember the music we made
And the love that we once knew?
In 1973 at the 401 Inn we drank
Apricot liqueur over ice
And I had ambitions then
That I would be your wife
But songs in your basement studio
Recorded on reel to reel tape
Are my still visible connection to you
The only commitment you'd make
Downstairs in the music room now
My piano stands unused
Everywhere I looked this year
Your name was in the news
Brian Eno was a gift from God
The Joshua Tree, U2
Do you remember when we discussed
What the future would hold for you?
When they filmed you in New Orleans
You smiled that mysterious smile
As if this journey had been preordained

And it had only taken a while
Danny, do you know that I had a son
And I called him Danny too?
I cried tears over opportunities lost
And hoped he'd be like you.
But I often wondered
If he was the son that we were meant to have
The thought continued to haunt me
Comforting me with mind salve
Had somehow by a twist of fate
Preordained plans gone astray?
As if to agree, the man who helped me to create him
Drifted quietly away.
I watched him grow to love music
Encouraged him in serious play
Followed him into nightclubs
And in a strange and curious way
I lost one musician Daniel
And gained another one in his place
And if the two should ever meet
It will be with God's good grace.
So please don't forget me, Dan
In your race to money and fame
I never forgot you through distance and time
I gave my son your name.

By 2005 I was a grandmother, enjoying a happy family life and well on my way to fully realizing my life as Maureen while continuing to successfully fulfill Nick's own hopes and dreams. At last in Calgary, I'd had the opportunity to become a working musician once more, only this time, without the drugs that had destroyed him. Between the years 1994 and 2004, I also began to focus more and more on my psychic abilities and turned them to advantage in working for several psychic telephone hotlines operating out of Calgary. This type of work I alternated with music and daycare work, so at that time I was juggling three balls professionally and making money from all of them. I was able to use my talent for astrology in combination with a newer ability to read the Tarot cards and showed some psychic ability for remote viewing.

Continuing in my research efforts to find Nick Jackson, I'd found a well-known American psychic to the celebrities on the Internet and had booked a telephone session with him to try and nail down some details about Nick Jackson. In that telephone conversation between us, he told me that Nick Jackson's father was Mexican and his mother was Afro American, that their last name had been Juarez, but Nick also went by his mother's last name Jackson because she was a single mother, who had been deserted by her husband. Maybe Nick had been able to speak Spanish. It had almost seemed that when I visited Mexico, I had had a natural affinity for the language and culture.

He advised me that Nick had grown up in the French Quarter of New Orleans and agreed with me that he had died of a heroin overdose, in New York City, contradicting Betty Riley's story but did not give me an exact birth or death date. He told me that Nick had also recorded his music and that deteriorating demos could still be found somewhere in the U.S.A. But where, and where exactly was his diary, if it hadn't turned to dust by now, and where were the demos?

He told me that when Nick died in New York, he *swallowed the heroin,* instead of injecting it, which explained why I've suffered from gut problems all of my life.

Although I continued to search the birth and death records for evidence, it seemed as though Nick Jackson was going to eternally be an unsolved mystery, but curiously, birth and death records from areas outside New Orleans did indicate several Nick and Jessup Jacksons, although none seemed to fit the estimated birth and death dates. The music continued to taunt me, by its very existence and continued to spontaneously appear. In 2010 "Catfish Stew" flowed through my fingers, while strumming the guitar and the lyrics provided instructions for making the popular Southern dish I'd never eaten. I headed directly into EK Sound Studios in Calgary with John Thiel on guitar, and we recorded it. A few years earlier, I also re-recorded "Morning Train," and they were added to the original songs of 1973. I'd never taken a single lesson on guitar, I didn't know what chords I was playing or what I was singing about, and I didn't have a clue that what I was playing was essentially inspired "Leadbelly" Delta blues, with a strong Creole influence.

Catfish Stew

Got a rumblin' in my tummy that jus' won't go away
There's no food in the cupboard since my daddy went away
Goin' down to the pond with a pole and a hook
Goin' to catch me a catfish, oh, Lordie, take a look
See the little stump frogs sittin' on a log
Lordie, catch the froggie, fore he jump into the bog
Catfish stew, catfish stew, gonna make up some catfish stew for you
Catfish stew, catfish stew, gonna make up some catfish stew for you
Crawdads skittle in the swimin' hole
Poverty engraves itself upon your Southern soul
Summer heat in waves from the dusty backroads
Lil black boys playin' with the brown swamp toads
Throw some 'taters' in the pot, fry the onions in the rue

A little bit of salt, put some pepper in there too
The fishie like the froggie, but the froggie swim free
Oh, froggie catch the fishie, gonna have some stew for me
See the little stump frog, sittin' on a log
Lordie, catch the froggie, fore he jump into the bog
Catfish stew, catfish stew, gonna make up some catfish stew for you
Catfish stew, catfish stew, gonna make up some catfish stew for you
Flies buzzin' through the old screen door
Daddies who don't come home no more
Mama sittin' in the parlor, lost in despair
Cryin' over money she knew was never there
Goin' down to the pond with a pole and a hook
Goin' catch me a catfish, oh, Lordie take a look
Fishie like the froggie, but the fishie swim free
Lordie, catch the froggie, gonna have some fish for me
Catfish stew, catfish stew, gonna make up some catfish stew for you
Catfish stew, catfish stew, gonna make up some catfish stew for you.

I puzzled over this song, but I'd always had a love for cornbread and remembered going to the cupboards as a teenager, whipping up rice and beans impromptu and delving into it, not knowing why I was drawn to this type of food, since my mother never made it. Now I experimented with Jambalaya and Gumbo, but I'd still never had Catfish Stew.

In early August of 2005, I was sitting on the front porch of my house in Calgary, playing "Morning Train," when suddenly I distinctly felt the soul of New Orleans calling out to me, like a terrified child anticipating trouble. Feeling the anxiety of the beloved home, I'd never seen but always felt invisibly linked to, I added a chorus to the song, and sang it over and over, as if to reassure New Orleans and myself that everything would be all right, although I didn't understand why I was comforting her.

Recording "Catfish Stew" at EK Sound Studios in Calgary, Alberta in 2010.

New Orleans, my fantasy, why do you call my name?
The south never changes, it never does
It will always be the same.
It will always be the same.

And at the end of August, 2005, Hurricane Katrina hit with a vengeance, and New Orleans stood fast through it all.

At the same time that Dan Lanois was achieving success with the music soundtrack from the film *Slingblade,* I also became interested in movie scriptwriting and finished a rough draft of my own story *Go Back Jack* in move script form. The logic behind this was that the movie would use the music soundtrack of all of

Nick's songs, as part of a complete package. In 2005 I flew to Hollywood and attended my first Fade in Pitchfest with high hopes of selling it. Unfortunately, although the idea seemed to generate a lot of interest among the producers, when I got back to Calgary, my phone was silent. I rewrote it, had it edited, consulted with TJ Lynch, a scriptwriter living in Los Angeles and flew back again in 2007, to the Great American Pitchfest, where I met producer Signe Olynyk, who advised me to write the book. As an adapted story, it might have more of a chance. With the soundtrack of Nick's music, it would make a dynamite movie!

Working with children in
Calgary daycare approx. 1998-2005

I walked out of this Pitchfest with lots of encouragement from the exec's but no takers. I settled into full-time work at the Calgary Herald, Special Edition Daycare in 2006 and for the next eight years, mingled with award winning writers and reporters, taking care of their children while discussing my writing projects and making trips to L.A. Proudly I could show them a few articles of my own that had been published in Canadian and American magazines and let them know that my movie script efforts had received some attention from the producers in L.A.

I had a one-page drawn up, rewrote the script again, and again to Hollywood in 2013. In the meantime, *Go Back Jack* had succeeded in reaching the semifinals in the StoryPros International Screenwriting Contest, not bad for a self-taught scriptwriter who had begun at middle age. This time, several producers walked away with a hard copy of the story, and I never heard from them again. At this point, I despaired of ever selling my story or music to the public, but I would never give up trying. An urge arose within me to return to New Orleans and explore Nick's childhood home.

Chapter Twenty-Five

Return to New Orleans

Southern Nights

I crave a summer so hot

The sweat drips down

From flushed and clammy foreheads

Bayou bogs, still air, breathless

In the dusty, street corner alleyways

Filled with the aroma of Creole gumbo bubbling deliciously

In the evening kitchens of New Orleans

I crave Mississippi blues

American soil, where the heart beats true

A life lived so vividly

Red, white, and blue, catfish stew

I remember palm tree breezes

Whispers sway, white sand, spinning fans

Spanish phrases interjected

Unbroken into the busy afternoon marketplaces

Ocean murmurs, Miami nights

Pulsing with the beat of laughing Latino drums

And I know that I must return

To a memory that still burns

And leave this cold, Canadian land

With a suitcase in my hand.

Finally "home again", walking along the shores of the
Mississippi River in New Orleans, Louisiana in 2013,
revisiting past life memories.

The last song that floated into my mind was a strange story of
New Orleans that my fingers found the chords and lyrics to on
guitar, and again my guitarist John Thiel and I headed back to EK
Sound Studios to record it in 2013. I would sit for hours,
strumming this song over and over again because it seemed to
lay my soul bare for all to see and told the whole story in explicit
detail. I wasn't sure if it should be called "Ten Miles West" or
"South of New Orleans," which led to my examining a map of
New Orleans to see what would be located west or south of the
city. West would take me to the area surrounding the Louis
Armstrong Airport while south might take me to the St. Bernard
Parish area. Given that Jessup's dialect was of the St. Bernard
Parish area, he may well have lived more south than west.

Ten Miles West of New Orleans

Goin' down to the riverside
Ten miles west of New Orleans
There's a shanty, down by the water's edge
And a boy who calls for me
Papa goin' cry, Mama goin' cry
Sister goin' cry for me
I'm goin' away, you know I cannot stay
Mama don't you cry for me
Goin' down to the riverside.

In November of 2013, on my 61th birthday, I packed up my old acoustic guitar and wrote a big sign on the side, "This guitar is goin' to New Orleans" and headed for the Calgary airport. Passing through American Customs, a wave of emotion caught me in the pit of my stomach, and it was all I could do to stop the tears from flowing down my cheeks. I was really going home. I could still feel it in every bone in my body. "Chasin' ghosts" in every sense of the word. *Lord knows what I would find.*

I arrived in New Orleans in the dark of a November evening curiously drawn to Algiers Point, an area made famous for musicians' decades past, and pulled up in a taxi in front of a Bed and Breakfast called "The House of the Rising Sun." The driver, reluctant to go down into Algiers, kept babbling on about taxi drivers being murdered there, giving me some idea of how dangerous an area it could be.

I was welcomed inside by Kevin and his wife, Wendy, who parked my bags in the "Memphis Minnie Room," and I felt right at home there, given that my name was Minnie too. New Orleans, on first impression, struck me as a heavy-duty voodoo city, filled with incense burning and Caribbean culture always pervading. It was dark, mysterious, strange and full of secrets that seemed to taunt me by night and welcome me, sunny and bright, by daylight. I was finally home and felt eerily serene. I wandered down by the Mississippi River, watching the barges in the distance, begging passersby to take my photo with the camera I'd toted along. I took the pathway to the ferry, which would lead me across the river to the city, and penned this poem.

Lights across the Mississippi

Lights across the Mississippi, Algiers Point at night
Ships and barges steal to port, before dawn's breaking light
And I wish I'd come home sooner, but maybe now it's time
I lie in bed on Pelican Avenue and listen to the church bells
*   chime*
Canal Streetcar to the French Market, the voodoo temple
Up Rampart Street
Past the St. Louis Cemetery tombs
Where souls of the living and dead still meet
Beyond the Garden District gates
Where elegant mansions rule
And wandering through the French Quarter
To follow the Bourbon Street fools
Out on the River Road to Laura
The cries of slaves still haunt the cane
The fields of Oak Alley Plantation
Sweltering fields under a driving rain
Down by the Mississippi, I touch your waves that lap the
*   shore*
My friend, I must leave you now, but I'll return once more.

The urge to play music came over me, and I pounded the keys nightly on Kevin and Wendy's upright piano in the living room and played "The House of the Rising Sun" for them and "Ten Miles West of New Orleans" for me. I fought an even fiercer urge to take the guitar down to the streets and busk for the crowds, who would surely appreciate my love of this city that flowed through these songs. I knew that Nick had sung and danced on street corners, and no doubt, if I'd stayed long enough, I would have too, even at my age, but I only had a week off work. Not nearly enough time to enjoy the delights that New Orleans had to offer.

I explored every inch of the city by foot that I had time for and much of Algiers Point as well. I walked until I was stiff and sore and could barely walk anymore, and my spirit kept me going. I was on fire to discover the city, stopping only to grab the odd bite to eat or bottle of water to drink, boarding the hop on, hop off tour bus that wound its way through the narrow streets of the French Quarter, past the old St. Louis cemetery, up past the French Market into the Garden District, then circling back around, past the Superdome and the World War Two Museum and disembarking, to explore the French Quarter alone, by foot, past the mysterious Voodoo Palace, incense floating through its spooky doorway. Standing before the entrance, I summoned up enough courage to enter, and I was led past the back courtyard, chickens running freely, and a snake in a cage, to the voodoo alter. Offering some money to appease the spirits and soaking in the dark and mysterious Caribbean vibes, I stepped briefly into this strange and foreign world and, being the white witch that I am, resonated completely with it.

Another day, out the River Road by van to the Creole plantation, Laura and Oak Alley Plantation, I wandered into a gift shop, and standing in front of an antique kitchen pantry cupboard, my eyes scanned the shelves, examining old cookbooks and knickknacks. Suddenly, I was pulled back in time and heard these heart-wrenching words. It was Annie crying, "Nick, there's no food in the cupboards." The van outside was filling up with the tour group, intent on continuing, but I stood frozen, feeling only the helpless kind of sorrow that empty shelves can bring to an empty stomach, and again, for a brief moment in time, I was Nick again answering to his mama.

Someone snatched me out of my trance. It was Lisa, my tour companion, a friend I'd made en route, tugging on my shoulder. "Maureen, hurry! They're about to go!" Reluctantly, I pulled away, puzzling over the invisible voice I'd just heard, battling deep and familiar waves of nostalgia. The tour group guide, whose own ancestors had lived in Laura, led us through the old Creole plantation, originally founded by Guillaume Duparc, a French veteran of the American Revolution, entrancing us with stories of another era. But it was his remark about the custom of a Creole boy coming of age at thirteen and being declared officially a man that struck a chord within me. I had always wondered about the song "Morning Train" and why Nick had run off when he was just twelve years old. Now I completely understood that in this region, in those early days, it was taken for granted that a boy was no longer a boy when he turned thirteen, and Nick must have been almost thirteen when he left home.

The River Road had changed through time, or possibly I was still searching for the Catfish Pond and familiar bayous that were hidden from my sight. Flashes of memories still interrupted my reverie, the feel of scorching heat on my back, the smell of dirt in the cotton fields, scratchy hay in an old barn somewhere, sunlight filtering through particles of dust, Jessup's carefree laughter, the simplicity of poverty and, overriding it all, a profound faith in God, inspired by my mama, that somehow, some way, we would all survive. Music was the magical salve that had soothed the wounds of hardship which led to our assuming a spiritual state of being because the material world had failed us. It was a curious paradise where berry bushes and a neighbor's potato fields supplied breakfast and lunch, almost as if we still walked naked and unashamed in some sort of innocent paradise that was The Depression of the '30s.

This is what I experienced in New Orleans, but more so in the outlying rural countryside. Although it was November, I remembered the smothering heat of a summer day, the listless retreat of life, mist on the Mississippi, snakes and gators sunning themselves on the banks of the river, down by the church, a freshly dug grave, preachers looking for another soul to save, dreamlike movements in the humid night, of voodoo born witches chanting spells, still stirring their pots deep in the bayous and communing with the spirits of the dead. The air was permeated with the supernatural pressing to break through, and I felt it, just as Robbie Robertson had felt it, expressed in his song "Somewhere Down the Crazy River."

Finally, I understood why I had been drawn to the swamps of Ontario, why I'd spent my summer days wading through the muck, scraping off leeches, chasing frogs, stepping on snakes and swatting bugs. I'd never truly left the bayou. It was in my blood, that way of life, and even though I didn't really need those frogs to survive, like Nick did, it was a habit that had followed me through the grave. The south becomes a part of you, in some deep inexplicable way, the lingo, the people, the bond with the land, the food, the music; they all conspire to touch your soul somehow, in a powerful way that defies time.

But Hurricane Katrina had left her mark everywhere, in the buckling sidewalks of Algiers Point, and damaged, deserted, boarded up buildings forgotten and neglected, a taxi driver who recounted the horrors of trying to survive the hurricane, battling cottonmouth snakes who had swum up from the river; she droned on and on about how she had to jack up her house still higher and didn't know where she was going to get the money to pay for it. It was the south that I remembered, touched yet still struggling bravely to endure. I wandered by the shore of the Mississippi and spoke to her and to the ghosts that I had left behind.

"I came back, Mama. I came back," I murmured, as if trying to apologize to Annie Jackson and make amends for the errors of the past. Tears slid down my cheeks as the waves lapped the shore. "I have to go again, but I'll be back soon. You know, I'll always come home."

And I felt her forgiveness, the timeless Mississippi, smiling at me, saying, "And I'll always be waiting for you when you return."

New Orleans, Voodoo Child

New Orleans, I fell into your voodoo spell
On a pitch black night in a November taxi
In flight from Louis Armstrong Airport
Heavy and ominous, the calm before a storm
I dived into your alien, black streets
To seek refuge someplace warm
"The House of the Rising Sun"
And awoke to church bells breaking
The dawn facing the light
The pleasure seekers of New Orleans

Sin owns the night
Your ghosts still haunt these streets
Red Allen blows his horn
While barges float up the Mississippi forlorn
Here was every vice known to man
Hell's playground, indulgence staining the sand
And this gumbo mix of lust and love of life
Attracted me as a husband to a wife
Cutting the curtain like a machete knife
Like a moth to a flame
My enduring love for you has no name
Only a fascination.

Upon arriving back in Calgary, I wrote what may have been the last of Nick's songs, "Mississippi Lights" a fast-moving blues in A minor, sharing it with the poem of the same name.

Mississippi Lights

Comin' into New Orleans at night
Watchin' Mississippi river lights shine on me
What a pretty sight
River road rain cuts like a knife
And I've been wanderin' all my life, it's true
I've got the Mississippi Blues.
Chorus:
    Barges steal down the river way
    And the cold, dark waves meet the light of day
    The sun disappears and the sky turns grey
    And I got lost along the way
Louisianna bound and runnin' wild
Flowin' with the river little Delta child
Mississippi Lights, what a pretty sight

To cottonmouth country runnin' south
The past leaves a bitter taste in my mouth
It's true, you've got the Mississippi Blues.

June 24, 2015

In the heat of the city night, I was half walking, half running, eager to get to the National Music Centre in Calgary to hear my old friend Daniel Lanois, just in from L.A., scheduled to give a music workshop that evening. Part of me hesitated anxiously, reluctant, yet exhilarated. I was well past sixty now, and so was he, so why should I even care anymore? Was it some semblance of loyalty that motivated me to attend, or was I still wrestling with my heart? Dan was in town, and Dan would always be Dan to me–the same Dan who had introduced me to his family and recorded my songs in the basement of his mother's house. He was the only one I'd ever completely surrendered my heart to...but I was late, wasn't I?

I stood at a table set up in the front lobby, handing over my ticket, a little sheepishly, a little out of breath, and glanced up to see him. *Yes, it was really Daniel standing at the top of the stairs!* His meandering gaze fell upon me. He was startled and, for a moment, I wondered, "Is he afraid of me? This is a crazy coincidence, that we should both be standing here in the same room at the same time." It was almost impossible to catch a celebrity like Dan up close. "This is like one of those dreams," I marveled. Time had grown a bushy beard on his face and added years to his appearance, but the same brown eyes softened and knew instantly who I was.

"Hi, Dan," I smiled, as if it were yesterday.

I rushed up the stairs, past people arriving and amazed NMC staff and into an embrace that hugged me tightly. He whispered...

"Long time..." and I hugged him back, feeling his time weathered vulnerability with a heart still alive with embers and sparks glowing. The thought flashed through my mind– "Will it always be this way?" but I simply replied, "Yes, Dan, it sure has been."

Chapter Twenty-Six
"The Blues Challenge"

After 2015, Nick's songs continued to occasionally drift up from the subconscious that remembered them– "Lady Blue" and a song called "A Lazy Summer's Day in St. Louis." I didn't know that Nick had been to St. Louis, but the song certainly knew about the *"summer sunshine in my eyes, the sidewalk heat that fries–it's a lazy summer's day in St. Louis"* and if I didn't know about *"the wrong side of town where the forgotten people are found–down where all the cool cats play,"* I must have remembered listening to the *"randy blues"* and *"hearing all the backstreet news"* because he'd been there.

And how could I have known the heartache of being black in a time of prejudice and persecution, when I was born a white middle-class Canadian woman? "Sweet Blackness" would remind us all that *"we move in a shadow world, broken hearts in an unkind world,"* but *"before the One who saves we get down on our knees and pray because God loves all of us–sweet, sweet blackness."* And of course, I couldn't know about a *"Lady Blue who wandered down a back alley 'til she was out of sight, like a ghost who haunts in the middle of the night."*

These songs were pure magic, gifts from God, I reasoned. Every time one appeared, I thanked Him for the miracle.

In 2018, I finally finished, wrote and published the book *Go Back Jack* with the help of Bruce Moran and Total Recall Publishing, which had been one of the biggest goals of my life.

The book did come after the *Go Back Jack* script, after Hollywood producer Signe Olynk suggested it, and the music complemented them both.

I had taught myself script writing after the age of fifty. I'd never known I had the talent for it. I went on to write other scripts that won Quarterfinals with Page Awards International Screenwriting Contest and Story Pros International Screenwriting Contest, and received good scores and comments from the highly respected "Dr. Format" Dave Trottier and positive feedback from several screenwriting contest judges.

Performing on Stephen Avenue, downtown Calgary in 2018.

I wrote a script about Jimi Hendrix called *Jimi's Last Poem* which won a Quarterfinal, and even a comedy called *Idiot House* which received a "Consider" from the Hollywood execs. Who would have known?

After publishing *Go Back Jack,* I decided to go public and promote it and Nick's music by busking on the streets of Calgary. A friend of mine, Yvonne Duncan, joined me on guitar with her own originals, and before we knew it, we'd played on Stephen Avenue downtown, at the Marlborough and Southcentre LRT Stations, in Inglewood, and at church gigs. The gigs were plentiful in 2018. I became a Stagehand booking artist and played the Music Mile. I was simply repeating the past, but the irony was that I was making money from songs that Nick had written.

Yvonne Duncan and I "bringing down the house" at the Marlborough LRT Station in 2018.

Yvonne and I each bought collapsible wagons and pulled our gear with us wherever we went: amps, keyboards, guitars, microphones, you name it. I often travelled on the LRT system with mine. Our gear had to be battery operated in such informal settings, and we could set up anywhere, anytime.

In November 2018, the *Toronto Star* heard about us, sent a reporter to interview us and featured us in an article entitled "Busking duo bringing down the house at Calgary LRT stations."

At Mikey's Nightclub after the Road to Memphis Blues Challenge in Calgary in 2019.

The year before Covid turned the world upside down, the Calgary Blues Society afforded me an opportunity to perform at Mikey's Nightclub in the Road to Memphis Blues Challenge, and

I was finally able to showcase Nick's music on stage in front of the most discriminating crowd of blues lovers in the city.

That day, after Cindy McLeod had introduced me as a contender in the Solo/Duo category alongside fellow keyboardist Debra Power (who was reportedly the best blues keyboard player in Calgary at the time and had won the Road to Memphis Challenge several times over), I stood in front of the lights in a packed nightclub and told the story of *Go Back Jack.*

I told them what it had really been like and what the blues were all about. I told them about being barefoot in the Depression, hopping trains, and singing the blues because the blues were all that a black man had–God and the blues. I told them about catfish stew and how you often had to rustle up a dinner with what you had around you–a few potatoes, catfish from the pond, some onions, a bit of flour for the rue. It was a simple life, close to nature, but like Annie had often said, "The Lord will take care of you." And once more, the haunting melody of "Little Girl Blue" touched the hearts of those listening.

At the end of my performance, I heard the roar of applause and fans came out of the woodwork to congratulate me, buy me a meal and place bracelets on my wrist. The world of music is a strange place, and those who live for the spotlight are a breed apart. Now I knew what had driven Nick and why he had loved it so much, and I felt sad that he couldn't be there and share in the glory.

In August 2022, I performed at Stagehand's Car Free Sunday in Inglewood with Pete Johnson, a local guitar player. They had shut down traffic and people wandered up and down the street listening to bands play. We were one of them.

Playing "Stagehand's Car Free Sunday"
with Pete Johnson in 2022.

I wrote a children's book *The Leprechaun Who Was Not a Mouse* in 2021 and published it next.

I continued to work with children for the Calgary Catholic

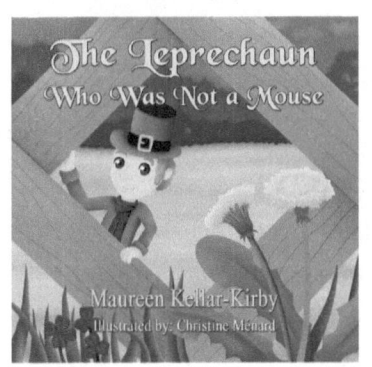

School District as a casual on call and brought my guitar to work. I was living my dreams over and beyond Nick, but I never gave up on him. I was still playing the bongos and sitting in on keyboards with bands who didn't realize that the talent I had for picking up songs by ear was directly inherited from him and his years on the road as a working musician. No matter. There was still a demand for piano players, and always would be. I vowed that I would continue to work on my musical skills and keep improving them.

In 2023, at the age of 71, I meandered off on a mission to create a new type of music called Celestial Rock. Continuing Jimi Hendrix's legacy in his songs about the astral world, I had already composed "Astral Wife" and now, "Wrapped Up in Karma." It was time, as Jimi had often said, to "wake up those sleepy people." In television and media, I could see people's eagerness to reach out and connect with the invisible worlds in their ghost hunting and paranormal adventures, which had become a passion of the times. They truly wanted to touch the Spiritual Worlds. They just needed to be pointed in the right direction.

I uploaded the *Go Back Jack* songs and *The Angel Music* on SoundCloud and YouTube for all the world to hear. Would the spiritual awakening my mother had spoken of result from the reading of my book *Go Back Jack* or from *The Angel Music*? Or would the Celestial Rock "Astral Wife" and "Wrapped Up in Karma" point them in the right direction? Only time would tell.

One of Nick's songs, "Puffy White Cloud," was about being

high on heroin, and I realized that I'd reached a turning point when I changed the lyrics, transformed it into a children's song and uploaded it to YouTube. This was followed by another children's song called "Fly A Plane," which is about all the possibilities of what you can do when you grow up. Now the children could watch, listen to and clap along with these songs in the classroom, and I got the word out to all the teachers I came in contact with. Perhaps these songs would inspire the children and bring people to a spiritual awakening that way.

I was no longer the original Nick in my lifestyle. I'd turned to health and vitamins instead of sex, drugs and rock and roll, and directed my energies into useful, creative and constructive work instead of addictions.

Sitting in with "The Vintage Express Band"
at the Jubilee Legion 286 in 2023.

I wasn't a teenager driven by my hormones and taking crazy chances any longer. I'd lived through it all, and it was truly a miracle that I'd survived to tell the tale. I was living a conventional life, married, with grandchildren; but ironically, in 2024 I was still battling to keep that front tooth that Nick had lost during the Great Depression. Some things never change.

My sister Kate, who had been instrumental in guiding me onto the path of *Go Back Jack*, retired from teaching and became a full-time musician. She released several CDs and kept busy playing gigs in a duo called Silverwood in the Vancouver, British Columbia area. Like Nick's friend Luke, her main instrument was flute, which she played beautifully.

Every time Kate and I got together, we played the *Go Back Jack* songs. She hadn't forgotten.

I also realized that my writing and musical ambitions and efforts of this lifetime would lead me into the next, so it was important to continue to improve my skills as a keyboard player, bongo player and singer-songwriter. I was also leaning toward writing movie scripts and soundtracks, with Hollywood in view.

By 2024, with four Final Quarterfinalist wins under my belt, I was in Coverfly's top ten percent. If I didn't live long enough to see success in this lifetime, I would hand the scripts over to my granddaughter Reegan, who also had writing ambitions.

As for Nick, Jessup's words had come true: "Could be two, could be ten, until you achieve dat purpose." No matter how long it might take, he'd known my destiny all along.

So, my Adventure Continues!

Author Bio

Maureen Kellar-Kirby lives in Calgary, Alberta, Canada with her husband and three cats where she volunteers for the Meow Foundation, taking care of neighborhood strays.

She continues with her love of the occult in her practice as a psychic-astrologer and works with children in schools, utilizing her Diploma in Early Childhood Education. She also continues to develop her talent as a writer of movie scripts, book manuscripts and as a songwriter and musician by recording her music and sitting in with other musicians in the Calgary area.

https://www.maureenkellar.com

https://www.soundcloud.com/maureen-kellar-kirby

Acknowledgments

I would like to express my gratitude to the special people who were as enthusiastic as I have been about delving into the truth and purpose of life itself.

Sigrid Macdonald, my editor, who patiently guided me through the trials and tribulations of my first book manuscript, always encouraging me, while being eternally fascinated with the content.

Signe Olynyk, writer and producer, who encouraged me to not only write the script, but also the book.

My sister, Kathy Kellar, without whose psychic work, this book would not have been written,

Daniel Lanois, world renowned producer and musician who gave me the chance to record the music.

Thanks to Bruce Moran, at TotalRecallPress.com for making my worldwide publishing dream of "Go Back Jack" come true.